Anne Anderson

D1799638

Wave Me Goodbye

Jura MacLean Sherwood

PublishAmerica

Baltimore

© 2002 by Jura R. Sherwood.

All rights reserved. No part of this book may be reproduced in any form without written permission from the publishers, except by a reviewer who may quote brief passages in a review to be printed in a newspaper or magazine.

First printing

ISBN: 1-59129-324-3
PUBLISHED BY PUBLISHAMERICA BOOK PUBLISHERS
www.publishamerica.com
Baltimore

Printed in the United States of America

Dedication:

Lest We Forget – *WAVE ME GOODBYE* is dedicated to the memory of the 83 British evacuee children who perished when the German submarine U48 torpedoed the *SS City of Benares* on 17th September 1940.

AUTHOR'S NOTE

The inspiration for this book is based on a little-known period in British World War II history.

In the summer of 1940 when Britain stood alone against the threat of a German invasion, I was seven years old and about to embark upon an adventure that profoundly changed my life. I was part of a little known British Government program called the Children's Overseas Reception Board (CORB): a scheme devised to save the children of Britain by sending them to the Dominions of Canada, New Zealand, Australia and South Africa.

Twenty-two thousand applications were made for evacuation, but less than twenty-three hundred children actually participated. I was one of those, and spent the next five and one-half years with two older sisters, but without my parents, in South Africa.

The CORB program was halted after only three weeks when two ships were torpedoed. The *Volendam* was first, although she did not sink. Many of the surviving children were then transferred to the ill-fated *City of Benares*. Bound for Canada with ninety CORB evacuees and ten children whose parents had paid for their passage, she sank with the loss of 83 children. Most of the *Benares* crew and the staff who had volunteered to accompany the children were also lost.

Some adult volunteers returning home to Britain after successfully accompanying other evacuees to Australia and New Zealand did not fare well either. They were attacked at sea by German Raiders masquerading as Japanese merchant ships flying the Rising Sun. This was more than a year before Japan attacked the United States and entered the war. One group of British volunteers who were taken prisoner spent two and a half years in a German Internment camp before being exchanged through the Red Cross. Another group was abandoned on an island in the Pacific.

Although my story is fiction, I researched the facts on which it is based in many sources, including the following –

The Absurd and The Brave – Michael Fethney, The Book Guild, 1990
Children of the Benares – Ralph Barker, Methuen, 1987
Atlantic Ordeal – E. Huxley, Chatto and Windus, 1941
Children In Flight – A.H. Body, ULP 1940
The Evacuees – B.S. Johnson, Gollancz, 1968
Exodus of Children – D. Johnson, Pennyfarthing Publications, 1985
Who Will Take Our Children? – C. Jackson, Methuen, 1941
The Singing Ship – M. Maclean, Angus and Robertson, 1941
Prison Life on a Pacific Raider – Sandback and Edge
No Time To Wave Goodbye – B. Wicks, Bloomsbury 1988
The Day They Took the Children – B. Wicks, Bloomsbury 1989
Borrowed Children – St. Leo Strachey, Murray 1940

CHAPTER ONE

September 1940

Priscilla Thornton flinched.

The banshee scream of an air-raid siren shattered the night—and her preoccupation with how to break her news to Ted.

"Make you jump, did it?" Ted chuckled and tightened his arm draped around her shoulders.

She laughed at herself. "Will we ever get used to it?" The siren reached a crescendo, held high 'C' for a few seconds, and then plunged down to a sinister growl. "But Jerry's late tonight," she said. "For once he let us enjoy the picture all the way to the end."

"Yeah, but I don't think you saw much of it, Cilla. You seem to be a million miles away tonight."

That was true. She'd paid little attention to what was happening on the screen. Instead, in the darkness of the theatre she'd tried to think how to best tell him her plans. It was no use. However she said it, he was going to make a scene, and she'd just as soon it wasn't in public.

Probing searchlights swept the moonless sky. The distant boom of an anti-aircraft gun over-rode the siren, and the night quivered in the responding echo.

"Come on. We'd better get to the shelter." Ted quickened his pace, urging her along.

Cilla stopped walking and cocked her head. "No. Wait. Listen!"

"What? What is it?"

"Ssh!" She tightened her arm around his waist to silence him. "Listen. The bombers. They're not coming this way."

"How do you know?"

"A year of air-raids taught me," she chuckled. "Listen, you can tell."

"You're right," Ted said, after a minute's concentration. "Sounds as if the Croydon Aerodrome's catching a packet though."

"And poor old London, again." She blew out an exasperated puff of breath.

"No matter what else he's after, that bloody Hitler always seem to include a few bombs on London, just for good measure."

Ted directed the shrouded beam of torchlight to guide them along the unlit street, past houses darkened by blackout curtains.

Rounding the corner onto the street where her home and his stood locked together by a single wall like Siamese twins, they almost collided with a steel-helmeted Air Raid Warden.

"Better get off the street, you two," he said as he passed.

"Right you are, mate. We live just down here." Ted gestured to the row of identical houses caught, for a brief moment, in the ghostly glow of a searchlight sweep.

"Goodnight, Warden," Cilla called after the dark form disappearing into the blackness. The wailing siren swallowed the warden's response.

The air-raid warning died to a long, quivering growl, and the night seemed to catch its breath before the howl spiralled up again. A few miles off, great flashes of gunfire zigzagged across the heavens. The thump of exploding bombs, and glowing sky over London, told the story playing out below.

Cilla shook her head slowly, imagining the human clamour erupting into shouting, screaming, cursing, ambulance bells clanging, and the terror as buildings crashed to the ground. "Those poor devils. I don't know how they can go through it, night after night."

"Come on." Ted tightened his hold on her shoulder and pulled her toward home. "Want a cuppa before you go in?"

"Is your mother home?"

"No, she's working." He stopped at the front gate regarding her quizzically. "What difference does it make?"

"Oh, nothing, really. I just wondered if we'd be alone."

Ted chuckled. "What did you have in mind?"

"Don't be cheeky. Or I'll go straight home, now."

"Oh, no!" He feigned a sob. "You wouldn't have a member of His Majesty's Royal Navy spend the last hours of his leave alone, would you?"

"I suppose not. Anything for the war effort. Especially if there's a cup of tea in the bargain." He guided her through the front gate. "A cup of tea, then I have to get my beauty sleep. I'm still a working girl, you know, even if some of us get to go on cruises to foreign ports." Her heart beat faster as she thought of her own impending voyage. *Here's my opening. My chance to tell him. No. No, I can't. Not yet. He's going to try to talk me out me. Say something, anything, quick!* "Any idea where you're going this time?" She walked ahead of him up to the front door.

"Cil...la." His voice stretched in mild chastisement. "You know better than to ask that. But to answer your question, no I don't. My orders reassign me to some admiral's staff. I don't even know the new ship's name."

The key clattered as Ted pulled it through the letterbox. Inside, he closed the front door and retrieved the string holding the key before he checked that the blackout curtain was in place, then turned on the light.

Cilla blinked and shielded her eyes from the sudden flood of light. She looked up and caught her breath as Ted's eyes locked with hers in the hall stand mirror.

He held her gaze for a long moment as he hung his sailor hat on the peg. A lock of dark hair fell across his forehead, reminding her of when he was a little boy, and people remarked on his beautiful dark brown eyes and long, thick lashes. He'd always been good-looking, even as a gawky teen, when she'd felt ugly and awkward in her changing body. He'd grown to a tall, handsome man who had an unsettling effect on her. The way he made her squirm at moments like this always disturbed her, and tonight, hiding a secret, she was especially vulnerable.

He frowned at her in the mirror.

"What? Why are you looking at me like that?"

"I'm just trying to sort out what's different about you tonight."

She watched the colour rising into her cheeks and quickly lowered her eyes and ran a self-conscious hand over her hair.

"Here! You aren't chucking me over for another bloke, are you?" He was grinning so she knew he was just teasing her.

"Not just any bloke. I'm running away with another sailor."

"That's all right then. Had me worried for a minute. Right. Tea or cocoa?" he said, turning and striding down the narrow hall to the kitchen. "Go on in," he called over his shoulder.

She knew the way. All her life she'd been coming to this house, identical to her own home. Two rooms downstairs, one the family lived in, the other used only at Christmas and when the vicar visited, and a kitchen large enough for only one person at a time to work. Upstairs were three bedrooms, one a small box above the stairs. A closet-sized bathroom and a separate loo stood side by side.

She took off her coat and tossed it across a chair. In the quiet little parlour only the steady ticking of the mantle clock marked the few minutes she had to compose how she would tell him of her plans to help the war effort. *I don't owe it to him to tell him. He doesn't have to know, but if he comes home on leave and I'm not here, he'll be hurt and angry that I didn't tell him.*

The kettle screamed, and a minute later Ted pushed the door with his foot. "Here. I made cocoa. Help you to sleep." He set the steaming beakers down and studied her with his forehead furrowed. "Hey. Cilla, you all right?"

"Oh,...yes. I was just thinking that tomorrow you'll be off on another voyage, and I was wondering when we'd see each other again."

He wrapped his arms around her, pulling her close and pressing a kiss on her forehead. "And you're going to miss me, right?"

With her head tucked against his chest, she could hear his heart beating under the rough fabric of his uniform.

Glancing at his face, she found him smiling down at her. She poked one finger into his ribs. "Don't flatter yourself. As a matter of fact I was wondering who'll go to the pictures with me. My brothers are gone to war and you won't be here."

"That's all? And here's me thinking you'll actually pine for me."

She heard the laughter in his tone as he nuzzled her hair. "Hmm. You smell good. Did I tell you that?"

"Yes, you did. Twice already this evening. It's the scent you gave me last Christmas."

"And you still have it?"

"Of course. I'm hoarding it. There is a war on, you know. And until it's over, I doubt that we'll see *Evening in Paris* for sale again."

"Well, then, I am flattered that you would spare a little for my benefit. I'll have to see about getting you some more the next time I'm in a foreign port. I may be able to get you some silk stockings, too."

"Is that the bait you use on the cheap tarts you pick up in those foreign ports?" She arched one brow.

"What!? What the hell are you talking about?"

She didn't miss his momentary chagrin.

"That's what I heard. You're trying to live up to a sailor's reputation and have a woman in every port."

"Who told you that?"

"Doesn't matter who told me."

"Ah, Trevor. Your little brother never could keep his mouth shut." He shrugged. As understanding registered, he faced her again. "So, that's what all this is about."

"What do you mean?"

"This funny mood you're in. You're being evasive. Acting as if you've got something to hide." He tilted her chin with his forefinger and looked directly into her eyes. "Cilla, whatever Trevor told you about me has nothing to do with you and me. We'll always be friends."

"Of course." She jerked her face away from his hand and smirked. "Friends."

"See what I mean, Cil? You're acting strangely. Don't pull away from me. Surely I don't have to explain myself to you, of all people."

The long one-note all-clear signalled that the raid was over. She turned away. "I should go home, anyway."

"Why? What are you so cheesed off about?" He ran one finger down her spine and tickled her ribs. "I know how to get you to laugh. You're not too old to be tickled, Cilla Thornton."

She jerked from of his grasp. "Stop it! When will you realise I'm not a child any more and start treating me like an adult? That stupid horseplay should have stopped ten years ago. We're not children anymore. Friend!" She spat the word at him.

"Wow, you do have your knickers in a knot." His eyes bore into hers and she read the hurt. He shook his head and sighed. "I'm well aware you're not a child anymore. Come on, I'll take you home." He snatched up her coat and held it for her. "I hope you're in a better mood the next time I get home."

She obediently slipped her arms into the sleeves and quickly turned to face him. "Ted, that's what I've been trying to tell you."

"What?"

"I...I may not be here when you come back." She fumbled with her coat buttons, not daring to look directly at him.

"Why? Where would you be?"

"I've applied to be a CORB escort."

"What the hell's a CORB?

"It's the Children's Overseas Reception Board. A government program to evacuate kids overseas?"

"Overseas? Bloody 'ell!" His breath escaped in a whoosh of exasperation. "What the hell did you do that for?" He rubbed the back of his neck. "That's what you've been hiding. Why didn't you tell me before now?"

"Because I knew you'd react in exactly this way. I've already heard all the reasons why I shouldn't do it from my dad. I didn't want you to rag on me, too. Not tonight."

He paced. "You can't go to sea in the middle of a war. It's madness!"

"And why not?" She placed her hands on her hips and glowered at him. "You are."

He stopped and faced her. "That's different. It's my job to go to sea, especially during wartime. But you don't have to. You have a perfectly good job here. Besides, school teachers are in short supply since the forces have taken so many."

Cilla thrust her chin toward him. "You don't understand, Ted. This is a way for me to do something more useful for the war effort than herd a bunch of schoolgirls into an air-raid shelter umpteen times a day."

He drew in a deep breath and enunciated each syllable. "Then join the bloody Land Army and help the farmers grow food for the kids!"

"Don't be ridiculous!" She spat the words through clenched teeth. "And stop shouting at me."

"Cilla." He sighed and assumed a more patient tone. "You worked so hard to qualify for your credentials. I remember how proud you were to be offered a teaching position at St. Margaret's. You said you'd grown to love *your girls*. What happened to all that?"

"A war happened! In case you haven't noticed. The country is on the verge of an invasion. The bloody Germans are bombing the schools, and half my girls have already been evacuated to the countryside." She jammed her hands deep into her coat pockets. "Anyway, if this government plan works out, in a few months there won't be any children in Britain to teach. They'll all be in places like Australia or New Zealand."

He put his hands on her shoulders and stared squarely into her face. "Listen to me, Cilla. I don't know what you expect, but crossing the ocean in the middle of a war is not at all like a glamorous peacetime cruise. Believe me, I know what it's like, and contrary to your snide remarks, I don't go on luxury cruises. There are long-range bombers, mines and submarines out there just waiting for a chance to sink our ships."

She shrugged his hands off her shoulders. "It can't be all that dangerous if the government is willing to send thousands of children across the ocean."

"Strewth! I wish I had your faith. Do you think the people sitting on their fat arses in London planning these evacuations even think about the consequences? Not a week ago, the Germans torpedoed a ship with children aboard."

Cilla sucked in her breath. "I didn't hear about that. Did the ship sink?"

"No, it didn't sink. But it was badly damaged and had to be towed back."

"What about the children?

"All the kids survived. And that's the only reason you didn't hear about it. A Navy destroyer picked them up and brought them home. But that's beside the point." He flicked his hand. "Somebody dreamed up this lunacy, and now they don't want to lose face by scuttling the plan."

She tossed her head defiantly. "That wasn't the first ship to sail with evacuees aboard. The rest of them made it safely."

"Cilla!" He blew out a long breath and tipped his head back as if expecting to read the right words on the ceiling. "How can I convince you that what you're planning is more dangerous than staying here and taking your chances with the German invasion or air-raids? I don't want to go back to sea worried about you."

"Well then, don't worry."

He suddenly gripped her shoulders so tightly she thought he would shake her. "Listen to me." His voice vibrated. "I know how you feel about children and that you want to protect them, but believe me, what you're planning isn't the lark you think it is."

She pulled from of his grasp. "Now, who's got their knickers in a twist? Anyway, I haven't actually been accepted yet. CORB may still decide against me. All the teachers I know about who've been accepted are in their late thirties and older. But if they offer, I'll take it."

"Cor blimey, you're stubborn!"

"Being stubborn has nothing to do with it. I made a commitment. You understand about taking responsibility seriously."

"Believe me, if I had a half a chance I wouldn't go back out there."

"Yes, you would. I know you. It hasn't even crossed your mind not to return to your ship. You'll do your duty."

He wrapped her in a hug. "Oh, Cil! I hope you know what you're doing, but I seriously doubt it. How long will this madness take you out of England?"

"I don't know. I think it depends on the length of the program. It only started a couple of weeks ago."

"I expect it depends more on the number of available transport ships than anything else. Well, you can always tell them that you've changed your mind."

"But I haven't."

"I know, but tell them that anyway. Tell them you're going to be married."

"Why would I tell them a lie like that?"

"It doesn't have to be a lie." He held her at arm's length and studied her expression.

Her jaw sagged. "What are you talking about?"

"I'm talking about us getting married."

"I can't believe this."

He tilted his head back and blew out a long breath. "Cilla, I'm sorry. That isn't the way I intended to propose."

"Of all things!" She ran her hand through her hair. "I don't believe what I just heard. Is this like when we were kids and used to joke about getting married?"

"It isn't a childish joke anymore, Cilla."

She ran the back of her fingers down his cheek. "Thanks. I appreciate what you're trying to do, but I don't need rescuing. Besides, how many times have I heard you say it was daft for people to get married in wartime?"

"I know. I know, too, there's a good chance I might not come back. But we might both survive the war and we will have wasted so much time."

"That's it? You're afraid of wasting time!"

"Oh, hell! I'm doing a bloody awful job of this. After all the years we've known each other, do I have to spell it out for you?"

"That might be nice."

He lifted her chin with one finger. "I've always loved you, Cilla. I thought you knew that."

"Perhaps I always suspected it, but it's nice to be told. Unfortunately, that's too little too late right now."

"Bugger it!" He pulled her to him and wrapped her in a hug. "Give me another chance to ask you properly." He gently patted her back and sighed. "This CORB thing is such a hare-brained scheme. Please don't go. Marry me on my next leave, all right?"

He seemed to be getting his motives tangled up with his emotions.

She buried her head hard against his chest and bit back an angry response. She'd waited half her life, or so it seemed, to hear him so those words, but she'd be damned if she'd be taken for granted. If he thought she could be blackmailed so easily, he was mistaken.

"All right, Cilla?"

She looked up at him braving a smile without answering. *Not on your Nellie, Ted Evans.*

CHAPTER TWO

The wail of sirens and the distinctive throb of approaching German bombers combined to drown out the gentle slosh of water against the Liverpool dock. Cilla sagged like spent elastic in a pair of old knickers. *Not another air raid!*

She rubbed her tired eyes and forced her weary limbs into action. "All right you lot! Let's get lined up and off to the shelter."

The children stirred, but grumbled at being disturbed. Scattered on the dock in small groups, they drank milk from half-pint bottles and munched on biscuits.

Cilla shared their brain-dulling exhaustion. In the three days since she'd arrived from London, she hadn't even had time to question whether accompanying two hundred and forty-one children to Canada was such a brilliant idea. By day she'd herded them to the shelters, and at night she'd helped carry the little ones to safety. Between raids she'd attended briefings, assisted harried doctors and dentists, settled childish disputes, and comforted children so distraught at leaving their families, they were physically sick. Assuring them the war would soon be over seemed to make matters worse, since they couldn't understand why, in that case, they had to go away at all. A handful of children, just too traumatized to be evacuated, had already been sent home.

Facing still another day of bombs and bedlam, Cilla began to think that going home wasn't such a bad idea.

"No peace for the wicked!" Ruby's young face reflected the weariness in her voice. The little Cockney's red-rimmed eyes, glazed with exhaustion, stared from her pinched face.

Bombed-out of their East End tenement the night before they left London for Liverpool, Ruby, and her little brother Freddie had lost everything, including the brand-new clothes bought especially for their evacuation. Briefed on their circumstances. Cilla knew it couldn't have been easy for their widowed mother to outfit them. Now, all they had left were the rags they stood in.

"Cor blimey. No' agin!" Freddie planted his stubby hands firmly on his hips and squinted down the river toward the sea.

"There'th the buggerth," he lisped, pointing at the specks skimming the River Mersey like giant dragonflies. "I wonder why they're coming in tho low."

Freddie's elbows poked through the holes in his dirty jumper, and pink flesh peeked through the seat of his short trousers. He wore no socks, and the soles of his dilapidated shoes flapped when he walked.

Ruby's tattered coat with a grimy black velvet collar was too small for her. The cuffs were halfway up her arms, and the half belt at the back rested just below her shoulder blades. Her old rubber Wellingtons were three sizes too large, and so tall the tops hit above her knobbly knees and prevented her from bending her legs. To keep from tripping, she mooched along, dragging her feet with every step.

Over the siren's incessant howl, the steady, belly-thumping throb of aircraft engines shook the ground, vibrated up Cilla's legs and trembled her spine.

"Come on. Get the lead out!" Her shouted words disappeared into the sudden thunderous roar of a nearby anti-aircraft gun.

"'Ere, I 'aven't finished me milk and biscuits ye'." Kitty Brown's shrill, indignant voice penetrated the racket.

"Leave your milk bottles. Hurry! Follow Miss Thornton to the shelter!" Anne Stansbury shouted.

The children picked up their luggage and queued up behind Cilla. Other adults herded the stragglers, trying to hurry them along.

At the shelter entrance Cilla stepped aside and urged the evacuees inside. "Come on! Shake a leg!"

The little ones, juggling suitcases, teddy bears and crumbling biscuits, scurried to keep up. Their gas masks, dangling from shoulder straps, bumped awkwardly against their bottoms and slowed them down.

"Come on! Move! Move!" Reverend Smythe urged. The little Yorkshireman peered anxiously at the sky and nudged several children ahead of him into the shelter.

A group of older boys, squinting at the approaching bombers, argued as they sauntered by.

"You're barmy, you are," said one and punched another boy in the shoulder. "A Blenheim's a British kite, and I know the sound of a Blenheim."

"Naw!" Another knot of boys jostled one another. "A Halifax has nine machine guns and can carry five and half tons of eggs."

"Well, eggs ain't gonna stop old 'Itler." The boy chuckled.

"Coo, don't you even know that eggs means bombs? Coo!"

Cilla urged them along by the shoulders. "Come on, boys, hurry up. The war'll be over before you get inside."

"We should be so lucky!" A gangly, dark-haired teen picked up an exaggerated pace and gave Cilla an impudent wink.

"Cheeky monkey!" She grinned and followed them into the shelter.

The children settled themselves on the rows of long wooden benches lining the walls and down the centre of the room.

"Right," yelled Father Hurley. "What'll it be t'day? "Run Rabbit Run?"

The children cheered. They had their own version of the popular song and delighted in bellowing, "*Run Adolf, Run Adolf, run, run, run. Here comes the British Tommy with his gun, gun, gun.*"

Cilla leaned back against the cold wall of the concrete bunker and wondered where Father Hurley got the stamina to walk up and down the rows, waving his beefy arms, beating time to the singing.

The evacuees had already formed a relationship with the big, sandy-haired priest, but Dennis Marlow was their favourite. Dennis, a huge, jovial man, volunteered as an escort while he waited for his commission as a Navy Chaplain. He expected to be back in England before it came through.

Scattered among the children were six more schoolteachers and one woman who had worked privately as a nanny. Two Salvation Army officers belted out the song, and their spouses, sitting opposite, rested their black-bonneted heads together and harmonised. Anne Stansbury, slight and middle-aged, strolled among the rows of children. Her high-necked blouse, tweed skirt and sensible shoes suggested she brooked no nonsense. Years as a housemistress at a girl's school in Kent qualified her for the job of Chief Escort.

The handsome American, Clint Jennison, sat alone in the far corner of the room. He was still a bit of a mystery, and Cilla wondered why an American would get involved in a British government scheme like CORB.

And why had Smythe, the little, sixtyish Yorkshire cleric, volunteered for what was turning into and exhausting job? He was the oldest of the volunteer adults, and Cilla reckoned at twenty-two she had to be the youngest.

The dockside ack-ack gun roared, trembling the bunker. Bare ceiling lights jumped and swung through the showers of loosened dust. Again and again the thundering anti-aircraft guns drowned out the weary voices, but undaunted, the chorus never missed a beat.

Cilla was much too tired to sing, but even if she'd wanted to, the emotional lump in her throat would have choked her. Tears welled in her eyes. The stalwart children who had already been through so much fear and danger, singing their heads off, made her ashamed of her own misgivings about what she was doing in their midst.

The letter from CORB accepting her as an escort had made her feel very noble. The chance to see something of the world had thrilled her, and her fantasies had soared. She'd imagined herself basking on the deck of a ship bound for South Africa or Australia. Perhaps she was destined for New Zealand or Canada! But as the time for embarkation drew closer, Ted's warnings about the dangers she faced weighed heavier than she'd imagined they could. Perhaps she shouldn't have dismissed his concerns so quickly. No, she shrugged off her fears. She simply could not believe the British government would deliberately endanger children's lives. Assured that all evacuee ships would sail in convoy under the protection of a Royal Navy escort, the parents had no fears. There was nothing to worry about—nothing, once they were safely away from the constant air raids on Britain.

A piercing single note signalled the end of the air raid. Cilla emerged from the shelter into the bright September sunshine and blinked, confused. A pall of smoke from a burning warehouse far down the Mersey was the only indication there had even been an enemy attack.

"For all that noise, they didn't do much damage, did they?" she said to nobody in particular.

The Salvation Army major rubbed his eyes and squinted toward the smoke. "They were so low, I reckon they must have been dropping mines in the river," he said.

The reek of smoke, carried up the river on the breeze, mingled with the tang of salt water, diesel fuel and wet rope. The smell of the sea evoked memories for some of the children, too.

"Coo, smells like Southend, don' it?" a freckle-faced redhead said.

Kitty wrinkled her pug nose and sniffed the air. "Yeah, reminds me of cockles and whelks."

Anne Stansbury clapped her hands. "All right. Line up and have your ration books and gas masks ready for Mr. Jennison and Mr. Marlow. We're going to get aboard the ship now."

The level of the children's chatter rose with their sudden elevated excitement.

Cilla pressed her hands against the flutter of expectation rising in her own midriff. Although she couldn't quite dismiss her apprehension about what she was undertaking, she was determined not to show it.

"What about our name tags?" The boy peering through thick glasses pulled on the cardboard strung around his neck.

"No. Keep them on until we're aboard the ship."

Clint Jennison, the charming American escort, smiled lazily at Cilla as he swaggered casually down the line, collecting the children's ration books. She watched his progression until he turned, then she flushed and looked away quickly, realising he had been quite aware of her scrutiny.

"Right. Let's have your gas masks. I know you can't bear to part with them, but you'll just have to sacrifice and give the British government back its pieces of smelly old rubber," Dennis yelled.

"You can have 'em. We won't need 'em no more." Ruby wrinkled her nose and held out her gas mask by the metal snout. "Good riddance to bad rubbish!" She yanked Freddie's gas mask out of the case. "We're goin' to keep our cases. Is it orright?"

"I don't see why not." He smiled at the children. "I'll bet your mum made those, didn't she?"

The children nodded in unison.

"Terry!"

It came as a scream more than a call. Everyone who heard it turned to face the woman separated from the evacuees by a high wire fence.

"Terry!" She screeched again.

"It's me mum!" The boy's eyes widened.

"What on *earth* is she doing here?" Anne Stansbury snapped. The woman dressed in dungarees and with her hair neatly tucked into a snood gripped the wire fence tightly with both hands.

Anne spoke quietly to the boy and, putting her hand on his shoulder, walked with him to his mother. The two women exchanged a few words, and the chief escort walked back alone, scowling.

"She works here on the docks, and when she saw the children, she took a chance that her son was one of them." Anne pursed her lips. "It would have been better if she hadn't seen him. She's quite emotional, and that's the very reason parents are not allowed to see their children off on the docks. Imagine the chaos if two hundred and forty more sets of parents were here." Anne Stansbury wagged her shoulders indignantly.

The boy's mother reached through the fence and clutched at his shirtfront. Her face contorted with the effort to control her emotions.

Some of the children began to sniffle.

The chief escort shook her head with obvious disgust. "I wish she'd leave. Just look at her! Her son can't comfort her and now he's becoming upset."

Terry's mother sagged against the barrier and sobbed as her son turned away. He took a few steps and stopped. Turning back, he called out, "Don't cry, Mum. Come on now, wave me goodbye."

He dragged his sleeve across his nose and jogged away to join the ragged line of children moving along the dock.

Cilla herded them past bales and crates of cargo. She urged on the stragglers staring at the huge cranes swinging booms of cargo overhead and into the holds of ships tied up at the quay.

"Get a move on. Don't dawdle. You'll be left behind."

Around the corner of the next large warehouse, a huge ship loomed. Cilla gaped. Excitement lit the children's faces.

Freddie stretched his gaze to the top of the ship's forward mast. His mouth slowly widened, exposing the gap in his front teeth. "Coo! Is 'at our ship, miss?"

"I think it must be." Cilla's pulse quickened.

"Ach, would ye look at the size o' it?" a little Scots lad said.

"By, but she's a big 'un!" A Yorkshire boy was equally impressed.

"Blimey, 'narf big innet!" Freddie said.

Anne Stansbury yelled down the line. "This is our ship, boys and girls. Lets get aboard. No pushing."

Cilla pulled herself up the steep gangplank and stepped onto the deck. She turned and stretched out her hand to help the child behind her.

"Cilla!"

She gasped, recognising the familiar voice calling her name. "Ted!" Her voice resounded with shock. "What are you doing here? I thought you'd be at sea by now."

She knew him as well as she knew her own brothers, and she thought she'd seen him in every conceivable mood, but she'd never seen him looking quite so angry! Muscles twitched in his tightened jaw and his chin jutted forward, accentuating the cleft. He wore a work uniform with the sleeves of his shirt rolled up above his elbows, exposing strong, lean arms crossed firmly over his chest. Thick brown hair peeked around the edges of his hat set jauntily just above his right eye. Imprinted in gold on the band were the letters HMS.

His shoulders tensed. "More to the point is what the hell are you doing here, Cilla?" His dark brown eyes, shrouded by a scowl, darted from her face to the children climbing the gangplank.

Thoroughly ruffled, she flushed at his accusing outburst and, biting her lower lip, stepped back as children began piling up around her. "I'm escorting these evacuees," she squeaked. *Bugger! She hadn't meant it to sound like an apology.*

"What? I thought we settled this the other night." He compressed his lips and looked quickly about him. "Oh, hell! I can't talk now. Meet me at...er...sundown, aft on the promenade. We have to talk." He threaded his way through the knot of children and continued along the deck.

She stared after him, fighting tears of embarrassment. "Ted, wait! What's an aft? And a promenade?" Her voice rose to a shout, but he gave no indication that he had heard her and disappeared through a hatchway.

CHAPTER THREE

"'Ere, look at 'em blokes. They're wearing skirts!" One of the older boys nudged another and pointed at the brown-skinned men hanging over the upper railing of the ship.

"Hey! They ain't got no shoes on," yelled another child. One after another the children began pointing and snickering.

"Don't stare." Cilla chastised the giggling children, but she couldn't take her own eyes from the small, dark-eyed men dressed in colourful sarongs. Their interest seemed centred on the children as they chattered and gestured.

"Good God! What's this?" A voice boomed overhead.

Cilla's head snapped up. An officer leaned over the railing of the top deck and stared, slack-mouthed, at the crocodile line of children streaming up the gangplank and spilling onto the deck.

"Sutherland!" The voice boomed again. "What's going on?"

"Sir!" A young officer at the head of the gangplank bellowed back. "Our passengers are coming aboard."

"Children? Nobody told me our passengers were children!" He banged his fist rapidly on the edge of the railing, hesitating, as if trying to decide what to do next. "Sub, take a rating and escort these ... er ... our passengers on an orientation tour of the ship while I sort this out."

"Aye, aye, sir." The young officer turned and smiled at Cilla. "I'm Sub-lieutenant Sutherland," he said to her. "If everyone will follow me, I'll show you around the *Punjohpur*."

The children suddenly seemed to forget their fatigue and jostled one another for position at the head of the crowd and began asking questions.

"What's the name of this ship?"

"The *SS Punjohpur*."

"That sounds Indian," Cilla said.

"You're right, miss. It is." Sutherland said.

One little girl pushed her way to the front. "'Ere, what sort of ship is this then? A destroyer?"

22

Sutherland smiled gently at her, but some of the older boys whooped with laughter.

The child ignored the guffaws. "My dad's on a destroyer. The *HMS Tornado.*"

"And a fine ship she is, too," said Sutherland. "The *Punjohpur* is a liner, though. She used to be a posh cruise ship sailing around Asia, before the war. She's meant to be a troop carrier now. This is her first voyage in these waters."

"Why do sailors always call ships *she*?"

Sutherland chuckled. "Must be because we spend so much time on them we think we're married to them. Right, let's have a good look at her."

He started the tour on the boat deck and included a quick look at the lifeboats, a peek at the bridge, then down metal stairs to the promenade deck. Cilla followed without sharing the children's enthusiasm. Tense days and sleepless nights were beginning to take their toll on her.

"'Ere, 'ow about showing us the engines," one of the older boys said.

Sutherland was doing his best to answer the children's questions, but his patience seemed to be wearing a bit thin.

"It's very dirty and noisy down in the engine room, and I don't suppose the young ladies would be interested. Perhaps when we get underway, the captain will allow you chaps to go down there." He hurried on. "These rooms are called the public area." Sutherland gestured with a sweep of his hand at a lounge. "They also serve as muster stations for lifeboat drills."

Traipsing through a mirrored lounge, Cilla sucked in a shocked breath, startled by her own dishevelled reflection. With her hair windblown and her eyes dull and purple-smudged, she looked what her mother would have called "an absolute fright." It was no wonder Ted looked so shocked at seeing her come aboard. The memory of his outburst still smarted, bringing colour to her face. He had no right to speak to her like that! He'd embarrassed her in front of her colleagues and the children.

The tour trooped to the sports deck then the upper deck.

"Why is it called the upper deck when we have to go down to it?"

If the sailors heard the child, they ignored it. "Here is where you will have your meals," the young officer said. "We'll go down to the main deck now. Your quarters are aft." He led them through a hatchway where the air was thick with a peculiar spicy smell.

"Ooh! What's 'at?" Ruby held the end of her nose between her thumb and forefinger.

"Whew! Don'narf pong, don't I'?" Freddie's face contorted into an exaggerated expression of horror.

Sutherland stopped in his tracks. "What? Oh. That smell?" He laughed. "It's called curry. You see, except for the officers, our crew are all Lascars. They're from India, and that's their lunch you can smell."

"Will we 'ave to eat it an' all?" a very small girl said.

Sutherland chuckled. "Oh, no," he said. "You'll have proper food."

Cilla pushed the cabin door open with the end of her suitcase and bumped into something solid on the other side.

"Just a tick." A mop of dark curls appeared, followed by twinkling brown eyes and a wide, warm smile. "Hello. Sorry to be in your way. I can see we'll have to take turns getting into the wardrobe." She was plump with a pleasant round face. "I'm Millicent Parkin. Millie. The girls' nurse." She held out her hand and chuckled. "There's hardly enough room for a proper handshake."

Cilla laughed. "Priscilla Thornton. I'm called Cilla." She quickly appraised her cabin-mate and noted she was a few years older and wore a gold band on her left ring finger.

Millie stepped back, and Cilla squeezed into the tiny cabin. The door almost touched the end of the stacked bunks, each with a reading light above it. A nightstand stood beside the lower bed, and the wardrobe was behind the door.

"Up or down?" Millie pointed to the bunks. "If I have a choice, I'll take the lower one. I'm a bit of a lump for climbing up top."

Cilla immediately warmed to her. "The top is fine with me." She unpacked her one small suitcase and shoved it out of sight under Millie's bunk.

"I'd better go and see if the girls are getting settled in all right." Cilla squeezed past Millie and out the door.

Children scampered up and down the corridor, eagerly inspecting each other's cabins, checking to make sure that the boys' cabins on one side of the corridor were identical to the girls' on the other.

Cilla poked her head around a cabin door "Is everything all right in here?"

"Ooh, yes, Miss." Three girls chorused.

Pamela Merryman collapsed onto a neat bunk and, laughing, flung her arms above her head. "This bed's got real sheets, and the blankets are so soft." She caressed the cover on her bunk. "It's going to feel lovely after that horrible hostel."

"No more straw mattresses on the floor and using your clothes for a pillow, eh?" Cilla grinned at the girls.

"And no more hairy blankets," said another girl.

"I'll see you later." Cilla backed out into the corridor.

"Miss! Miss!" Ruby plucked at Cilla elbow. "Is it orright if me bruvver stays wif me? 'Es all scared goin' wif those big boys." Ruby scuffed her large rubber boots while Freddie squirmed to be free of her grip on the back of his neck. He was a sturdy little boy with light brown hair and wide hazel eyes set in an angelic face. But Cilla knew that behind his innocent appearance he had a vocabulary that would make a docker blush.

Cilla sighed and rolled her eyes upward. "Oh, please don't let them start switching about," she muttered. "Ruby, I'm sorry, but Freddie will have to go to his assigned cabin for now."

"But 'es frightened, Miss."

"Ruby, please!"

"Miss, please Miss." Mary pushed between Cilla and Ruby and readjusted her battered felt school hat. "My little sister just wet her knickers." She draped a protective arm around the shoulder of a doll-like smaller girl. Flaxen curls tumbled around her elfin face, and her huge blue eyes brimmed with tears.

"It's all right, Jill." Cilla bent and wiped the tot's cheeks with her handkerchief. "Don't cry, we'll get you some dry knickers."

"We can't, Miss," said Mary, flicking one of her long blonde plaits over her shoulder. "We can't get her any clean knickers 'cause we don't 'ave none."

"Oh, that's right." Cilla rubbed the spot between her aching eyes, remembering that these two girls were also casualties of a recent air-raid on London. They'd lost everything, including an older brother to be evacuated with them. The experience had left Mary without any signs of emotion. Her sole, self-imposed duty now was the welfare of her five-year-old sister, Jill.

Mary pulled on the strap of her ever-present hat, oblivious to the grooves the elastic band made in her chubby cheeks. Her dulled eyes stared as she patiently waited for Cilla's solution to the problem.

"Mary, you know that you and Jill are getting all new clothes, don't you?"

When the refugees had arrived in Liverpool with nothing more than the clothes they were wearing, someone had contacted the owner of a large department store who agreed to donate clothing to the bombed-out evacuees.

Mary nodded. Her solemn expression never changed.

"Well, they should be delivered to the ship any minute now. Take Jill to the cabin and take off her wet knickers. Wait there until the new clothes arrive." Cilla sent them on their way.

"Miss."

Cilla pushed a long strand of hair from her face. "What is it now, Ruby?"

"Wha'cher gonna do about Freddie, then? 'E wants to stay wif me and I promised me mum I'd look after him. 'Ow can I look after 'im if he's in anuvver cabin?"

Cilla let her breath escape in a noisy sigh. "Ruby, let him go to his cabin, at least until he gets his new clothes. In the meantime, I'll have a word with his escort, and we'll see what we can sort out. All right?"

"But, Miss!"

"Now listen, Ruby. The cabin assignments have been carefully arranged so that young boys like Freddie will be looked after by the older ones, and little girls will be in cabins with older girls to look after them."

The Cockney waif glared through her straight black fringe at Cilla and gave Freddie an impatient shake before she released her grip on his neck. Freddie scampered away.

Cilla matched each of her girls' names with their assigned cabins. "All right, girls." She checked her watch. "I have to go to a meeting, but I should be back in about thirty minutes. Stay in your cabins. While I'm gone, Pamela Merryman is in charge, but Mrs. Parkin is in my cabin to help, if you have a problem."

"Ladies and gentlemen, may I have your attention?" Anne Stansbury said. "Before I outline your duties, I'm afraid I have a bit of bad news."

The hum of conversation drifted into absolute silence.

"As you know, the Germans dropped mines in the Mersey this morning, so Captain Near informs me the ship will not sail at noon today as scheduled." The Chief Escort held up her hand to silence the loud groans and complaints before she continued. "The river is being swept at this moment and the captain believes we will sail at mid-day tomorrow."

"Tomorrow!" Cilla sucked in a breath and clapped her hand over her mouth.

Anne Stansbury scowled at her. "What's the matter, Miss Thornton?"

"Tomorrow is Friday the thirteenth!"

"That's superstitious nonsense! And don't you let me hear you frightening the children with it."

Chagrined, Cilla slunk in her chair, her cheeks burning. She'd never been one to challenge superstition. Spilled salt called for a pinch thrown over the left shoulder. Never walk under a ladder or turn a horseshoe upside down. She wondered what the crew thought about sailing on such a foreboding day. Ted had told her that even in peacetime, few seamen relished starting a voyage on the ominous date. Surely in wartime it was a deliberate thumbing the nose at fate.

"We have a further problem," said Anne Stansbury.

Cilla's stomach began to churn with apprehension. This voyage was not starting out as well as she'd hoped. By the muttering around her, the other escorts were having similar doubts.

Anne laughed. "Don't worry. This is something over which we do have control. It appears that nobody at CORB thought to plan activities for the children, so it will be up to us to keep them occupied and entertained." Cilla joined in the explosion of loud groans and tension-relieving laughter.

"Please. We must get on," Anne begged for their attention. "You've met Sub-Lieutenant Sutherland. He will explain the 'Abandon Ship' procedures in case we are torpedoed."

Cilla shifted uncomfortably in her chair and giggled nervously.

"God in Heaven!" the priest said. "Doesn't anyone have any good news?"

"'Fraid not," Sutherland said. "But knowing children, this should give you a chuckle." He handed each escort a piece of paper, and as they read it, they began to snicker.

Dennis Marlow exploded with laughter. "You surely don't expect that we can actually enforce these 'Rules for Children'." He read aloud.

Children must not put their heads out of portholes.

Children will not be allowed on the upper deck during the hours of darkness or when coming alongside.

Children must not climb on the ship's rails.

Before she even reached the cabin area, Cilla could hear the sounds of squabbling. Freddie, with his hair slicked down and dressed in new, short, grey trousers and a dark green jumper, flailed his arms at his sister. "Thod orf, Ruby. I don' wanna be wif no flamin' g'ewth." Ruby jumped back, avoiding a kick from his shiny new shoe. "You bet'er bloody well let me go."

Ruby protested. "I'm gonna tell on yer, Freddie."

"Stop it, you two. What's going on?"

"He won't stay wif me. He wants to go in the boys' cabin now." Ruby screeched and gave her little brother a thump on the shoulder.

Clanging bells drowned out any further protests. "Saved by the bell!" Cilla said.

"What's it for, then?" Mary wore a new skirt and jumper, with the precious hat still perched on her blonde hair. Jill, dressed in a new white cardigan over her blue frock, presumably wore dry knickers.

"It means we have to go up on deck to find our muster stations for a lifeboat drill."

Cilla and her girls were assigned to Number Three Lifeboat. A tingle of satisfaction sped down her spine, though after Anne Stansbury's admonition, Cilla wouldn't admit out loud her belief that it was a good omen.

Kitty Brown, who held no such reservation in expressing her superstitions, blurted out, "Coo! Lucky number free!"

At the far end of the deck, away from the evacuees, a knot of sailors, including Ted, stood with an older officer. He had several gold stripes on his sleeve, and by the way the sailors laughed politely at something he said, Cilla thought he must be important.

She tapped a nearby officer on the shoulder. "Excuse me. Is that the captain?" She pointed to the naval officer.

"No, Miss. That is Admiral Meacham and his staff. They're Royal Navy."

"I don't understand. Aren't you Royal Navy?"

"Oh, no, Miss." His back stiffened slightly. "The officers of the *Punjohpur* are Merchant Navy."

"I see. I didn't know there was a difference. Thank you."

The look he gave her suggested she'd committed a serious blunder.

Asian stewards walked barefoot along the deck, handing an orange life jacket to each passenger. In a flurry of swaps, everybody ended up with a life jacket that almost fit him or her. Still, some of the smallest children seemed to disappear behind the unyielding blocks of cork. Cilla wrapped the long strings around Jill's waist and tied them in a big dangling bow at the back. She gave a loud exasperated sigh and stared at the excess ties hanging down Jill's legs and dragging on the floor. "I think we shall have to cut these off."

An officer, making his way from group to group inspecting each child's jacket, stopped. "No! Don't cut the strings." He tugged on the ties at Mary's back. "They must be tied tightly in front," he said. "You can see this is particularly important with children. Otherwise they could be throttled jumping into the water or break their necks if they hit the water from any height."

Millie gasped and shot Cilla a horrified look.

"In the case of very small children, like this one," he pulled on Jill's life jacket and, as the strings came untied, she almost disappeared inside it, "it may be necessary to stuff a pillow or some clothing between the chest and the jacket. And see that the strings are secure." He moved on to the next group.

"We'll have to remember to grab a couple of pillows the next time we have this drill," said Millie and began to retie Mary into her life jacket.

Cilla wound the long strings of Jill's life preserver around her tiny waist and tied the ends firmly together in front of her.

"Do you believe that garbage?" Clint guffawed.

Cilla turned her attention to him. "What?"

"That guy's trying to tell us that fifty people are supposed to fit in that puny little boat." He pointed to one of the twelve wooden lifeboats swung by stout ropes out over the side of the ship.

"I know. I wondered about that when I saw the assignments. Your group and mine are all in together. Millie, the nurse is with us too."

"Yeah, plus three British officers and fourteen Lascars. How many is that?"

"Fifty. Just as they said. Imagine us all trussed up like sausages in these miserably hard life jackets, sharing those wooden seats." She felt no joy in her giggle.

"It'll never happen." Clint dismissed the whole ridiculous idea with a flick of his hand.

"Well, let's just pray we don't have to put it to the test."

Cilla turned her attention to the sailors checking tins of condensed milk, corned beef, sardines, ship's biscuits and water. She craned to see over the heads of the children as the crew packed the provisions, blankets, flashlights, signalling flags and tools back in the locker of each lifeboat.

The 'Abandon Ship' drill went well until, for practice, two of the lifeboats were loaded with children and lowered over the side.

A howl burst from one small girl on the deck. "Larry, Larry," she screeched and ran toward the disappearing lifeboat.

A crewman scooped her up, but she fought and kicked to get free. "I want to go with my brother."

Her screams alerted others. As if on cue, several more children began to wail at the sudden realisation they were assigned to a different lifeboat than a brother or sister.

Cilla did a quick check of her girls. Only Ruby and her little brother, Freddie, had different lifeboat assignments. The thought must have already crossed Ruby's mind. Her black eyes blazed as she glared at Cilla through her fringe of black hair.

CHAPTER FOUR

Ted rested his arms on the railing aft of the promenade deck and sniffed the distinctive mixture of bunker-C, creosote and hemp. The reek was as familiar to his senses as the constant dockside racket. The roar of machines, iron and steel clanging, the hiss of welding arcs and the sudden punctuation of staccato riveting-guns filled the air in a frenzied pace.

Approaching rhythmic boot steps echoed above the din, and a contingent of marching sailors in stark white webbing belts and gaiters marched into view.

"Guard. Halt!" Boot leather crashed against concrete, resounding like a blacksmith's anvil. On command, the armed sailors took the place of those who guarded the entrances to the offices crowding the edge of the shipyards. Fixed bayonets glinting in the sun, the old guard, relieved from watch, marched away.

Shore duty was all right for some, but not for Ted Evans. He loved the sea and everything connected with it. He turned, and leaning back on his elbows against the railing, studied the *Punjohpur*. She had a graceful yacht-like hull, a raked and rounded stern, two tapering masts and two elliptical funnels. Even in her buff and black wartime camouflage, she was a beautiful vessel

He checked his watch. It would soon be dark, and he wondered if Cilla would even come. He couldn't blame her if she didn't. Furious at seeing her come aboard, he had, as usual, handled it all wrong. He should never have yelled at her in front of the kids and ordered her to meet him. He really hoped she'd come. He wanted to apologise, but more than that, he was desperate to make her to go home. He'd have to be careful how he approached her. She was so bloody stubborn.

Sailors crammed on the deck of a ship in the adjacent berth suddenly began cat-calling and whistling. Ted turned to see the object of their interest making her way along the deck toward him. A smile tugged at the corners of his mouth.

Cilla's usual peaches and cream complexion glowed red and rosy under the admiration of several hundred sailors. Ted didn't blame them. She really was incredibly sexy and attractive, and one of the things he'd always loved about her was that she didn't flaunt it, like some others.

"Cilla." He took her hands and studied her lovely dark blue eyes. "Thanks for coming. I wasn't sure you would after the way I yelled at you this morning."

The wolf whistles grew intense.

She pulled her hands from his and, smoothing her long honey blonde hair clasped as the nape of her neck, glanced at the ship beside them. "Can we go somewhere else?"

He couldn't suppress a grin at her embarrassment.

"You sadist!" she hissed. "You're enjoying this, aren't you?"

"Every bit as much as they are. Come on, let's go on the other side." As he took her elbow and turned her away from the railing, he stretched his arm over the side of the ship and gave the cheering matelots the 'two-finger salute.'

Once they were out of their sight behind the bulkhead, the jeering subsided.

"Why does that ship have such a large crew, anyway?"

"They're not crew, they're passengers going to Canada. The Americans are trading us Caribbean bases for fifty obsolete destroyers. That mob will crew them back to Britain."

"Oh, I see." She turned to face him. "Sorry I took so long. The girls had to have baths before I could get them settled in their beds. They're probably asleep now. All the children were so tired after being kept awake every night with air-raids. Anyway, they had a marvellous dinner. Crikey, you should have seen the massive helpings of ice cream they put away. And..."

"Cilla! Stop rattling on and tell me what you're doing here. I thought you agreed to give up the idea of escorting these kids." It was an effort to keep the frustration out of his voice.

"I didn't agree to any such thing." Her eyes widened and she pursed her lips. "I never intended to give up the idea."

"Oh, so you were just placating me."

"That's not true. I didn't tell you I would. I honestly didn't think I'd be accepted because of my age, and if you remember, that's what I said."

"Look, let's not get cheesed off at each other."

"I'm not angry. You are. You're cheesed off because I didn't do what you wanted me to."

"I'm not angry, I'm worried about you and I don't know how to convince you that the Atlantic Ocean is a dangerous place, full of mines and U-boats."

"Well, if it's dangerous for me, then it's as dangerous for the children. So

don't lecture me. Anyway, it's too late now. I'm committed and I'm here."
She leaned her arms on the ship's railing and stared off into the distance.

On the deck of the *Punjohpur*, in the gathering dusk, Ted studied Cilla's
profile. Over the years he'd watched her face evolve from chubby baby cheeks
and button nose, to high-rounded cheek-bones and a small, straight nose.
She'd always had beautiful wide, innocent eyes and full lips that smiled
easily. She wasn't smiling now, and it seemed like aeons, not days, had passed
since they'd had this same argument. He had no idea what she was thinking
and didn't know if he could explain his anxiety for her safety.

One of the qualities he'd always liked about her was her independence,
but she'd gone beyond independence. That bloody stubbornness could kill
her. He inwardly shuddered at the thought. Everyone on the ship faced the
same danger. He couldn't do anything about all those little kids sleeping
below decks, but he could still do something about getting her out of harm's
way, if only she'd listen to him. She was always headstrong, but he'd give it
one more try.

"You know, Cilla. Until the ship sails, you can still change your mind.
Nobody will think any less of you."

"Don't be so daft! I told you I have no intention of changing my mind."
She didn't even turn from the railing.

He chewed on his lower lip and shook his head at her. "Will you at least
think about it overnight? We don't sail until noon."

"For God's sake, Ted! Give it up! If you have nothing more to say to me,
I'm going to bed. I'm really tired." She started to turn away.

"Yeah, you do look knackered, but please, don't go yet."

"Well, all right. But no more nagging." She sighed and leaned back against
the railing. "Actually, I saw myself in a mirror earlier today. I look pretty
awful." She grinned and looked over her shoulder at him. "Wouldn't my
mother do her nut if she could see me?"

He leaned over the railing beside her and stared off at the horizon. "How
do your parents feel about this?" He glanced over at her and let out a controlled
breath. It was all he could do to keep his voice level and act as if his insides
weren't churning with apprehension. He wanted to wrap his arms around
her. To let her know how very much he loved and how desperate he was to
keep her from going on this dangerous journey. In her present mood, though,
this was neither the time nor the place.

She smiled and shrugged her shoulders. "They weren't happy about it, of
course, but they still love me." A pleasant laugh erupted from her. "Dad's

always proud of everything and anything I do. And you know Mum. But she'll get over it. I'd bet she'll be down at the next Ladies Guild telling all the old dears..." Cilla drew herself up to her full five foot three inches, looked down her nose, and in a perfect imitation of her mother, said, "My daughter, Priscilla, is engaged in important war-work."

Ted chuckled. He'd seen Mrs. Thornton in that same pose many times. "Do Nigel and Trevor know?" he asked.

"What...? Oh, no. How could they? It all happened so fast."

"Your brothers would've tried to talk you out of it, too."

"Yes, I know. You're all *so* protective of little Priscilla."

"Don't be sarcastic, Cilla. We care about you. Is that so terrible?"

He ran the back of his hand along her cheek and gently kissed her lips. She didn't object, but she didn't return his kiss, and he thought they were more like new acquaintances than childhood friends who had shared their first tentative sexual awakenings as teenagers. Not that he'd ever got very far with her, and if he knew her as well as he thought he did, no other bloke had either. "So you're still cheesed off at me, then?"

"No, I'm not. I just don't want you, or anyone else for that matter, telling me how to run my life. I can make my own decisions."

The determined way she tilted her head made him back off. His efforts to make her see reason only made her angrier. "Well, if you're not cheesed off at me, why won't you kiss me?"

Cilla ignored the question. "Does that noise ever stop?" She indicated the frenzied activity on the dock.

"No. They work around the clock. We've lost so many ships lately they can't keep up with the demand for more."

Her quick smile showed the irony hadn't escaped her.

A cool breeze blew across the deck. "Brrr." She hugged herself.

"Are you cold?" He wrapped his arms around her and he felt her stiffen her back under his touch. Perhaps after all it was a good thing she was here with him on this voyage. It would give him the opportunity to tell her again how much he loved her and to propose properly before they reached Halifax.

The remains of the day slid into the horizon, and the first star appeared.

Cilla clenched her teeth in frustration. Oh, damn! It was so unfair. Why did he have to be on this ship? It would have been so much easier if he'd sailed away unaware that she'd gone to Canada. He hadn't mentioned any more about them getting married. Now she wasn't sure if he was serious or just blurted out the proposal in the heat of trying to persuade her to give up

CORB.

"Cilla," he breathed into her hair.

Darkness descended over the dockyards of Liverpool. Lights disappeared behind blackouts, and Cilla could just make out Ted's features as he lowered his lips to hers. Wrapped in his arms, feeling the strength of his body pressed against hers, she couldn't help responding. She weakened and returned his kiss.

"Who's there?" a male voice demanded. Unseen and unheard amid the commotion on the docks, a figure had approached.

Ted dropped his arms to his side and stiffened his spine. "Leading Signalman Evans, sir."

Captain Stephen Near, master of the *Punjohpur,* peered at Cilla, then at Ted. "Are you on my crew, Evans?"

"No, sir. I'm on Admiral Meacham's staff. Sir, this is Miss Priscilla Thornton. We're neighbours at home."

"Good evening, Miss Thornton. I trust you won't make a habit of going about my ship without your life-jacket."

"Oh, no Captain. I thought since we were still in port..."

"Humph." The captain clasped his hands behind his back and continued on his way.

"Goodnight, sir." Ted called after the receding shadow.

"I must go, Ted." Cilla rubbed the top of her arms. "It's turning chilly and I need to check on my girls."

"So you've a whole new collection of girls to call your own, eh?"

"Yes. The oldest is fifteen and the youngest is just a baby, really. She's only five. It's a terrible thing their parents have had to do."

"It's a terrible thing you do."

"Don't start that again!"

"Oh, all right! Come on. I'll walk you back."

They walked in silence to the corridor leading to the evacuee quarters. He stopped. "This is as far as I'm allowed to go."

"Well, goodnight, then," she said, still seething.

He pulled her to him and kissed her lightly on the forehead, just as her dad always did. "Goodnight, pet," he said and turned abruptly and hurried away.

Cilla slowly walked to her cabin, wondering how she and Ted had arrived at the point where he couldn't even kiss her and she couldn't even let him.

CHAPTER FIVE

Captain Near walked the decks of his ship in the evenings, weather and work permitting. He'd never been slim, but in the last couple of years as his sandy-red hair thinned and turned to grey, he'd noticed a thickening of his waist. He hoped this limited walking would help to halt the spread of his middle. This time alone also gave him time to think, and tonight he had a great deal on his mind. He took one more turn around the deck, then checked in with the bridge before making his way to the wardroom.

"Cha, sah?" The Asian steward, dark and impressive in his starched white jacket and trousers, cocked his head and smiled deferentially at the captain.

"Yes, thank you, Cootay."

The door opened, and First Officer James Darroch, with his ever-present briar clenched between his teeth, came through. "Hello, Captain." He swung into a chair across from the skipper, calling to the steward. "Make that two, Cootay."

"Very well, sah." The steward gave a compliant bow and disappeared into the galley.

"How'd it go, sir?" He removed the unlit pipe and placed it on the table.

"She's in great shape," the captain said.

The *Punjohpur* had just undergone a full overhaul for renewal of her passenger certificate. Her machinery, boilers and emergency generator were all checked over. Her lifeboat's equipment examined and each boat tested by lowering into the water.

The steward deposited two mugs of steaming tea on the table.

"What's the Old Man like?" Jim Darroch splashed evaporated milk from a tin into his cup and stirred in a spoonful of sugar.

"The admiral? He's a stuffy bastard. Knows it all." The captain, Chief Engineer and First Radio Officer had met Admiral Benjamin Meacham for the first time that afternoon, at the convoy conference at the local Admiralty offices in the Royal Liver Building. The captain smiled wryly at his friend. "You know the type. Retired from active service eight years ago, but the

Royal Navy is so desperate for officers, they've called him back to service. Now he thinks the navy can't manage without him." The captain leaned his elbows on the table and cupped his hands around the mug.

"Is he the cause of the frown? You look like thunder." Darroch lifted his cup of scalding hot tea to his lips and blew across it.

Captain Near stared at his friend's rugged face. His skin was coarse and deep wrinkles—the product of years of squinting at thousands of horizons—etched themselves around his bright blue eyes. His thinning white hair had been fair when they first met as fifteen-year-old naval cadets. Over the years their paths crossed and recrossed until the present arrangement had evolved. It suited them both perfectly. They had a mutual trust and respect for each other's competency, but Darroch still always called the captain "sir." The captain thought Darroch should have had his own command long ago, but the First Officer was happy being just "Number One."

The skipper shook his head. "Was I frowning? Oh, well...the admiral's only part of the problem. It's not his fault, but our escort will be limited to 17 degrees West."

"Christ a'mighty! That'll leave us right in the middle o' the bloody U-boat activity with no destroyers for protection." Even after an absence of forty years, Jim Darroch's speech still reflected his West Highland roots.

"Yes, but the navy just has too few ships to escort the convoys, and sailing a day late will cost us a day of protection. But it can't be helped." He shrugged. "The escort is scheduled to rendezvous at 22.00 hours on the sixteenth, with a convoy from Halifax. I don't have to tell you the incoming convoy needs all the protection the Royal Navy can give it to get through the Western Approaches."

It was no secret that the German submarines operating out of captured bases on the Bay of Biscay and taking advantage of the Irish 'neutrality' were able to range far into the Atlantic.

Near thumped his fist on the table, and the mugs wobbled, sloshing tea over the side. His stomach had been in knots since he'd received his orders from the Admiralty.

"I'd feel a lot more confident about this whole voyage if our passengers weren't little children. And on top of that there's the added responsibility of the *Punjohpur* leading the convoy."

Darroch wagged his head. "Aye, Captain. And I'm glad it's no' my responsibility. But the convoy will disperse when the escort leaves. Then we can make a run for it, alone."

The captain's shoulders sagged. "No, Number One. The orders are to disperse the convoy at mid-day on the seventeenth."

"The seventeenth? Wait a wee while! They mean to keep us in convoy for fourteen hours without an escort?"

The captain blew out a long breath, nodding. "It's just a bloody cock-up any way you look at it, Jim." He swallowed a mouthful of tea. "If we could take off alone and maintain our full speed, no bloody U-boat could catch us, submerged or on the surface. But holding the *Punjohpur's* speed down to accommodate the slowest vessel in the convoy...I don't know."

"Aye, and I just saw the list of convoy ships. My God, Sir. It's as though they scraped the bottom of the barrel to come up with that fleet of tramps, whalers and banana boats."

"You aren't far wrong, Jim. Have you seen the tonnage lost in the last month?" He slowly shook his head. "Just since June over three hundred and fifty ships have been sunk off the top of Ireland alone. If these losses continue, we'll be down to using fishing trawlers."

"Sah?" The Lascar fidgeted at the captain's side. His eyes were wide.

"What is it, Cootay?"

"Air-raid, topside, sah."

"Thank you, Cootay. We're as safe here as anywhere."

The steward scurried away into the galley, and the captain returned his attention to Darroch, who absent-mindedly jammed the pipe-stem back between his teeth and chewed on it.

"Who the hell dreamed up this hare-brained scheme to send thousands o' kids across the Atlantic in the middle o' war, anyway, Skipper? And what the hell is wrong wi' the parents to agree to it?"

"Ah, you can't blame them, Jim. With the invasion imminent and the damn blitz, they're desperate to save their kids. But I think the government duped them."

The First Officer frowned. "How?"

"You know how the British feel about the Royal Navy? British tradition— the Senior Service and all that? Well, the parents of the evacuees were assured that the Royal Navy would safeguard their children, and I doubt many of them would have even considered sending their kids overseas without that reassurance."

"How do you know?" Darroch frowned.

"My youngest daughter brought home a letter from school about this CORB plan to send children to the Dominions."

"Ye didna' want her to go?"

"I'd as soon put her hands in a fire! And the letter said the children would not travel in convoy with military personnel or weapons, and they'd have a naval escort all the way. With the admiral and his staff and the navy gunners on board, we're a bloody war ship, not a passenger liner. And the convoy ships are carrying troops."

"No wonder you're frowning, Captain."

Startled by a terrible thought, the captain's head snapped up and his shoulders straightened. "My God, Jim! The government couldn't deliberately be sending children on warships in hopes that the Germans won't attack, could they?"

"Using bairns as shields, Captain?" Darroch shook his head. "Oh, no. They wouldna' do such a callous thing."

"You can bet Jerry knows all about the scheme, and it would certainly account for their being less concern about the safety of our passengers than for the incoming convoy."

"I canna' believe such a thing." Jim Darroch pulled the pipe from his mouth, drained the last of his tea and stood up.

"Good-night, Captain."

"Good-night, Number One, and thanks for the ear."

Darroch nodded and swung out the door.

Millie slept soundly in the bunk below, but Cilla lay wide-awake with her thoughts in a tangle of the day's happenings. She was deprived of sleep during the air raids and physically exhausted, but her fears kept her awake.

She would never admit it to Ted, of course. She was much too stubborn for that, but she had begun to have misgivings earlier during the 'Abandon Ship' drill. The children's terrified screams as their siblings in the lifeboats disappeared over the side of the ship finally registered the enormity of what she was undertaking.

She thought of asking Ted tonight to tell her more about the torpedoed evacuation ship, but she didn't want him to know she'd even given his warnings a second thought. That would only have given him a reason to start nagging at her again.

The children had reached the point of no return. Little Jill, and Mary in her battered school hat. Cockney Kitty. And Pamela Merryman, shapely and mature beyond her fifteen years. Ruby, her little brother Freddie, and all the rest were counting on the adults, and she was determined not to let them see her apprehension. There would be the inevitable homesickness, for her as much as for them, but whatever they experienced, she would, too. She would not let Ted and his paranoia keep her from honouring her commitment.

Having settled that argument to her satisfaction, she settled more comfortably into the unfamiliar narrow bunk and allowed her thoughts to wander to what she hoped would be the best part of the voyage.

Ted. She'd loved him for as long as she could remember. He and his parents had moved into the house next door to Cilla's family just before she was born, and he was just a toddler. He'd gone to sea as a fifteen-year-old cadet, and she'd been devastated thinking he was gone from her life forever. Life in the Royal Navy agreed with him. He grew from a good-looking little boy into a tall, handsome man with ruggedly chiselled features and a devastating cleft in his chin. The ocean winds and sun had bronzed his sinewy arms and lightened his thick hair that tumbled over his forehead.

It's true they had grown apart for awhile, but since the war began and he'd come home to see his mother more often, Cilla discovered her schoolgirl crush on him had turned to passion. She wasn't aware of when his feelings for her had turned to love, but she had no doubt they were genuine. She didn't doubt either that he was serious about marrying her. She just wasn't going to be coerced, she told her self defiantly. Volunteering for CORB had given her the opportunity to see something of the world before she settled down, and she intended to make the most of it. She snuggled closer in her blankets and wondered if she would take another assignment if CORB offered it.

She had told Ted that her parents weren't happy about her decision to cross the Atlantic in war-time. That was a bit of an understatement! Her father had supported her decision right from the start, but her mother was not as stoic.

Cilla had applied to CORB even though she thought they'd turn her down as being too young. The letter telling her she had been "selected for duty" arrived the day after Ted left, and gave her only forty-eight hours to get to Liverpool.

Her mother had whimpered, "Priscilla, how can you think of doing such a thing? Isn't it enough that your brothers have had to go to fight this dreadful war? Tell these CORB people you've changed your mind. Please, don't go, Priscilla." After her mother had used all her arguments and left Cilla completely overcome with guilt, she stomped off up to her bedroom. She didn't appear again until it was time for Cilla to leave for Liverpool.

At the train station, her mother had lifted the veil of her funny hat and dabbed her brown eyes with a lace handkerchief. "Oh, Priscilla," she wailed, "do be careful, darling, won't you?"

Cilla's father, wearing his best navy-blue suit and white shirt, shook his head and rolled his eyes skyward as if pleading to heaven. "Leave the girl alone, Maude. She's made her decision." He gave Cilla's shoulder a reassuring squeeze.

Cilla stepped back to see tears glistening in her father's deep blue eyes. He was of medium build but always carried himself erect, making him seem especially tall. His once thick, wavy blonde hair had turned grey in the last couple of years, and a definite bare spot shone on his crown. Rimless spectacles seldom left his straight nose. She wrapped her arms around his neck, grateful for that special father-daughter bond they'd always shared. "Oh, Dad. I do love you."

He folded Cilla in his arms and hugged her to him, as he had done when she was a little girl. He'd kissed her forehead and whispered, "I'm not sure this is an entirely safe venture, Cilla." He held her at arm's length, his eyes searching hers. "But I'm very proud of you. Mum and I will miss you, love, but we raised you to be independent, and I'm sure you're quite capable of taking care of yourself."

"Of course, Dad. I'll be fine." She'd turned from him and gave her mother a hug. "Mum, please don't cry. Be happy for me. I'm off to see a bit of the world."

"That's what frightens me." Her mother's voice rose, drawing the attention of several people standing nearby. "Having you go off to the ends of the earth in charge of somebody else's children. We don't even know where you're going, let alone when you'll come home again." She smoothed her cornflower-blue dress over her plump hips.

"Mum, please keep your voice down." Cilla kept her voice low but firm.

"Yes, Maude," her father whispered, "do be quiet. People aren't supposed to know about the overseas evacuations. You could be endangering Priscilla's life."

Her mother's tear-filled eyes widened, and her long, tortured wail was swallowed up in the sudden whistle from the train engine.

Pushing her suitcase in ahead of her, Cilla jumped into the compartment and slammed the door. She let down the window and leaned out. The train shunted, then stalled and finally began to roll. "Goodbye," she had called, "cheerio," and blew one last kiss before the train picked up speed.

Tears began to gather in the corners of her eyes. She knew the worry and anxiety her parents would suffer until their only daughter was safely back in England and felt sorry for that.

Would her brothers have attempted to talk her out of it? She'd never know now. Nigel was somewhere in the Middle East, an officer with the Royal Artillery, and eighteen-year-old Trevor was in flight training with the Royal Air Force. They had no choice but to serve when called into the forces, but she had volunteered for what could turn out to be hazardous duty!

CHAPTER SIX

Friday the 13th! Cilla shivered as much from the ominous date as the cold wind that blew up the River Mersey from the bay.

The *Punjohpur* moved into the river and anchored early in the day. The evacuees' anticipation built, but as the scheduled departure of noon came and went, the children became increasingly agitated. Some were wild with exhilaration, others emotional with homesickness.

Then, as the day drew to a close, a flurry of activity signalled the final preparations for the ship's sailing with the next tide.

Cilla leaned over the deck railing watching canvas bags of mail being tossed from the ship into a small motorboat. Among them was her letter to her parents and the quick note she had written to the headmistress of St. Margaret's.

The children's biggest concern about the letters they wrote was that their parents wouldn't find reason to fault their spelling and grammar. Mary wasn't taking any chances and had asked Cilla to check her letter for spelling.

> *Dear Mum and Dad,*
>
> *It is very lovely here on the ship. I wish you were here with us. We have lots of dark men from Bombay to clean our shoes and clean our room for us. They do all the work when we are on deck. You have to laugh at the way they are dressed. Some have their shirts hanging out. They have no shoes. Some wait on us when we go into a big room for meals and we have silver knives and forks, table napkins and three different kinds of knives and forks. We have a menu card in which we can choose what we like off the card. There are about a dozen different things on it.*
>
> *We had our photo taken as we were coming on the boat. Our boat is in the middle of the river. We are eager to start off.*
>
> *While we were on the boat last night there were two air-raid warnings, but we were asleep.*

Me and Jill are sharing a cabin with another girl called Pamela.
She is fifteen. She is a bit posh but very nice.
I will write to you again when we reach Halifax.
Your loving daughter, Mary

Across the bottom of the page, Mary had carefully added a row of Xs.

A smile tugged at the corners of Cilla's mouth as she remembered Mary's observation of the Asian stewards. The polite and helpful Lascars had completely disarmed the children by pushing their chairs up to white linen-covered tables. The array of eating utensils confused most of the evacuees, but having choices off a menu delighted them. After wartime rations of eight ounces of sugar, eight ounces of fats, one egg, two ounces of cheese, a couple of ounces of bacon per week per person, each meal aboard was a banquet. Having meat at every meal astonished the children.

A sudden bustling and commanding shouts startled Cilla and brought her from her thoughts. The mail boat revved its motor and shot across to the dock. The *Punjohpur's* engines vibrated, and the watertight doors slammed shut. Deck stewards scurried along the boat deck swinging the lifeboats to the outboard position, and as the ship slewed her bow toward the bay, the air became charged with frenzied suspense.

The *Punjohpur* moved slowly down the River Mersey, and the children, caught up in excited anticipation, shouted to dockworkers and waved at the sailors on ships still anchored in the harbour. Cheering echoed back at them. Tugs sounded their horns. Somewhere aft, a group of children began singing "Wish Me Luck As You Wave Me Goodbye." The song was picked up by successive groups of children. By the time they got to "Roll Out The Barrel," they were all singing at the top of their lungs.

"So much for not letting the enemy know of our departure," Cilla said to Anne Stansbury. They had come to Liverpool under sealed orders and sworn to secrecy.

Infected by the excitement, Anne and Cilla waved and joined in the singing, and for the time being, Cilla forgot her earlier trepidation.

The proud *Punjohpur*, her pennants flying in the stiff breeze, followed the channel down the Mersey. As if to make amends for the grey blustery day, the setting sun reflected off the clouds and touched the water with a rosy glow. Cilla looked back and glimpsed the gilded birds atop the twin spires of the Liver Building, gleaming in the sun's last rays.

"Red sky at night, sailor's delight," she pointed at the sky. "We'll have good weather for the voyage."

Anne studied the pink-tinged clouds. "It certainly looks promising. Well, I must be off. 'Bye, Cilla."

A minute later Freddie let out an excited whoop.

"Look! Look Mith Fawnton. It floath juth like they thaid it would." He stood on the railing holding the top rung by one hand and pointing at the water with the other. A melon-slice grin lit his face, while his life jacket bobbed away on a swell.

"Freddie! Oh, no! Your life jacket!" Cilla screeched at the boy. "Get down off that railing at once, you little monkey!"

Freddie jumped to the deck and scurried away, laughing.

Cilla drew a deep breath to calm her pounding heart. If the children got up to this much mischief before the ship even got to sea, the staff were going to have their hands full.

A hand settled on her shoulder.

"Hi, are you ready for our great adventure?" Clint Jennison flashed her his perfect smile.

"Hello, Clint, I haven't seen much of you since we got on board."

"Yeah, well, it's been a bit hectic getting settled, and one of my kids might have chicken pox. I had to get him checked into the sick-bay." He sagged against the railing in exaggerated fatigue. "I'm beat. I got raked in for organising a boxing match for the boys this afternoon." He straightened. "Anyway, how are you, Cilla? What have you been up to?"

"I'm fine, but tired. We organised games for the girls this afternoon, too." She laughed. "But I thank God for the dear man who sent us all those games and toys."

"Yeah. Typical government operation…this CORB thing. Trust them to forget the most important part—occupying the kids. Where'd all that stuff come from anyway?"

"I heard it came from Marks and Spencers. We are so lucky. Things like boxing gloves, skipping ropes, and especially playing cards and notebooks have been as scarce as hen's teeth since the beginning of the war. Whew!" She propped herself against the deck railing. "I'm knackered after the workout I had playing ball with the girls this afternoon. And now I know why the CORB interviewers were concerned with my agility! I expect we'll spend most of the voyage organising or supervising games."

"Yeah, I guess so."

Cilla chuckled. "You don't sound very enthusiastic, Clint."

He shrugged. "Playing nursemaid to a bunch of kids is not how I planned to spend my time on this voyage."

"Really. I thought that's what we signed on for."

He gave her a sidelong glance without responding.

The sun had disappeared behind the clouds, and when the ship moved out of the Mersey and into Liverpool Bay, the wind picked up and the sea turned choppy.

"It's turned cold." Cilla hugged herself. "We'd better begin to round up this mob before it gets dark and get them inside where we can keep an eye on them," she said.

"Yeah, okay." Clint levered himself wearily from the railing, then brightened and turned to Cilla. "Hey, want to take a walk around the deck later?"

She hesitated. If Ted saw her with Clint, it would only make things between them that much worse. She shrugged. That was nonsense. The American had asked only that she join him for a stroll around the deck. Besides, how could he possibly see her on the passenger deck? "Yes, all right. I'll meet you here after I get the girls settled."

"Yeah, I gotta get the terrorists to bed, too. See you here in about forty-five minutes."

Settling the children was easier said than done. Many of them, keyed up with excitement, bounced off the walls. Others were feeling the effects of too much ice cream and rough sea. Cilla braced herself for a night comforting seasick girls.

"I expect Clint will be having the same problem with his boys, so it won't matter if I don't show up."

"You don't have to stay, Cilla," Millie said. "If the kids are going to get seasick, I'll take care of them. After all, that's what I was hired for."

"You can't manage them all by yourself."

"Don't be silly. Go on. You'll be spending plenty of time with the children before we get to Canada. Besides, nobody is actually sick yet. Take the break while you have the chance."

"All right. Thanks, Millie. To tell you the truth, I'm curious about Clint."

"Oh?" Millie's eyebrows arched.

"No. Not in that way. I mean I'm curious about what he's doing here. Millie, don't you think it's funny that a healthy young man like Clint isn't in uniform? That's what struck me about him when we first met at the train station."

"Did you travel with him?"

"No, the hostel people sent him to meet me. Right from the start, he seemed so self-centred. Not the sort of bloke you'd expect to find looking after children. He has some other reason, and I'd like to know what it is."

"Well, go on with you, then. I'd like to know about the mysterious Mr. Jennison, too."

Cilla struggled into her life jacket, adjusting it over her coat. "Cor, I can hardly move in this bloomin' thing. Wish we didn't have to wear them all the time."

"Well, at least we don't have to sleep in them."

"That's a blessing since the captain says we have to sleep fully clothed. But I don't like the sound of that."

"Oh, I'm sure it's just a precaution. Off you go, then."

"I won't be gone long, Millie. Cheerio."

The sea turned rougher. The middle of the ship remained relatively steady, but on the outer deck Cilla had difficulty keeping her balance. She doubted Clint would be waiting outside, but if he wasn't on deck, she'd go to the lounge and get a cup of tea. Sooner or later, she intended to get answers to the questions that had bothered her since she'd first seen him on the platform at Liverpool station.

She'd been excited but very nervous when the train huffed in, and before it even lurched to a stop, the carriage was a flurry of activity. Passengers lifted suitcases from the racks above their heads or dragged bags from beneath their seats.

Her anxiety heightened when she seemed to be the only one who didn't know where she was. There were no station markers. They'd all been removed, along with the street signs and village signposts, in preparation for the expected German invasion. It was meant to confuse the enemy, but even schoolboys reckoned the Germans were bound to have pre-war maps.

"Is this Liverpool?" she said to a naval officer sitting opposite her. He seemed comfortable with the surroundings.

"Aye, lassie. Liverpool it is." He grabbed the broad leather strap to let down the window and in one smooth movement opened the door. He hefted his kit-bag and stepped out, to be swallowed into the sea of uniforms spilling onto the platform.

Cilla's long hair had come loose from its clasp at the nape of her neck, but the crush of people trying to get past her to the open door prevented her from refastening it. Pushing the unruly strands over her shoulder, she grabbed her suitcase and eased onto the platform. The first whiff of salt air, laced with the coal dust from the train, sent a tingle of excitement coursing through her. She looked about, needing to find the 'Ladies' to wash the train-grit from her hands and to smarten up before she searched for a telephone kiosk to call the hostel. She had no idea how to get there, even if she knew how to find it.

"Miss Thornton? Miss Priscilla Thornton?"

At the sound of her name spoken by a silky American voice, Cilla spun around. "Yes."

He was absolutely gorgeous—an Adonis. He towered over Cilla. He was deeply tanned, and his navy-blue blazer and silk ascot set off his tawny hair and astonishingly green eyes to their best advantage.

Flustered, Cilla smoothed her hair and quickly trapped most of it in the fastener.

"Hi. I'm Clint Jennison." A wide smile exposed a perfect set of teeth. "The folks at the hostel asked me to meet you."

A half-smile that didn't quite reach his eyes confirmed that he was quite aware of the impression he created.

Feeling gauche and unsure of herself, Cilla stuck out a grimy hand. "Hello. You're from the hostel?"

"Yeah. It's a madhouse tonight." He shook her hand. "They're expecting a bunch of kids in tomorrow so they're pretty busy organising sleeping arrangements." He reached for her suitcase and lifted it as though it were empty.

"But aren't you an American? I don't understand."

"I'm an escort, too. This way." He steered her out of the station. "We'll have to walk, but it isn't far. Just a couple of blocks." He sounded just like the American movie stars...

As she stepped through the hatchway onto the deck, a sharp gust of wind snatched her breath. She grabbed the bulkhead to steady herself and turned into the gale.

Clint stood at the railing, his hands jammed deep in the pockets of his camel-hair overcoat and his chin tucked down into the top of his life jacket. He stared out at the whitecaps.

Cilla yelled as she came up beside him. "The ocean looks really stormy. I've never been to sea before. I wonder if it always gets like this at night."

Clint turned to her. Utter misery clouded his face, and he didn't look nearly as handsome with a red nose. His purple-tinged ears protruded above his upturned collar. "Jesus, if I'd known it would be like this, I'd have opted to stay in London and take my chances with the goddam bombs."

Cilla fought her hair against the wind and grinned at him. "You look completely frozen. Come on. Let's go inside and get a cup of tea." She slipped her hand in the crook of his arm and clung to him as the wind forced them into a run.

Once inside the warm public room, Clint became his charming self again, asking Cilla about her family, but she had the distinct feeling that he wasn't really listening to her. He gazed around the room making eye-contact and smiling at the other women escorts.

Turning the conversation to Clint, a subject of much more interest to him, Cilla said, "I still don't understand how you came to volunteer as an escort for the evacuees."

"It's simple. I got stuck in London and couldn't get back to the States. So, I volunteered to escort kids to Canada 'cause I figured I can get home from there."

"Did you tell the CORB people that?"

"Hell, no. CORB pulled a fast one on me, anyway. They didn't tell me I'd have to amuse fifteen snot-nosed boys all by myself. Geez! I don't know the first thing about kids. I figured I'd just have to, you know—be there." He shrugged. "Aah! What the hell. Each knot or mile, or whatever that we sail, is that much closer to home. It's gotta be better than being trapped in London with falling bombs."

"How did you come to get stuck in London, then?"

"I went over in June of thirty-nine on a one-year contract. By the time June of forty rolled around, the war was in full swing and I couldn't book passage back to the States."

"What do you do for a living, Clint?"

He flashed her a brilliant smile. "I'm an actor." He threw back his head and laughed loudly. "I should have got an Academy Award for my performance in persuading the CORB folks to take me on."

Cilla glared at him. He was exactly the opposite of what CORB told her they wanted. During her own interview, they had stressed their choices be dedicated, have some experience in dealing with young children, and not be along just for the joy-ride—or looking for a cheap passage home. She glared, thoroughly disgusted with him.

He shrugged. "You don't approve. Well, you know how it is. If you don't look out for number one, nobody else will."

Completely turned off, Cilla rose from her seat. "I'd better be getting back. Some of the girls were beginning to get seasick before I left."

He followed her. "Yeah, I turned a couple of kids over to the doc before I left. Damned if I was going to clean up their puke."

Cilla hurried along the corridor to her cabin. "Goodnight, Clint," she said over her shoulder.

He swung her around and crushed his lips to hers. His kiss was warm and well-practised. Completely unexpected, it caught Cilla off guard.

"We'll have to do something about meeting somewhere where we don't have to wear these passion-killers." He chuckled, indicating their life jackets.

"That won't be necessary," she snapped.

A movement in the shadows at the end of the corridor caught her eye. In the dim light, she saw Ted's scowling profile before he turned and left

CHAPTER SEVEN

On the bridge of the *Punjohpur*, Ted leaned on his signal-lamp and steadied his binoculars, staring where the dark sea merged into an equally black sky. He lowered the glasses and, letting them hang around his neck, rubbed his gloved hands together to restart the circulation through his fingers.

Overhead the mast rolled through a slow arc against the night sky. The wind suddenly blew the clouds apart, and moonlight bathed the ship in a clear bluish glow. Visible in that brief illumination, Admiral Meacham, braced against the railing, stared through his binoculars, and Captain Near leaned far over the bridge rail, as if the extra few inches would increase his vision. The Officer-of-the-Watch and two lookouts, one on either wing, peered ahead.

The cold had penetrated Ted's oilskins. He flexed his back and stamped his feet. The hollow ring of his boots against the metal grating startled him. This was not his first voyage across the Atlantic in wartime, but for the first time, he experienced real fear—not for himself, but for Cilla. Thinking about her made him remember that flaming Yank kissing her. The vision brought a flush of anger that tingled his cold cheeks. He'd have smashed his fist into that dandy's chops, except for Cilla's shocked expression. He consoled himself thinking the American had caught her completely off-guard.

First Officer Darroch turned to him. "Anything, Signals?"

"Nothing yet, sir," Ted leaned against the lamp and squinted through his binoculars.

Darroch began to whistle softly, then stopped. "Bit raw, eh?" He jammed his hands deep into his pockets and hunched his shoulders inside his duffel coat.

"Yes, sir."

"Where are you from, Signals?"

"Surrey, sir." Ted wondered at the officer's interest, but like the rest of the cold, tense men on the bridge, he was probably just trying to keep warm and alert.

"Married?"

"No, sir." His answer brought immediate thoughts of Cilla. For the hundredth time he wondered what else he could have said or done to persuade her to leave the ship before it sailed. He'd failed, but maybe having her aboard wouldn't be all bad! He made up his mind that before they reached Halifax he would have her promise to marry him when they got back to England.

He'd grown up imagining he'd marry Cilla someday. But he'd lacked the confidence to ask her, reasoning that if he didn't tell her how he felt about her, she couldn't reject him. Then the war came along, and the possibility that he might not come back from one of these voyages gave him the perfect excuse not to think about marriage. Instead, the war had matured him. Other blokes got married in spite of the war—or because of it. He regretted now his arrogance in taking it for granted she would be in England, and waiting, when he got back from this trip. He had it all planned out, until this CORB thing. Bugger!

Before the clouds refolded themselves over the pale moon, Ted glimpsed the outline of the mist-shrouded hills of the Mull of Kintyre.

Darroch began his quiet whistling again, and Ted smiled to himself as he silently put words to the tune.

"Westerin' home and a song in the air
Light in the eye and it's goodbye to care…"

"Are you from one of these islands, sir?" he ventured.

"Aye. A long time ago. This is as close as I get to it these days." The First Officer swept his arm to the right. "Islay should be away north of starboard about now, and the beautiful island of Jura beyond it." He sang softly, "*At hame wi' my ain folk in Islay.*" Then he fell silent.

The ship swept on through the North Channel between Scotland and Northern Ireland. Ted's back ached continually from leaning over the lamp, but the rolling of the ship made it impossible to focus the binoculars without steadying himself and further bruising his thighs.

Raithin Island, at the tip of Northern Ireland, where the *Punjohpur* was to rendezvous with the rest of the convoy, lay dead ahead. Suddenly a flicker of light in the distance caught his attention. He straightened. "Flashing light ahead, sir."

The men on the bridge stirred. Flurried movements in the darkness told Ted that the admiral, the captain, the First Officer and the lookouts were adjusting and focusing their binoculars to catch the flicker that he'd seen.

If it was the vessels from Bristol and the Clyde of Scotland assembling for the long uncertain journey ahead, the admiral would now take command of the *Punjohpur,* and Ted tensed for the expected order.

"Evans!" the admiral barked.

"Sir!"

"You know the challenge and response."

"Yes, sir."

"Send it."

Ted flashed the challenge signal and called out the ship's numbers as they responded in turn. Admiral Meacham's next order was a long signal about the organisation of the convoy. A mishmash of nineteen British, Dutch, Norwegian, and Greek freighters, whalers and tankers made up the convoy. The ships formed into the appointed formation of eight columns of two vessels each, and a ninth column of three, with the *Punjohpur* in the lead—the focus of the convoy—and enemy submarines.

Ted's pulse began to pound. The convoy, heading due west into the Atlantic along the Irish coast, was entering the most dangerous stretch of water in the world. Unlike the First World War when Britain had the use of Irish naval bases in Southern and Western Ireland, she now claimed neutrality. The subject came up often among the men who sailed these waters. Neutrality, like hell! Ireland allowed German ships to use her ports and U-boats to hide off her coast. His adrenaline pumped. He knew from previous crossings that he would not sleep again until the convoy had traversed these treacherous waters.

The dark silhouettes of the nearest ships were visible in the intermittent moonlight. The others stretched behind somewhere in the darkness. He strained his eyes through the binoculars for a glimpse of the navy destroyer, *HMS Royal Windsor* zigzagging two miles ahead. He couldn't see her but he knew she would be listening through the pinging of her submarine detection device for the presence of the U-boats known to lurk off the coasts between Scotland and Ireland. Two stocky sloops flanking the destroyer were the sole protection of the convoy, and Ted wondered whether their ability to depth-charge U-boats would be sufficient to fend off an attack. German submarines no longer attacked singly, nipping at the heels of defenseless ships on the edges of a convoy. They'd begun to collaborate and they weren't called wolf-packs for nothing!

Morning brought thick black clouds scudding across a pewter sky, and the wind whipped the water into foamy sea horses. The ship pitched and rolled as she sliced through the angry waves. Seasickness had taken its toll, and the dining room was almost empty at breakfast.

Cilla steadied herself against the deck railing. She swept her wind-blown hair from her face and watched Clint scolding two unruly boys. He really wasn't cut out for supervising children.

"Ain't it smashing, Miss Fawnton?" Excitement shone in Ruby's dark eyes as she skipped by. The wind moulded her coat against her thin back and blew her black hair out in front of her.

A group of boys as frisky as young colts charged along the deck, yelling into the wind.

"Slow down, boys. You'll collide with someone." They didn't even hear her warning.

One boy tripped, and laughing, they tumbled into a heap against the railing. They picked themselves up and ran on, shouting into the wind at each other. Well, at least they had their sea-legs, but it won't do them much good if they get blown overboard!

Ships of all shapes and sizes, spread out behind and on either side of the *Punjohpur,* pitched and heaved in the towering waves. Cilla sucked in a sharp breath as through the spindrift she watched one of the small ships completely disappear into a trough. Seconds elasticised into a minute before the ship popped like a cork shot from a champagne bottle back into her view, and she let out a relieved sigh.

A Lascar steward, with his arms full of bread loaves, stepped through a hatchway and onto the deck. Smiling and gesturing at the screeching seagulls circling the ship, he handed the bread to the children.

"What? Give this to the birds?" Horror and disbelief registered on Jocelyn's chubby face.

An officer, passing by, stopped and smiled at the children. "It's quite all right," he said. "We can't save what we don't eat, so it gets tossed over the side."

"What a waste of good food. Why bake so much?" Jocelyn stared at the bread, while the screeching gulls circled overhead. The officer shrugged and went on his way.

"Like this." Cilla took one of the loaves and broke off a piece. She tossed it into the air and the seabird caught it on the wing.

The children squealed. "Let me," yelled Ruby. The gulls chased the wind-tossed bread into the waves.

"Let me 'ave a go." Freddie grabbed chunks of bread and heaved them skyward.

An alarm bell clanged, signalling another lifeboat drill.

"Come on. We must get to our muster stations." The wind stole the urgency from Cilla's voice.

The evacuees knew the drill by now and saw no reason to hurry. They hung back until the greedy birds had fought over the last pieces of bread and biscuits.

The weather continued to worsen, keeping the medical staff busy. More seasickness meant fewer children to supervise. It also struck more adults, so those still on their feet had to pick up the slack.

Although the ship seemed steadier inside the middle section, the children soon discovered a rolling ship made a good excuse to cheat at Fiddlesticks.

"'Ere, that weren't my fawt," protested Kitty, the street-wise Londoner. "It was the ship rollin' wot made that stick move. Ain't that right, Miss Fawnton?"

"Narki'. You 'narf a cheat." Ruby had been watching Kitty intensely ever since she accused her of cheating earlier at Old Maid.

"Oh, do shut up, you two. Let's play snakes and ladders. You can't cheat at that." The well-spoken Jocelyn, whom Ruby referred to as "that posh g'ew," took charge.

Ruby's black eyes flashed as she pointed an accusing finger at Kitty. "Be'cher she can. But don' cher worry, I'm keeping my mince-pies on 'er."

Cilla laughed at the Cockney jargon rolling so easily from Ruby's mouth.

Millie had found the note shoved under the cabin door when they came back after breakfast. "It says *'Truce? Same time, same place tonight. Love, Ted'* Must be for you. I don't know anyone named Ted on the ship." She raised her eyebrows and grinned mischievously.

Cilla took the note and read it herself.

"Well? My curiosity's killing me. Don't keep me in suspense," Millie urged. "Who is he?" Millie egged her into confessing who Ted was and what the note meant.

"The last night of his leave we had a row about my becoming an escort. He was livid when he saw me come aboard. The night before we sailed, he tried to get me to leave the ship and was furious when I wouldn't. So I'm surprised he's so eager to make up. Especially since he saw Clint kissing me last night."

"Uh-oh! Better be careful, Cilla. I don't think this ship is big enough for you to play games with both of them."

Cilla chuckled. "Don't worry. I don't have feelings for the American. And there's no comparison between Clint and Ted. Clint is a shallow, narcissistic bloke, but he is such a handsome devil." She threw herself backwards on Millie's bunk. "But, do you know, I actually flirted with him."

"You and every other woman on this ship." Colour crept into Millie's cheeks and she giggled. "So, now that there's no turning back, are you going to patch things up with Ted?"

"I certainly hope so." She chuckled. "If he wants a truce, it will definitely make the voyage a lot more pleasant."

As night fell, the storm grew steadily worse. Cilla staggered along the corridor, bumping into the bulkheads with each roll of the ship. As she stepped through the hatchway onto promenade deck, the wind slammed her against the door and almost knocked her off her feet. She groped her way through almost total darkness, doubting as she went that Ted would actually be waiting for her in such weather.

He stood huddled next to the bulkhead with his back toward her. With his hands jammed deep into his pockets, he stamped first one foot and then the other. A chin-strap held his hat in place, and his coat collar protected his ears. Cilla came up behind him and put her arms around his waist. "Hope you didn't freeze waiting for me," she yelled above the wind.

Ted turned to her, scowling. "No, I'm as warm as toast."

She caught his sardonic look. "Whatever's the matter with you?"

"Well, how the hell do you expect me to be warm? There's a bloody gale blowing. Or are you too wrapped up in that flamin' Yank to notice?" His drawn cheeks were blue-tinged.

"So that's what you're cheesed off about. You saw me with Clint Jennison. Well, you've got a bloody cheek. If you hadn't been spying..." She cupped her hands around her mouth, directing her words at him.

"I wasn't spying on you. I was looking for you." He was almost screaming.

"You were?" Her voice rose with surprise. "Why?"

"Just tell me what he means to you." Ted raised his voice and spoke directly into Cilla's ear to make himself heard above the howling gale.

She lifted her mouth to his ear and shouted back, "He doesn't mean anything to me. He's just a friend." The ship rolled and she staggered into him, but she stepped back quickly to put distance between them.

The wind momentarily quieted. "Friends don't kiss friends the way he kissed you. Strewth, Cilla! I saw him, and if you hadn't been wearing your life jacket, who knows where it would have ended?"

"Well, I was wearing my life jacket and so was he. Nothing happened but a kiss." She screamed the last words as the wind gusted again.

"Humph! Some kiss! I thought he was going to eat you."

The wind blew her hair across her face. She tossed it away angrily, pulling strands from her mouth. "What has it got to do with you, anyway? And what's this about a truce? This doesn't sound to me like you want to make up. I'm off." She turned to go.

He yanked her to him, crushing her life jacket against his. His grip on her arms was bruising. "It has a lot to do with me." To prove it, he kissed her with much more conviction than Clint could ever have mustered. It left her breathless. "That's to prove I love you, Cilla." The wind snatched whatever else he'd said.

"What?" Her mouth had dropped open. She could feel her chin resting on her life jacket. "What did you say?" Surely, the wind had distorted his words. His grip continued on her arms like a vise.

"Let go! What's the matter with you all of a sudden, Ted?" She tried to pull away from him, but he held her firmly.

"I'm trying to..."

Whatever he said disappeared in a gust of wind, and Cilla snickered.

"Cilla? What's so funny?" He gave her a little shake. "What's the joke?"

"I can't understand you!" She had to shout over the shrieking wind. "It's just that we're yelling at the top of our lungs." She laughed. "I'm getting a sore throat shouting over this gale-force wind."

Suddenly he released his grip on her arms and, taking her hand, dragged her after him through the hatchway.

She stumbled on the sill, but he steadied her and slammed the door behind them, shutting out the gale. In the gloom of the passageway, he glanced at his watch. "I have to go soon." Pressing her back against the bulkhead, he placed a hand on either side of her head.

"We shouldn't be here, Ted. Isn't this area off-limits?" His hands slipped to her waist and he stopped her protest with a kiss so full of urgency she gasped. His eager body, hard against her thighs, betrayed him. She freed her arms and looped them around his neck. If he didn't worry about breaking the rules, she certainly wasn't going to object.

At last the kiss ended and Cilla opened her eyes to lock onto his gaze. "Tell me again what you said outside," she said and caressed the back of his neck.

He closed his eyes and, pressing his cold cheek next to hers, spoke softly into her ear. "I said I love you."

"I know, but what else did you say?"

"Never mind." Fiercely he pulled her to him, and crushing her to him, buried her lips under his warm kiss.

He was very good at this, but then he'd had lots of practice, if what her brother had said was true. She nestled very close to him and, following his lead, she returned his kiss, finally pulling away to breathe.

He reluctantly ended the kiss with a final tug on her lower lip. "Now, let's have that truce and start all over again." He looked directly into her eyes. "Cilla, sweetheart. I bungled my last attempt, and this isn't exactly how or where I planned this, but...will you marry me?"

"But I thought...Are you sure you're not just?... You're really serious."

"I'm asking you to marry me. As soon as we get back home. Say yes, Cilla."

Lead weights seemed to have taken up residence in her lower belly. "Why do I get the feeling you're in some sort of a hurry now? Is it because of Clint? Because he means nothing to me."

"No. I don't think he does. But I want to make sure you know how I feel about you. And I want your promise that this will be your last voyage. If you marry me, I know you'll be home, safe and waiting for me."

He kissed her again. Tenderly this time. Suddenly he lifted his lips from hers and straightened. He dragged air into his lungs. "Oh, Chrikey," he moaned, blowing out the air. "Cilla, I'm sorry."

"Sorry? What for?"

He stepped away from her and peered at his wristwatch. "Because I've got to go. I've got the watch and I'm late." He cradled her head in both hands and kissed her lips. "Cor, Cilla. This is going to be the longest voyage I've ever taken to Canada."

"Do you have duty tomorrow night?"

"I have the early watch, but then I'm free."

"Good! Meet me in my cabin at ten o'clock."

He cocked his head and regarded her with a quizzical smile. "What about your cabin-mate?"

"I'm sure I can persuade Millie to find something to do for an hour or so."

"Right, and I'll ask you for your answer then." At the hatchway he turned and grinned. "And stay away from that bloody Yank."

CHAPTER EIGHT

With the swimming pool boarded in and tables set along one side, the sports deck was transformed.

Cilla bobbed her head and Anne Stansbury tapped the toe of her shoe in time to the music blaring from a gramophone.

The music suddenly stopped, and Bobby wrestled the last vacant chair from Jill. Only three players and two chairs remained.

An hour before, the tables had been piled high with sausage rolls, sandwiches, fruit, punch, a gigantic cake, and a seemingly endless supply of ice cream. What remained looked as if a swarm of locusts had been through it.

Cilla worried that the children would get sick from eating so much, but Anne assured her that they were having too much fun.

"Miss. Miss Fawn'on." Ruby dragged Freddie by his collar over to Cilla.

Freddie squirmed. "Pith orf, Ruby. Leave me 'lone." He flailed his arms and lashed out with his feet at his captor.

Cilla stepped out of range of the flying feet. "What's the problem, Ruby? Freddie? Having a good time?"

"Ooh yeah, ta. Ain't it smashin'? An' what a lo' of loverly grub!"

Ruby held her brother at arm's length and solemnly turned him around for Cilla's inspection. "I wan'ed yer to see Freddie's new clobber. Doan' he look a trea'?" With her free hand, she flicked an imaginary speck off his shoulder. Freddie scowled and shrugged her hand away.

Slicked and scrubbed, Freddie wore short grey flannel pants and knee socks, a white shirt and a maroon blazer with a matching tie. Cilla doubted he'd ever had any clothes like them in his life. Ruby's mouth turned up in a rare grin. She was obviously very proud of his appearance.

Cilla looked him over. "You look very smart, Freddie. And I see you have a new life jacket."

He grinned at her.

"'Ere Freddie, show Miss your new teggie."

Freddie dutifully wrinkled his nose and rolled back his lip, exposing the corner of a new tooth shining like a wet pearl through his swollen gum.

"Oh, yes, I see it, and I expect it will be completely in by the time we get to Canada."

The gramophone blared out a rousing polka, signalling the start of the battle for the last chair.

Freddie broke loose from his sister's grip and scampered away, but Ruby hung back. "Miss. Do you fink the captain was 'aving us on when he said the RAF sho' dahn all them Jerry planes?"

"No, I don't think the captain was exaggerating, Ruby. That's why he gave permission for this party. He said one hundred and eighty-five planes were destroyed, and you know the Germans regularly sent that many and more at one time to bomb England."

"Well then, does that mean the war'll soon be over? One of 'em big boys said he 'eard we was turning round and going home."

"I haven't heard that, Ruby, but I do think it will be over by Christmas, and then we'll all go home again."

The little girl lowered her head and stared at her feet.

"And Ruby, Freddie isn't the only one who looks smart. You look very pretty."

A shy smile played at the corners of Ruby's thin lips. Millie had trimmed her fringe, and her long straight hair, having had a good wash, gleamed like black satin. Under her life-jacket she wore a red plaid dress with a white collar, and no longer forced to shuffle along in large Wellingtons, she skipped away in black patent leather shoes and white anklets.

The gramophone needle suddenly screeched across the record and the music stopped. The party halted and a burst of spontaneous applause greeted Captain Near.

He waved, smiling at the children as he made his way to Anne Stansbury, and began talking quietly. Cilla inched closer.

"I'm so sorry to have to bring this celebration to a close, Miss Stansbury, but we have just received word that a U-boat is following us," the captain said. "I'd like to explain it to the children."

The chief escort clapped her hands and commanded in her best housemistress' voice, "Quiet children! Captain Near has an announcement to make."

"Having a good time, boys and girls?" The kids shouted their approval. "Good. And I'm glad to tell you, I just got word that the RAF has downed fifty-six more German bombers."

The children responded with cheers and whistles, and the captain, grinning, raised his hands to calm them. "Now, I'm very sorry to have to bring this celebration to a close, but I must ask you all to return to your cabins."

A chorus of loud groans drowned out his voice. He raised his hands and silenced the protests. "I have received information that there is a U-boat in the area and that a Focke-Wulf Condor is patrolling nearby."

The children whispered comments to one another.

"Wha'th a Fork Wolf, when ith at 'ome, then?" Freddie yelled and stuck out his chin.

"I'll bet you can tell us." The captain pointed to Terry.

"Yes, sir! A Focke-Wulf Condor is a long-range converted airliner that acts as spotter for U-boat targets. And sometimes they bomb ships themselves. Mr. Churchill says they're the scourge of the Atlantic."

"You're absolutely right, and I'm very impressed, young man." He smiled broadly at the boy. "Now, we don't want to get caught unprepared, so please keep your life jackets on and your coats handy."

A murmur of young voices echoed around the room.

"This is just a precautionary measure," the captain continued. "We are not in any immediate danger," he assured them with a smile. "Nothing to worry about, really. But while I have you all together, I'd like to thank you, on behalf of my crew and myself, for your good behaviour and co-operation during all the lifeboat drills. Still, a bit more practice won't do us any harm, eh? So, I'm going to call another one in a little while. Thank you all." He touched his cap in salute and, turning to Anne Stansbury, lowered his voice. "I've ordered extra lookouts on the bridge, in the crow's nest and on the fo'c'sle head, but it might still be a good idea if they slept fully dressed tonight, too."

"Yes, all right, Captain." The chief escort looked worried.

Cilla clamped down on her trembling lip as shivers of fear ran up her spine. Determined to keep the disappointed children from knowing the full extent of the captain's concerns, she forced a smile. "We'll have an even better party after we get closer to Canada, won't we, Captain?" she said in a loud voice.

"Quite right, miss." The captain turned back to the children, smiling. "That's a promise." The room exploded with wild cheering.

Cilla studied the happy faces. The children were so brave, innocently trusting the adults to keep them from any harm. Tears burned the back of her eyes, but with great effort, she hid her emotions and fear.

At 22:00 hours, Captain Near read the message flashed from the Senior Naval Officer aboard *HMS Royal Windsor* to the convoy Commodore. *"U-boat operating ahead west of Longitude 2O degrees West. Goodbye and good luck."*

And we're going to need all the bloody luck we can get, thought the captain.

"Signaller!" the admiral bawled.

"Sir?"

"Respond—'Thanks for your help and goodbye'."

Captain Near checked the luminous dial of his watch. Fourteen hours to go before the convoy could disperse.

He made his way to his cabin and stretched out, fully clothed, on his bunk. He closed his eyes and drifted into a fitful sleep. Each creak and groan of the ship, in conflict with the elements, disturbed him. What was that? He sat bolt upright and strained, listening for alarms or the sound of running feet. Noon the next day couldn't come quickly enough for him, and the *Punjohpur* could be off at its top speed with his precious cargo.

Most U-boat attacks in the Atlantic occurred within three hundred miles of the north-west Irish coast, and that area was fast disappearing astern of the convoy. So why was he so tense? He'd had a knot in his stomach all day.

He thought of the party. It was the first time he'd seen the children all together. He chuckled to himself recalling their deafening cheers when he announced the RAF's successes. Their fierce patriotism brought a lump to his throat.

He closed his eyes and finally drifted into a shallow sleep.

By the next morning, the wind had risen, and the black clouds scudding overhead brought stinging sleet. Great grey waves towered above the *Punjohpur* as she bucked and rolled first to port, blocking the light through the starboard portholes, then reversed the process.

Cilla struggled to keep her breakfast plate from sliding down the table. Most of her coffee had slopped into the saucer. She peered anxiously through the sleet at the mismatched convoy vessels struggling to keep their appointed place in the formation. "What must it be like on board those small ships?" she said. She strained her eyes across the heaving waves and stiffened. "Where's our naval protection?" Her voice rose with the question.

Clint pressed his nose against the dining room window. "Jesus Christ! They've abandoned us in the night."

The escorts rushed to the windows for a verifying look, then stared dumbly at each other.

"Let's keep this to ourselves. We don't want to frighten the children," said Father Hurley.

"I don't understand this." A deep scowl furrowed Anne Stansbury's brow. "They promised. Do you remember the letter that was sent to the parents?"

"What letter?" The Salvation Army woman peered down her nose.

"The one that was sent after the press and the news on the wireless stirred everyone up by telling them that the navy didn't have enough ships to adequately protect seavacuees."

"I didn't see any letter." The Salvation Army woman waggled her shoulders as if to indicate that if she hadn't seen it, there couldn't have any such letter.

"It more or less said not to take any notice of the rumours, and that if the navy said they couldn't convoy the children, then the sailing would be...cancelled." Anne Stansbury's voice faded and her eyebrows drew together in a deep, thoughtful frown.

"Yeah, and convoy means a Royal Navy warship escort. So where the hell is it?" Clint turned from the window accusingly.

"May God be with us," uttered the priest, almost as a prayer.

Cilla drew in a deep breath. Her legs buckled and she sank into the nearest chair.

"Are you all right, Miss Thornton?" Reverend Smythe put his hand on her shoulder and studied her face. "You look a bit pale. Don't be frightened. I'm sure we're well away from danger now."

She managed a smile. "I'm all right, really. It's just the storm. I've done well so far, but I feel a little queasy just now." The buffeting waves and pure fright combined in a wave of nausea, and Cilla bolted from the room.

CHAPTER NINE

Kapitanleutnant Erich Kruger scanned the choppy grey waves from the conning tower of his *Unterseeboot.* He checked his watch. Noon. He'd had an early breakfast, so he was hungry and looking forward to lunch. The cook usually put on a good meal on Sunday.

He adjusted his powerful binoculars and once more scanned the uneven horizon before he went below to eat. Suddenly, he stopped. His heart began to pound. He pushed back his cap for a clearer view and shifted his weight. He held his breath and refocused the glasses. There was no mistake! "Franz!" His breath escaped in one word.

"*Kapitan*?" First Officer Franz Keipling turned from his own lookout. The two wore identical heavy wool jerseys, with their turtle-neck collars up around their throats, sea boots and reefer coats. But the first officer wore a dark blue cap tilted at a rakish angle, while Kruger sported the white summer cap cover adopted on many U-boats as the badge of the commanding officer.

Kruger clamped hard on the cigar wedged between his teeth and grinned. He pointed across the rough pewter sea.

The first officer trained his glasses in the direction of the captain's stubby finger. "*Gott in Himmel, Kapitan.*" He smiled broadly. "What a wonderful sight!"

"Did you see the liner leading the convoy?"

"*Ja*. She looks a juicy prize. She's probably carrying troops." A frown knitted his eyebrows. "I didn't see any destroyers." He raised his binoculars and swept his gaze far ahead of the British convoy, then carefully studied the ships.

"*Nein,*" said the captain. "The escort could be off chasing one of ours. Or it has left already." He grinned. "Perhaps they still don't know we can range this far. *Ja?*"

"So! What is the plan, *Kapitan*?"

"We can't attack here on the surface. We're too far away, and any closer, they'll see us." The captain ran his experienced gaze over the water. "A submerged attack is impossible in these seas." He raised his binoculars and studied the convoy again. Lowering his glasses, he said, "But she's worth waiting for. We'll follow until dark." He checked his watch. "About nine hours." He didn't miss Franz Keipling's disappointed scowl. The dark-haired, handsome, twenty-seven-year-old Keipling had made no secret that he thought the captain entirely too cautious. But Kruger was a patient predator who measured his successes as much by his boat's survival as his satisfactory attacks on British ships.

A feeling of elation surged through the skipper. If he could add this liner to his string of kills, he'd add the Oak Leaves to his Knights Cross. His heart pounded, and he sucked in a couple of deep breaths to calm himself. At thirty years of age, he was not the youngest U-boat captain—and he didn't actually have the Knights Cross yet, but he'd earned it! This was his first patrol in command of the submarine. He'd already attacked one convoy off the north-west coast of Ireland, sinking two steamers and one of the escorts—and he'd only been out twelve days! His crew worked well as a team and deserved much of the credit. When the boat returned to their base at Lorient, he'd give his men a celebration they'd never forget. He licked his lips and imagined the taste of schnapps searing his throat as it slipped down and warmed his belly.

"Post a look-out—post two look-outs. I want that convoy watched for any change in course. I can't believe they have no escort. Must be our lucky day, eh, Franz?" He grinned and clasped the First Officer's shoulder in a gesture of jubilation.

Kruger and Keipling went below to the chart room and pored over their maps and ship descriptions. "I would guess she is about 12,000 tons," Kruger said. "What do you think?"

"That's about right, sir."

The skipper jabbed a stubby finger on the silhouette of the *Punjohpur*. "I'd also guess she is the commodore ship." He rubbed his hands together and grinned. "And nothing panics a convoy more than the loss of the commodore ship. So now we wait for darkness."

The rain stopped for a few minutes, and just before the sun set, it created a rainbow. The children had raced along the deck, laughing excitedly as the bright colours disappeared into the ocean.

Now they were safely in their cabins preparing for bed while most of the adults relaxed in the dining hall. Soon they would tuck the children in for the night.

Cilla set her empty teacup in the saucer and grinned at Millie. "No. I don't know why Hitler doesn't ride a motor bike."

"Because, when it starts up it says, Brrritain, Brrritain." She could hardly get the words out for laughing.

"Who makes up these silly jokes?" Cilla chuckled.

"I don't know, but the boy who told it to me said his friend heard it from someone on the docks." Millie looked past Cilla's shoulder. "Hello, what's this?"

"Good evening, everyone." The purser beamed.

Cilla turned in her chair. "I wonder what he's so happy about," she said.

Millie shrugged. "I don't know. But it looks as if we're about to find out."

"Captain Near has asked me to tell you that the area of U-boat activity is now far behind us, so you can relax. He hopes you enjoy the rest of the voyage," the purser said.

"That's a relief," Cilla let out an exaggerated sigh.

The atmosphere in the dining room charged immediately with exhilaration. The women hugged and kissed each other. The men shook hands and thumped one another on the back.

"This calls for a celebration," the doctor said. "Nine o'clock, my cabin."

A four-hour watch on a storm-tossed ship was exhausting, and Ted's relief came not a minute too soon for him. He was hungry and cold, and his leg muscles ached from bracing against the rolling ship. He took the stairs down to his quarters two at a time.

Loud voices carried through the half-open door of the chart room.

"Sir, I must protest."

Recognising Captain Near's voice, Ted paused in the gangway to listen.

"That signal from the Admiralty warned us that the U-boat is believed to be still in the vicinity of our 12.00 location. You told me yourself the convoy was to disperse then, and here it is almost 22.00 hours and the convoy is still in formation and not even zigzagging. We should scatter now."

The admiral sounded tired. "No, Captain. We won't disperse. I halted zigzagging because the danger of collision in the darkness is far greater than a U-boat attack in these seas."

"But we're sitting ducks plodding along at seven knots. The *Punjohpur* is capable of twice that speed."

"We'll wait until midnight. The longer the convoy stays together, the more protection we can offer the slower ships."

"Admiral. Not a fortnight ago another liner, acting as the convoy commodore ship and carrying British child evacuees, was torpedoed less than two hundred miles from our present position."

Ted sucked in a breath and, cocking his head to catch every word, took a step closer to the door.

"That ship lost no passengers, Captain. What's your point?"

"The point, Admiral, is the rescue was a nightmare. I spoke with the skipper of the rescue vessel. He told me that they had rough seas and children in the lifeboats were wet through. They were so cold they couldn't even hold on to the rope ladders. The crew had to climb down into the lifeboats and haul the children aboard by ropes around their waists. And did you know that while the rescue was under way, two more ships in the convoy were torpedoed? My point is, sir, that should the *Punjohpur* suffer a similar attack, we cannot even expect rescue."

Ted's pulse quickened. Being on the admiral's staff, he was privy to certain information, so he knew the captain was correct. The convoy had orders to scatter at the first sign of attack and not to stop to rescue survivors.

"Sir, let me make a run for it." Captain Near pressed. "No U-boat can catch the *Punjohpur* when she's going flat out."

The admiral's voice vibrated with anger. "Captain Near. You may be master of this ship, but I am in command of the convoy and I have made my decision. The commodore ship will lead the convoy until I give the order to disperse, and I don't intend to give that order until midnight. Do I make myself clear?"

"Yes! Sir!" Frustration rang in the captain's voice.

Ted sagged against the wall. The captain would never question the admiral's decision without good cause. It could only mean he had good reason for his concerns.

Cilla! She was in danger and she didn't even have to be here. He clenched his fists in frustration. There was absolutely nothing he could do to protect her or those poor little kids sleeping in the cabins below. He'd always thought if he survived the initial attack on a ship, he'd be able to save himself. He was a good swimmer, and ships carried plenty of lifeboats and rafts, but he'd never reckoned on little kids.

The door flew open. Ted stepped back as the captain stormed out.

Kapitanleutnant Kruger drained the last of the bitter black coffee and set the mug down. His breath escaped in a whoosh. "I hate the waiting, Franz."

"Not much longer now." A sardonic smile crossed Keipling's handsome face.

Kruger realised that had it been up to the impetuous first officer, the U-boat would have attacked the liner hours ago and perhaps sunk a couple of tankers for good measure.

Kapitanleutnant Kruger now knew the name and the history of his intended victim. She was probably carrying troops, but her cargo put him under no restrictions. He knew the German battle orders by heart—"Fighting methods will never fail to be employed merely because some international regulations are opposed to them." The *Punjohpur*, by virtue of heading the convoy, was legitimate prey.

A blue forage cap appeared around the door, and a young sailor knocked on the outside at the same time.

"*Ja,* Schumm?" The captain welcomed the diversion.

"Wireless message from Grand Admiral Raeder's office, sir." He handed a piece of paper to Kruger and withdrew from the room.

"What could the Chief of the German Naval Staff want with me?" He scanned the paper. "Ah, not just me. *'To all German vessels in the vicinity of the British Isles.'* He smacked the paper with the back of his free hand. "*Donnerwetter*! Franz! Listen to this. '*The enemy air force is by no means defeated. On the contrary, it shows increasing activity. The Fuhrer therefore has decided to postpone Sea-Lion indefinitely.*' That damn Goering sat around on his fat behind waiting for good weather, then when he got it, the Luftwaffe couldn't knock out the RAF."

"So! That is the end of the invasion of Britain, eh, *Kapitan*?"

"*Ja*. But not the end of the war. Let's take out that liner." The captain put on his heavy wool reefer coat and headed for the conning tower.

At dusk the wind had grown to gale force. Sleet showers battered the men on the conning tower of the submarine, soaking their specially-treated leather coats and trousers and saturating the wool lining. Kruger planted his feet and braced his legs as he peered through the darkness for a glimpse of the convoy. Periodically the clouds parted and gave him a clear view of his target in the moonlight. "We'll attack from ahead of the port bow. That position should give us a clear run for the torpedo."

Keipling nodded. "And after her, the rest is easy pickings. *Ja?*"

Kruger checked his watch. "Almost 22:00 hours. It is time."

He lined up on the *Punjohpur* slowly ploughing through heavy seas, and inched as close as he dared. The clouds suddenly parted. "Damn the moon!"

As though shying from his curse, it ducked behind a cloud, and Kruger let out a long breath of relief. He'd welcomed its pale glow shining on his distant target, but now when his boat was so close to her, he feared the *Punjohpur's* lookouts might see the submarine. "We'll move ahead and prepare for the attack."

The captain lowered his binoculars and ordered the U-boat into position. He studied his target again. "Prepare to fire!"

"Prepare to fire!" repeated the torpedo man. "Number one tube flooded."

"Target speed?"

"Seven."

"Range?"

"650 metres."

"Fire!"

"Torpedo running."

Kruger held his breath and waited, listening for the tell-tale boom. When it didn't come, he blew out the breath with the certain knowledge that the single torpedo had passed harmlessly in front of the *Punjohpur*. He swore. He had overestimated the angle on the bow.

He smacked his fist into his palm and chomped on the stub of a cigar. "Battle position!" he bellowed. He manoeuvred the submarine for another clear torpedo run.

"Mark!" He took one more reading on the bow of the target. He couldn't afford to waste another torpedo.

CHAPTER TEN

Cilla tucked her girls in their bunks for the night and joined the rest of the CORB staff already packed tightly into the doctor's tiny cabin.

The priest raised his glass. "To the children," he said.

"To the children." They chorused and sipped their drinks.

"And congratulations to all of us," the doctor said.

Clint raised his glass. "Yeah, to us. We made it."

"Well, not quite," the doctor laughed. "Let's not count our chickens yet. We still have a few hundred miles to go."

Clint scowled and downed his drink in a single gulp, then reached for the bottle and refilled his glass.

For almost an hour, the men and women who'd volunteered their time to escort the children to safely celebrated in jovial conversation.

Just before ten o'clock, Cilla checked her watch for the umpteenth time. Her excitement mounted. Ted would probably be waiting for her by now. "I'll take a turn around the cabins and check on the kids," she said, sounding more nonchalant than she felt.

"Good idea," yelled the priest over the sounds of merriment and clinking glasses. "Make sure the little buggers aren't up to any mischief, eh?"

Across the noisy cabin Millie grinned and gave Cilla the unobtrusive thumbs-up. Cilla winked at the nurse and slipped out into the corridor.

She peeked inside the first cabin. A shaft of light shone on little Jill. Her arm rested outside the covers, exposing her frilly nightie. Pamela lay snuggled deep in her blankets, and Mary breathed steadily in sleep. Cilla quietly closed the cabin door.

This was their fourth night at sea, and someone, nobody seemed to know who, had said that since the ship was finally out of danger, there was no longer any need to sleep fully clothed. The news that they could shed their lifejackets had brought a wild cheer from the children.

In the opposite cabin, Freddie sported striped pyjamas. A tuft of hair was all that was visible from either of his cabin companions. Cilla closed the door on the sleeping boys and stepped back into someone.

She turned. "Oh! I'm sorry, Clint. I didn't know you were behind me."

He reeked of alcohol. "Thought I'd give you a hand." He smiled charmingly.

"Thank you, but it's all right, really. I can manage." She had to get rid of him.

Clint reached for the next door handle. Cilla placed her hand over his, staying him. "That's my cabin. There's nobody in there."

He turned the handle and in one swift movement crowded her inside. He flicked on the light and leered at her. "So, at last, Cilla." His emerald green eyes were brilliant and wild.

"Clint!…Have you gone mad? You've had too much to drink! Let me out of here." She tried to push past him, but he wrapped his arms around her, holding her fast.

"Cilla, Cilla," he murmured against her throat. "You don't want to go. That's why you told me this was your cabin, isn't it?" He caught the sides of her head in his hands and entwined his fingers in her hair. His mouth covered hers in a bruising kiss, and the tip of his tongue probed between her lips. Her stomach revolted at his fetid breath.

"No…" She pulled her head free and pushed hard against his chest to force him away. "Let me go!" she yelled. Fear gripped her belly. He was so strong, and who would hear her shouts?

He leaned into her, shoving her back against the metal upright of the bunks, and kissed her with his mouth wide. With one hand still gripping her head, he fumbled with the buttons on the front of her jumper until he reached inside and clasped her breast, holding her in place.

She pulled her mouth free of his and pummelled his chest, but her fists were ineffectual against his hard body. "Stop it!"

She winced as he squeezed her breast. He released her head and yanked at the waistband of her slacks, forcing his knee between her legs.

"No!" she screamed, more frightened than she had ever been in her life. When the pressure on her breast eased, she twisted away and, losing her balance, landed on her back on Millie's bunk.

With a triumphant cry, Clint fell across her, clawing at her clothing. Suddenly, the cabin door flew open.

"You bastard! I'll knock your bleedin' head off," yelled Ted as he yanked Clint backwards out the door.

Cilla got to her feet and, straightening her clothing, rushed out into the hallway.

"I'll bloody well kill you, Yank." Ted took a swing at the American, but in the confines of the narrow corridor, his blow glanced off Clint's face.

Children poured into the passageway, gawking. Father Hurley grabbed Ted, and Dennis Marlow pushed himself between the fighting men.

Clint pulled from the priest's grasp and threw an ineffectual punch at Ted. Ted drew back his fist.

Cilla screamed. "No, Ted! Don't! He's not worth it."

Ted's eyes blazed as he sent a crashing blow to Clint's chin.

The *Punjohpur* shuddered, and from her bowels came a muffled thud, followed by a horrendous explosion. Cilla lost her balance and staggered against the wall.

"What the hell was that?" Clint massaged his jaw.

Alarm bells sounded over the creaking of wood and the tinkling of glass.

Ted turned his attention from Clint and grabbed Cilla by the shoulders. "That was a torpedo. Hurry. Get your life jacket on. Get to the lifeboat deck as quickly as you can. I have to go to the admiral, but I'll find you later," he said and sprinted away down the corridor.

A pungent, sulphurous smell filled Cilla's nostrils and burned her throat. She coughed. The lights flickered once and died. In the pitch-blackness of her cabin she felt for her coat and forced her shaking hands to tie on her life jacket.

Out in the corridor between the sounds of retching and gagging, children called to each other.

"Mike? Michael, where are you?" A young boy searched for his brother.

"Shirley, give me your hand! Stay by me!"

Cilla pawed through the blackness. Her hand made contact with a bony little shoulder covered only by the thin fabric of a nightgown. "You're not dressed."

"But I've got my lifejacket," the child offered. By feel alone Cilla tied the little girl into her life preserver.

"I'm cold," said another small voice.

"Oh, where are your coats?" Cilla suddenly realised all the children wore only their nightclothes. "Never mind, you can't go back to your cabins now." She might never find them again in the dark. Damn! This wasn't a bit like the routine drills they'd practised in daylight. "Stay together and hurry up to your muster stations." She sent them on their way.

Led by the terrified voices of children trapped behind cabin doors, Cilla's hand closed over a handle and she pushed, but the door wouldn't budge. "It's all right, I'll have you out of there in a minute." She rammed hard with all her strength, but only succeeded in bruising her shoulder. Young voices from the adjoining cabin cried out for help. Cilla felt her way to the door handle, turning it and pushing at the same time. The door was as unyielding as the first.

"Pull the door when I push against," she shouted. The combined effort had no effect. Everything happened so quickly she hadn't thought to question what had become of the other adults.

"Clint! Help me! Where are you?" She threw her shoulder against the cabin door and let out a sob of frustration.

"Cilla. Is that you?" The priest's voice penetrated the bedlam of screaming children, creaking timbers and clanging bells.

"Father! Oh, thank God. The cabin doors are jammed. I can't get the children out."

"Mother of God, it's blacker than the inside of a cow! Come on, Dennis. Stand away from the doors, children," the priest yelled. "Ready, Dennis? On the count of three. One, two, three..."

The two men slammed themselves against the timbers, grunting each time their bodies made contact.

On their third attempt, the door splintered. Children spilled from the wreckage.

"Cilla." The priest gasped for breath. "Take as many children as you can gather and get them up on deck. Dennis and I will bring the rest."

"All right, Father." Cilla took the hand of the child nearest to her. "Join hands and follow me." She probed her way through the blackness. Behind her, the two men grunted and hurled themselves against another jammed cabin door.

Leading the chain of children, Cilla groped her way through the dark, smoke-filled passageway. Children's voices coming from somewhere ahead penetrated the pandemonium.

"Who's there?" she shouted and was suddenly banging into the group of children she'd sent ahead. "What on earth are you doing here? Why aren't you at your lifeboat station?"

"We can't get through, Miss. It's blocked."

The nauseating smell of oil, smoke and explosives permeated the trapped air. Cilla stretched out one hand ahead of her. A solid wall stopped her progress, and she jerked back her hand as something sharp jabbed her. "Ouch!" She sucked her finger and tasted blood. Cautiously she ran her hand over the obstacles again and recognised sheets of panelling wedged against each other. "It's the walls," she told the children. She touched metal and some sort of cord and jerked back her hand, unsure if the light fixture still carried electricity. "Stand still and try not to touch anything."

The little hand she held suddenly wrenched away, and Cilla realised she had been squeezing it. All sense of direction had vanished, and a claustrophobic panic gripped her gut, but her sense of survival predominated. "Stand back, kids." She rammed the flat of her foot against the obstacles, kicking until she'd forced a hole. Oblivious to the pain in her hands, she tore a gap large enough to climb through—into ankle-deep icy water. Dismissing the panic that gripped her belly, she pulled the children, one by one, through the hole.

"Miss. I can feel water. Is it the ocean?" a frightened little voice called out.

"No. I'm sure it's just from broken pipes in the cabins." *Please God, don't let it be the ocean.* "Don't stop. Keep moving."

They reached the boat deck just as the emergency lights came on, illuminating a huge crater in the middle of the deck.

"Stay together and watch where you're going." Choosing her steps carefully, Cilla guided them around the hole. The seawater gushing in below under tremendous pressure made a dreadful sound.

Shivering, bewildered children milled about the muster stations. Frantic crewmen and CORB staff did their best to organise the children and ready them for the lifeboats, but the wind and chaos worked against them. As one adult would gather a group of children, another would try to separate them into their assigned location. All the while storm-driven waves crashed against the side of the stricken ship, spraying everyone with needles of icy water.

Some of the Lascar stewards, dressed only in their native wrap-around skirts and light shirts, had already launched a few lifeboats, with disastrous results. They clamoured and fought each other to grasp the davits and hasten their escape from the doomed vessel. Their efforts sent the lifeboats crashing into the sea.

"Please, Miss. I belong to Mr. Jennison and I can't find him. What shall I do?" A shivering boy of about seven tugged at Cilla's coat.

"Stay here with me." She rubbed the boy's bare back. A few feet away, Clint grabbed his stomach and retched.

Cilla couldn't tell if he was scared or just drunk, but he'd made no attempt to check on his boys. Disgusted with him, she turned her back.

Anne Stansbury dashed up. "Cilla, have you accounted for all of your children?"

"I've only got eleven of my fifteen girls, but I have four boys. Father Hurley and Dennis Marlow are bringing more up, but Heaven only knows how they'll find all the children. It's pitch-black below." Anne was already hurrying away to the next group.

The Fourth Officer charged along the deck, bellowing, "Clear away the boats, man the falls, and stand by for lowering. But wait for the word!"

The chief escort came back again, counting children.

"Has everyone been located, Miss Stansbury? Have you found my missing girls?" Cilla said.

"Yes, everyone is accounted for." The chief escort's chalk-white face revealed shock and anguish. "Pamela Merryman is dead, and Mary Westfall and Jocelyn Hammersmith are both very badly injured. One of the boys has been killed too." She squeezed Cilla's shoulder and went on to the next group.

Cilla fought the bile rising in her throat. Tears flooded her eyes. Pamela dead! Anne Stansbury's announcement had so shocked Cilla that she had forgotten to ask what injuries the other two girls suffered. The vision of Mary in her battered old school hat and Jocelyn, who had set herself the task of correcting the Cockney girls' speech, flashed through Cilla's mind. She flicked away the tears. She needed to show control.

The children seemed frightened, but too shocked to react. No one panicked or cried.

Since most of the CORB adults were still at the celebration when the torpedo hit, they were fully dressed. A few had managed to find their coats. Some didn't even have lifejackets.

Cilla wore slacks and a sweater under her wool coat, but only two of her children had managed to grab their coats. The others jumped up and down, hugging themselves, while they shivered in the cold wind. *If only they had slept fully clothed for one more night!* Cilla rubbed their bare arms and snuggled them around her. "There'll be blankets in the lifeboat. Just hang on. All right?"

"Coxs'n—pipe Abandon Ship."

"Aye-aye, sir." The coxswain complied, then walked along the deck bellowing, "Abandon ship! Abandon ship!"

The Lascars jumped to obey and, in a desperate attempt to launch the boat, fouled the lines, ripping one davit loose and upending the lifeboat.

Craning her neck over the side of the ship, Cilla watched in horror as the lifeboat swung crazily by one short rope and one long. Terrified children gripped the gunwales and each other to maintain their seats.

"No! Oh! No!" Cilla yelled a spontaneous warning.

The children's screams rose above all other noises as they plummeted into the icy sea.

"Oh, dear God, no!" Cilla wailed.

Another lifeboat, spewing bodies, crash-dived. One young boy, his mouth and eyes wide with terror, clung to the gunwale and stayed with the lifeboat until it smashed into the sea and pitched him headlong into the churning waves.

Other boats, launched only half-full, left others to slide down ropes that trailed from the lifeboat davits. Cilla, paralysed with horror, could do no more than gape. Many of the children, unable to hang on, fell into the sea. She could hardly bear the pitiful calling and crying from those in the water. Since the cold wind penetrated her dry wool clothing, she knew those inadequately-dressed children in the water could not possibly survive for long. She choked back a sob. Why was this happening? What good were all those lifeboat drills now?

A little girl began to scream. *"Larry! Larry!"* The children waiting on the deck had seen the catastrophe, and many of them had siblings in the swamped and overturned craft.

Boats that reached the water on an even keel tossed about like corks on the heaving waves.

Cilla's heart pounded in near panic. She clasped the children closer to her and wondered if they would all suffer the same fate.

The injured girls were carried on deck slung in blankets and were gently placed on the floor of the swaying lifeboat. Millie Parkin applied pressure to Jocelyn's bleeding shoulder where her arm had once been. Watching, the other children gasped.

"Where is Mary hurt?" A blanket covered the whimpering girl. Her pain was evident in her tightly shut eyes and her teeth clenched on her lower lip.

"The force of the explosion threw her from her bunk. She landed on her knees and shattered her knee caps."

Cilla clamped her hand across her mouth, successfully stifling a sob. Pallid and pinched, Jill walked numb and wide-eyed in the wake of the pathetic procession. Relieved to have found her missing fourth child, Cilla picked Jill up and carried her into the swaying lifeboat. The little girl had wet her knickers.

Sub-lieutenant Sutherland tried desperately to supervise a textbook launching, but on the slanted wind-blown deck, the falls became twisted and the blocks jammed. The lifeboat dangled forty feet above the black, forbidding ocean. Cilla crouched in the bottom of the boat, frozen with fear. She gripped the gunwale with one hand and Jill with the other. The bow dropped with a violent jerk, leaving the stern upended. Her own screams added volume to the terrified cries of the children.

CHAPTER ELEVEN

A feeling of uneasiness had driven Captain Near to the bridge early in the evening. He was still there when the *Punjohpur* shuddered from her mortal wound. His immediate reaction was to ring the engine room. "What's the damage down there, Chief?"

"We're up to our waists in water, sir."

"Get out now and go to your boat stations."

"Right you are, sir," said the Chief Engineer. "Time to go, lads," he yelled to the engine crew before he rang off.

Darroch's head appeared at the top of the ladder. The captain had been expecting him. He knew the First Mate would make straight for the bridge when he realised the ship had been torpedoed. He always slept fully clothed, like the rest of the crew who sailed these dangerous waters.

"Number One, check the extent of the damage."

"Aye, aye, sir." Darroch slid back down the ladder and disappeared aft.

Captain Near could do nothing more until he had a report of the damage, except to alert the rest of the convoy. He lit a flare and watched it arc through the dark sky. Immediately, the ships strung out behind him began to change course and scatter. Each vessel would save itself, if it could, and independently make its way to its destination.

Darroch clambered back up the ladder to the bridge. "Sir," he stopped to catch his breath, "the watertight door to the tunnel has been blown away and the engine room is flooded."

"Right." The skipper nodded grimly. "Did we get a distress signal off?"

"Yes, sir. The radio operators report a shore station in Scotland has acknowledged it. The operators are still at their posts maintaining radio contact."

"Thank you, Number One." The skipper peered down the length of his ship. "She's listing to port and sinking by the stern now. Any word on the passengers?"

"I checked all the public rooms and made sure everyone alive has gone to their boat stations."

A horrendous explosion immediately astern of the *Punjohpur* suddenly blotted out the sounds of creaking timber, sirens and the pathetic screams from the sea. The captain spun around.

"Oh, Christ!" Startled, Darroch thumped his fist on the bridge railing.

Flames from the merchantman lit the water and silhouetted the seaman frantically diving into the sea.

Only two lifeboats were launched before the ship slipped quickly beneath the waves.

"Poor bastards." Captain Near shook his head and turned his attention back to the First Officer. "What about the children?"

"I couldn't get a full report. Two killed outright. Several badly wounded. The launching isn't going well, Captain."

"I see that. Poor little devils. They're not dressed for it, and I expect if the sea doesn't get them before they can hope for rescue, the cold will." He sighed and turned back to Darroch. "Thank you, Number One. You can't do any more. You'd better make for your own lifeboat."

"What about you, Captain?"

"It's my duty to stay. I can't even consider my own survival." He indicated the scene off the side of the ship. "Good luck, Jim."

Darroch gripped his friend's outstretched hand. "Goodbye, Captain." His blue eyes brimmed with tears as he turned and hurried to his lifeboat station.

Lowered at the dangerous angle, lifeboat number three suddenly righted itself as it touched the water, saving it from the swamping the other boats had endured. Everyone had managed to hang onto his or her seat, and none had pitched into the oil pouring out of the stricken ship.

A fierce wind whipped the sea into rough waves that slapped against the hull of the lifeboat, sending icy spindrift over those huddled in her. The two injured girls shivering on the wet floor soon had their blankets soaked through. Dressed only in their nightwear, the other children shook with cold and their teeth chattered.

Cilla debated which one she should give her coat to. Should she give it to little Jill—or perhaps Kitty and Ruby who huddled together, deserved the warmth more than the others? If she gave up her coat and died as a result, she wouldn't be of any use to any of them. But if a rescue ship didn't come soon, the argument would be moot. In the end she reached for the two nearest blue-lipped children and snuggled them, one on either side of her, under the coat.

Clint, slumped with his head over the side, suddenly came to life. "Look, there's a ship come to rescue us," he croaked, pointing to a dark craft much larger than the lifeboats. Its spotlight swept the water, illuminating the dreadful scene of men and women, boys and girls struggling in the cold Atlantic.

Children rose from the bottom of the lifeboat. Every head turned toward the ship that offered them warmth and life. The wind suddenly didn't feel quite so cold, and the children began to murmur among themselves.

"The Royal Navy's come."

"We're gonna be orright, now." One by one they began to cheer and wave at the dark shape.

First Officer Darroch's voice shook with anguish. "Yon's no here t' rescue us. It's the U-boat that sunk us."

"Oh, God! What's going to happen to us?" Clint's whine contrasted with the children's sudden stoic silence, and anger overwhelmed Cilla.

"Don't just sit there!" she screamed at Clint. "Put a couple of children under your coat."

He glared at her in silence and deliberately pulled the coat tighter around him.

"Ye'd best do as the lassie says." Darroch's tone suggested that Clint had no options. The First Officer had already given his own coat to a couple of ill-clad boys.

"Do it! Do it!" Cilla clenched her fists in frustration and anger. "Or I'll personally throw you out there." She gestured at the swells and troughs illuminated by the submarine's light.

Clint jerked his head over the side of the lifeboat and relieved his stomach of its contents. He wiped his mouth and splashed sea-water on his face.

"I'm sick. It's these damn waves," he groaned.

"You're drunk, and I don't care how sick you are, you will help with the children." Cilla suddenly warmed with anger.

By the submarine's searchlight Clint's face appeared ashen, but he reached out and grabbed two children and tucked them inside his coat.

The U-boat captain watched the merchantman directly astern of the *Punjohpur.* A horrendous explosion suddenly lifted her out of the water.

"She's down," he said, allowing his binoculars to hang from his neck. The crew let out another cheer. Their second kill.

"Let's go in for a closer look at the liner," said Kruger. "No sense wasting another torpedo if she's done for."

The distance between the submarine and the crippled *Punjohpur* floundering and wallowing in the battering waves closed quickly.

"*Kapitan! Kapitan!*" The strangled cry of the lookout sent a chill through the U-boat captain.

"*Was ist los?* " He ran to where the young sailor stared through binoculars. "What the hell's the matter?" In the flickering light of the burning target, Kruger could see the look of incredibility on the young seaman's face as he pointed toward the *Punjohpur.*

"*Kinder, Kapitan.* There are children in the water." His voice cracked.

Kruger lifted his own binoculars and focused them. "*Gott in Himmel!* The British must be mad!" For a full minute he could not take his eyes from the ghastly scene. The young man beside him sniffled and, lowering his head into his hands, began to cry softly.

"We can't take prisoners, you know that." Kruger lowered his glasses and laid a hand on the boy's shoulder. He cleared his throat and resumed his professional voice. "Keipling! Note in the log that the target sank in thirty-one minutes."

The spotlight vanished, and the black submarine glided away as silently as it had appeared, leaving its victims to the uncertain night.

"Cilla. Cilla!" She peered across the choppy waves. By the lights of the condemned ship she saw Ted floundering in the water.

"Ted! Oh, thank God."

He swam toward her with one hand, holding an oil-coated, limp child with the other. Willing hands from the lifeboat took the unconscious boy. Ted immediately pushed off again, his arms moving slowly as if weighted down with stones.

Millie touched the child's neck and shook her head sadly. "Too late. He's gone."

Ted reappeared, dragging a little girl coated in thick black oil. They lifted her in to the lifeboat just as she choked one last time on the poisonous crude. Tears burned Cilla's frozen cheeks as she cried over the limp little body.

Twice more Ted made the arduous journey, and Cilla held her breath, pulling for him, but he was expending the last of his strength rescuing dead children.

"Ted, please come in now. You're exhausted." He gripped the gunwale in both hands and, resting his head between them, retched. "Ted, darling, please." Cilla tugged at his wrist in a futile effort to help him climb into the lifeboat.

Tears and drenching spray stung her eyes. She lowered her lips and kissed his ice-cold hand.

He raised his head and gazed at her. "I love you, Cilla."

"I love you, Ted. Please come into the boat now."

"No. It's already too full." He looked past her to Clint wrapped in his warm wool coat, huddled in the stern of the lifeboat. "Hey, Yank." Ted's voice rasped. "Take good care of my Cilla." He pushed off against the lifeboat and swam slowly away.

Cilla screamed his name above the wind, but if he heard her, he was too exhausted to respond. She watched until he disappeared into a swell.

Swallowing her sobs, she turned her attention to the injured girls, and a new wave of terror and frustration gripped her. "Oh, God! Millie, the girls." While everyone else's attention had been on Ted and his attempts to rescue the floundering children, the injured girls had quietly died. Mary and Jocelyn were ice-cold. Jill, slumped like a rag-doll over her sister, was dead.

It was almost more than Cilla could bear. She tried to be stoic and strong for the sake of the other children, but the dam of emotion broke and sobs racked her.

Millie hugged her. "Come on, Cilla, I need you to help me. We have to take their clothes for the other children before we put them over the side."

Cilla nodded. It was the practical thing to do, and she steeled herself to the task. "All right. I'll lift them, you get the clothes."

In the bucking, heaving boat it was a gruesome undertaking. Millie solemnly handed over the girls' pyjamas, but Jill's little nightie was too small for any of the other children. The Asians scrambled for the two sopping wet blankets, but Cilla grabbed them up and gave them to the boys.

Standing in the pitching boat was impossible. The waves crashed against the hull, lifting it up, then dropping it into troughs. The purser crawled forward and muttered a prayer over the three little girls, then one by one slipped them, as gently as the angry seas permitted, over the side.

Darroch wrapped his arms around the two devastated women. "You're a grand crew, lassies. Nobody could have done more in these conditions."

Cilla blinked her tears away and wiped the ocean from her cheeks. Millie ventured a grateful smile.

"Right," said Darroch. "we don't want to lose any more." He sounded gruff, but even the wind couldn't hide the emotion in his voice.

"Sutherland. You man the tiller," Darroch told the fourth officer.

"Aye, aye, sir." Sutherland clambered into the stern.

"And we need volunteers on the propelling gear," Darroch said. "We have to keep the boat head-on into the waves to keep it from swamping."

Millie raised her hand. "I'll do it. Show me what to do."

Sutherland pointed to two long handles standing up from the floor between each pair of seats. "These have to be pushed forward and back in unison. That revolves the shaft and turns a screw under the rudder. That will propel the boat forward."

"I can do that." Millie jostled her way to the nearest handle. "I'll pretend I'm pumping beer in a pub." Sutherland smiled at her attempt at humour.

The oldest of the evacuee boys was a skinny fourteen-year-old named Brian. He wore only pyjama bottoms and a life jacket. His hair lay plastered against his head, and water ran in rivulets down his bony shoulders. "I'll...I'll have a g...go, sir," he volunteered through chattering teeth.

"Good lad." Darroch moved aside to let the boy pass. "What about you, Yank?"

"Who the hell put you in charge?"

"My rank, son. I'm senior officer here. Now, we all have to take a turn. What about it?"

Clint grumbled, "I'm not your son, but I suppose if I have to, it might as well be now while I still have the strength to pull the damn handle," he mumbled and clambered to the nearest handle.

"Oh, Christ!" The blasphemy exploded from Darroch. "If ye don't want to be sucked to the bottom, you'd better pump like hell. Look at that, will ye," he yelled, pointing at the *Punjohpur* ablaze with lights and looming over the lifeboat.

Darroch's fears soon registered. Even though the ship's engines stopped when the torpedoed struck, her own momentum propelled her forward. The lifeboat was in danger of being pulled under when she went down.

The purser grabbed a pump handle and began working it.

"I'll help." Cilla began to unwrap the children.

"No, miss. You take care o' the bairns," Darroch told her.

The Lascars made no move. The First Officer climbed among them, waving his hands for emphasis. "Come on, ye heathen bastards. Ye'll have to help if ye expect to survive." A wave smashed the lifeboat broadside. The Lascars shrieked, and Darroch staggered, losing the grip on his pipe.

Under different circumstances, the look of utter disbelief on Darroch's face would have been amusing. His chin dropped and his mouth stretched open as his eyes followed the slow arc of the pipe into the sea. "Bugger it!"

he yelled.

The Indians stayed glued to their seats. Hanging on to each other and chattering incessantly, they passed acrid-smelling cheroots from mouth to mouth. The glow as they drew on the cigarettes lit up their bland coppery-coloured faces.

"Ach! Can ye no' see the danger we're in?" Darroch pressed his argument, staring into one pair of dark eyes after another, but they just glared back. "All right, then." He lifted the bottom of his heavy wool jumper. The handle of a revolver jutted out from the waistband of his trousers. "Ye'll help or go o'er the side. Now!"

The Asians had Cilla's pity. They had not exactly surrendered to the sea, but they seemed to have stopped caring whether they lived or died. Most of them had been stewards on the *Punjohpur* and weren't really sailors at all. Dressed only in thin shirts and without shoes, they cowered together, shrieking each time a wave washed over the lifeboat.

They looked to one of their own named Ramboon for direction and stirred only after he spoke to them. He turned to Darroch. "You do not have to shoot us, sir. We will take our turns."

"That's more like it. All right, the rest of you bail." He glanced up at the hull of the sinking ship bearing down on them. "And hurry!" he yelled.

CHAPTER TWELVE

Ted's limbs ached as he swam away from Cilla's lifeboat. His leaden arms moved through the icy water with no conscious direction from his groggy brain. All his exposed flesh was numb, prickling with needles of pain. Oil-coated swells washed over him, clogging his nostrils, filling his ears and burning his throat.

Children flailed in the water around him, and fuzzy plans for heroic rescues played around the edges of his mind, but he couldn't think how to carry them out. He let his life jacket support him while he rested.

Cilla! She was in a lifeboat. Why wasn't he in the lifeboat? He forced his numbed brain to remember—the lifeboat, crowded—full of Asians and officers, women and kids. And one of those women was Cilla. Cilla was safe. That much he could remember, nothing else seemed to matter. He rested his head on his life-vest and drifted, welcoming oblivion.

Suddenly, over the roar of the waves and the howling wind, he heard someone shout his name. "Evans! Evans! Over here!"

Admiral Meacham's order brooked no disobedience. Ted trod water and looked about him, listening for the direction. A swell filled his throat with the oily saltwater and blinded him.

"Evans! This way. Over here." The wind shrieked across the waves, carrying the admiral's command. Ted tried to obey, but his body no longer had any feeling. So cold...so cold. He must obey the admiral. A dark shape loomed above him. With his waning strength he forced himself away from the hull of the dying *Punjohpur* to the welcoming lifeboat. He grabbed the gunwale gasping, too exhausted to speak.

"Get in. You can't do any more." Admiral Meacham grabbed Ted under one arm. "Give me a hand here!" he yelled over his shoulder.

As if obeying the admiral's command, a swell lifted Ted and washed him over the gunwale to land in an exhausted heap among the admiral's staff. He leaned against a thwart, gasping and retching up oily water.

"Push off," yelled the admiral. The sailors, armed only with wooden oars, pushed the lumbering craft away from the hull of the sinking liner. Hurled back by the backwash against the ship's side, the oars snapped like matchsticks.

"Bugger it! Now how the hell are we going to push off?" The gunner stared, stupefied at the remains of the last broken oar.

"Use your hands," grunted another as he struggled to make headway against the rapids and mill-races swirling round the bow of the ship.

The *Punjohpur* loomed almost vertically above them, her bow cant in the air. Frantic to escape being dragged under when inevitably the stricken ship sank, even the admiral paddled.

The lifeboat had travelled only yards when there was a muffled explosion deep in the ship's belly. Still ablaze with lights illuminating Captain Near on the bridge, the once beautiful *Punjohpur* slowly, reluctantly slumped stern first beneath the stormy Atlantic and plunged the sea into blinding, impenetrable darkness.

As Ted's eyes became accustomed to the sudden blackness, he had his first sight of the lifeboats launched on the far side of the ship. Like fireflies on a summer night, torchlights flickered from one boat to the other.

Fifty yards separated the lifeboat and the capsizing ship when the tidal bore, created by the sinking liner, hit the lifeboat broadside. It lifted the boat up on a precipice and threw it upside-down into a deep trough. A tremendous force plunged Ted down, down, down. His lungs threatened to burst. The pressure on his ears caused excruciating pain.

The ocean suddenly came alive with sounds of ghostly moaning and screeching. The *Punjohpur*'s tortured hull complained as her plates twisted and collapsed.

Ted lost all sense of direction, and suddenly he felt warm, as if the sun's rays had found him. In that moment he gave himself up. A brilliant glow danced enticingly before his eyes, and his father urged him to follow the light...His father? That made no sense to him. He didn't even remember his father. Nothing made any sense. It didn't matter. He just needed to reach the light where he would find warmth and rest.

Whatever force had driven him down, now suddenly propelled him upward. His flesh prickled with a million icy darts. His lungs were at the point of bursting. A blue glow shimmered above him, and his head broke through the surface into the moonlight.

He gasped for air and swallowed a mouthful of oily water for his trouble. His ears rang and the cold penetrated to his bone marrow while hot tears of disappointment filled his eyes. He really didn't want to do this anymore.

The moon played hide-and-seek around the storm clouds, illuminating a small raft just yards from him. Fate had brought him back from oblivion, and with strength and energy he didn't know he had, he pulled himself to the raft.

Two British seamen Ted recognised, a gunner named Martin and another signaller called Shaw, reached over the side of the tiny raft to pull him aboard. The two Lascars who huddled at the other side of the six-by-three-foot raft had other ideas. The Asian sailors yelled and kicked their bare feet at Ted's face. One tried to loosen Ted's grasp on the side of the tiny raft. He hung by sheer instinct to survive.

"Bugger off!" Martin smashed his fist into the face of one Lascar and shoved the other almost into the sea. Between them, the two British sailors hauled Ted aboard.

"Thanks, mate," Ted croaked. The howling wind reached through his wet clothes, and he shivered. "Christ, it's cold!" He retched up poisonous oil from his stomach and collapsed on a corner of the raft, gasping for breath.

"Let's get to hell outta here," the gunner yelled. He had the only oar and he began to paddle the raft away through the flotsam of broken oars and containers of fresh water and food.

A young sailor in a nearby boat grabbed a bucket from the debris and began to bail the water from the bottom of the craft. Waves crashed over the heads of those sitting up to their waists in water. Children struggling to keep their heads clear floated out over the gunwales. The adults snatched them back and, using the ties of their life jackets, lashed them to the thwarts and mast.

"Oh, God! Can't we help them?" Ted's sense of helplessness overwhelmed him.

Faster and faster, the sailor threw the water out of the swamped lifeboat. Finally he dropped the bucket and collapsed onto a thwart, defeated.

A little girl floated past the raft, her hands tightly clenched around a piece of wood. The moon's last glimmer, before it disappeared behind a cloud, shone on her upturned face and blank eyes.

Ted reached for her and missed. He rose to dive into the swell after her.

"Forget it, Evans." The gunner stayed him with a grip on his shoulder. "It's no use."

"God Almighty!" Ted recoiled at the sight of several children's bodies being tossed about by the waves like so much flotsam. Had any of these children been in the lifeboat with Cilla? Tears stung his eyes and burned channels down his cheeks, but with the sea washing over them, Rob Shaw and Johnny Martin couldn't see him crying.

"We can't get far with one oar." Martin moved them slowly through the water, away from the bubbles still rising to the surface from the sunken ship.

The two Asians muttered together through chattering teeth. Their cotton skirts clung to their thighs and they wore only singlets under their life jackets. Between whispers they threw suspicious glances at the British sailors.

"Keep an eye on those two." Shaw squinted at the Indians. "They'll have us over the side quick as you like."

"God, my throat is raw. Let's see if we have anything to drink." Ted braced himself against the force of the waves and the wind and opened the watertight locker. Inside were food, a container of water, a couple of blankets and a bottle of rum. He passed the rum to Martin, then to Shaw. Ted licked his salt-crusted lips and spat the brine into the sea before he took a deep swallow. The liquid warmed his belly. He offered the bottle to the Lascars, but they shook their heads.

"They won't touch it, Ted. Their religion forbids it," Shaw said.

"Yeah, I know they're Muslims, but I'm sure Allah would forgive them on a night like this." He held out a blanket to the barefoot Lascars, which they eagerly accepted and wrapped around the two of them.

Ted snuggled in the other blanket, but within seconds it was soaked through. He threw it off in disgust and took another sip of rum.

"We should try to stay close to the other boats. Our SOS was received in Scotland, and they'll be sending out a rescue ship," Shaw yelled over the shriek of the wind.

"Right. I wish we had a torch-light." Ted glanced helplessly at the supply locker. It hadn't contained one.

Numbed by constant immersion and lambasted by blinding spindrift, the sailors clung to their only hope of salvation. Martin pointed across to where the other craft bobbed like toys in a bathtub. "We'll take turns watching the lights from the lifeboats. Then we can tell if we're getting blown too far from them and paddle back. I'll take the first hour."

A twenty-foot wave smashed into the tiny craft, and a Lascar screamed as he slid off the raft. Ted lunged and grabbed the fabric of his skirt. "Help me!" he yelled to his crewmates, but the force of the wave snatched the cloth from his grasp, and the Asian slipped beneath the water.

The wind drove the raft high on foam-speckled waves, then plunged it into a trough, jarring the men's spine against the hard seating.

"Cor, blimey, my arse don't 'alf hurt." Shaw tried to rearrange himself and took over the torch watch as they'd begun call it.

They didn't ask the Lascar to help. He'd started muttering to himself since his companion had died, and they didn't trust his competence.

All night the three sailors talked, sang dirty songs and told every joke they had ever heard to keep themselves alert until morning—until the rescue ship would come.

Dawn reluctantly shed enough light to tell the sea from the sky. To their relief, ten other boats and several rafts floated within their sight. Without warning, a savage storm of hail hammered their skulls and battered their shielding arms with bruising stones. When it was over, the Lascar was dead. They rolled him into the waves, and Ted thankfully stretched his cramped legs into the few extra inches vacated by the Asian.

Exposure to the wind and immersion in cold seawater had taken its toll on the other vessels, too. Each had lost its share of passengers, but it was the children's bodies being laid over the sides that most affected the three war-hardened sailors. Ted swallowed hard, but he couldn't stop the hot tears. He stole a glance at his companions, touched to see them biting their salt-cracked lips and crying openly.

Ted scanned each boat through his brimming eyes, searching for Cilla, silently pleading with the Almighty that she had survived the night.

The sun broke briefly through the clouds even though the sea still buffeted them without mercy.

"Let's eat. What's in the locker?" Martin said.

"Bully beef and ship's biscuits." Ted handed the rations to his companions and hefted the water container. His heart sank. While they'd kept a careful watch on the other craft all through the night, their precious water had been leaking through a hole in the corner of the canister.

"What the hell do we do now?" Shaw was flagging.

"We'll have to make do with condensed milk," Ted said. "There's still a swallow of rum for each of us." He tapped the bottle in his pocket.

CHAPTER THIRTEEN

A night spent in purgatory could not have been worse for the huddled mass clinging to the gunwales of lifeboat number three. Buffeted by the relentless wind and pounded by the heaving waves, the thirty-foot craft bucked and pitched in constant combat, drenching the passengers in icy spray and warm vomit.

The lifeboat plunged into the troughs as solid walls of foam-topped waves towered overhead. From the crests of the mountainous waves, occasional moonlight glimmered on other lifeboats. Their flashing torchlights offered the only comfort that they weren't alone, and several times Cilla thought she heard shouts above the roar of the storm. Sometimes a bobbing head or a tossing raft whirled by.

The three British officers, Clint, Millie and Cilla each snuggled two half-naked children under their coats and, throughout the night, periodically replaced them with two others. Even the children helped rub life back into each other's frozen hands and feet and massaged cramped muscles. The Lascars withdrew and refused to take or offer any help.

"We must all try to stay awake," Millie said. "Children, it is very important. If you feel sleepy, tell someone." She addressed the Asians, but they were already dozing. "Mr. Ramboon, please tell the men they must stay awake." Ramboon shrugged.

The children remained full of hope, urging each other into singing and acting out *The Spreading Chestnut Tree* to circulate the blood through their limbs. As the night wore on, they began to ask about the convoy ships coming back for them. Cilla had no answer for them. She wondered why their own convoy ships hadn't picked them up.

Ruby had a different concern. "Miss. Do you fink everyone wha' fell into the ocean from them tipped up boats was saved?" Ruby's black eyes bore into Cilla's face.

"I don't know, Ruby. Certainly many of them were taken on other boats. I saw them." She had also seen an empty lifeboat rise up on the crest of a wave and threaten to crash down upon them before it turned turtle and plunged again. It didn't take much imagination to guess what had happened to the passengers.

"Did you see Freddie, Miss?" Ruby's voice disappeared into the gale.

Cilla remembered the little boy with the angelic face and the foul mouth. "No, Ruby. I didn't see Freddie, but I'm sure he was picked up." *Oh, God, she prayed, please let that be so.* She had seen so many dead children floating in the water. The warning about the life jackets came back to her, and she wondered how many had died because their life jackets had throttled them or broken their necks when they hit the water.

Cold and exhausted, Cilla forced herself to stay awake, concentrating her efforts to warm the children and keep them awake. But even if she had wanted to sleep, she could not have ignored the nausea, and her torn and bleeding hands burning with each saltwater dousing. Nor could she escape the propelling gear handle driven into her back at the end of each stroke, all through the endless night.

A grey, morose dawn reluctantly appeared to reveal the brutal seas that had bounced them about in the darkness. The waves, like tormented mountains, picked up the little boat and smashed it down, jarring already bruised and battered bodies.

The first streaks of light revealed the dead. Seven Lascars, and the two youngest girls and one little boy, had succumbed during the torturous night.

The Indians insisted on putting the bodies of their countrymen over the side themselves.

Nobody spoke as Cilla and Millie stripped the dead and handed the clothing to the solemn, grateful children

The purser bowed his head. "Gentle Jesus..." he prayed as he gently placed each lifeless child in the water outside the boat. Tears brimmed in Cilla's eyes, and she swallowed the lump in her throat. Her heart felt like a stone in her chest. She wondered, if she survived this ordeal, would she ever forget this dreadful scene? Millie put her arm around Cilla and together they wept.

"Purser. I think we should have some breakfast, please." Darroch rubbed his blue hands together. "Then we'll get ourselves sorted out." His gruff show of apathy couldn't quite hide his grief.

One of the older boys had climbed up on the locker and was scanning the horizon. "'Ere, where are them other lifeboats, then?"

The Lascars, huddled in the bottom of the boat, seemed to sense from the boy's tone that something was not right. They rose, craning their necks and chattering, then fell silent as they stared at the empty ocean.

"We seem to have drifted away from them in the night," said the young fourth officer. He quickly looked at Darroch.

The wind muffled Clint's shout. "Goddam it, Darroch, you insisted those handles be pulled all night. Now we've gone too damn far and we'll be missed by the rescue ship."

"Mr. Jennison. Be quiet!"

"But any fool knows the first rule when you get lost is to stay where you are. Back home we were always told that," Clint spluttered through a mouthful of seawater as another wave slapped his face.

"We are not *back home*, we are in the Atlantic, and we are not lost. Listen, everyone!" Darroch stood in the stern and yelled. "Contrary to Mr. Jennison's assertions, we are not lost. It's true; the other lifeboats are no longer with us. I believe that's because we didn't swamp and fill with water like most of the other boats. We retained much more freeboard exposed to the wind, and the force drove us eastward at a much faster rate than the others."

"What's freeboard?" The tiny voice held a note of hope.

"It's this area from the gunwale to the waterline." He banged his hand against the outside of the hull. "This isn't a bad thing, and I've decided we'll keep heading eastward toward Ireland."

"And do you have any idea how far that is?" Clint's question crackled with sarcasm

"Aye. About six hundred miles."

"Six hundred miles! Are you out of your goddam mind?"

Darroch ignored the American.

"All right. Now we have to sort ourselves out. Purser, what about that breakfast while we rearrange things?"

"Aye, aye, sir," said the purser.

The British crew and Clint took the stern with the fourth officer at the tiller. Darroch ordered two of the propelling gear handles removed from their sockets in the bow. This made more room for Millie and Cilla, the remaining three boys and nine girls, but it was still very cramped.

When everyone settled, the purser passed a ship's biscuit topped with a sardine to each one, and two ounces of water to wash it down. "Here's breakfast fit for the King himself," he said.

"Cor blimey! Is 'at all we're going to get, then?" Kitty frowned at the meagre meal.

"That's all 'till the next time."

The long day loomed ahead.

About mid-morning, Darroch suggested further adjustments to the bow section where a large locker took up most of the space.

"Sutherland, you and the purser give me a hand. We'll rig the canvas over yon locker. It will give the women and bairns a little more room."

The awning provided a shelter over the storage container, and the children soon discovered that two of them at a time could fit inside it. They created their own system of taking turns in the cramped locker away from the wind and lashing waves. The rest settled themselves on the top or along the thwarts.

The Lascars had the middle section of the lifeboat. A canvas rigged between them and the bow provided some blessed privacy when the women and girls had to use the bucket.

The miserable day dragged on, and Cilla and Millie did their best to protect the children from the elements. They massaged wet, frozen feet and legs and tried to sound cheerful and positive.

"Let's sing." Cilla's throat was dry and scratchy, but she couldn't think of any other way to entertain the cold, bored and battered children.

A few weak voices took up "Roll Out the Barrel," but they soon drifted into silence.

"You know," Millie spoke up, "when I was a little girl in Buckinghamshire, a witch lived in the next village to mine."

The children lifted their eyes to Millie, and she began to tell them the most outrageous story. Each time Cilla thought the story had ended, the children begged for more and Millie continued. They didn't even notice the inadequate meals, but Millie hardly took a break all day.

By the time the sun set, her voice was hoarse. "That's all for tonight."

"Aw, finish the story."

"Yeah, how we gonna know wha' happened?"

"Tomorrow morning," she croaked, "after we've washed our faces and had breakfast, I'll tell you the rest."

"Washed our faces! That's all that's happened since we got into this boat. The sea's washed our faces!"

"Yeah, an' our 'ands and feet."

"And our bums."

The children snickered.

Cilla caught Millie's eye and smiled. Millie spluttered.

"That's enough now," Cilla said. Suddenly she began to laugh. "Millie, your lovely hair. It's caked with salt and standing up on end. How does my hair look?"

"Dreadful. It's white from the salt. Good thing Ted can't see you now. He'd think you had aged overnight." Millie laughed and patted her own hair. "Ooh, it feels all sticky."

As night drew in around the little lifeboat, the wind picked up force. Cilla had a hard time ignoring her physical discomforts. The gale howled until her ears ached from the sound. The palms of her blistered hands bled from working the propelling gear. Her muscles ached and she longed to stretch, but in the cramped lifeboat, that was impossible. Her eyes burned from the constant bombardment of saltwater.

Salt! Salt-caked eyes. It caked lips and hair and skin. It penetrated open wounds and seared like a red-hot poker.

Cilla steeled herself to endure another night on the open sea, and while the wind shrieked like a banshee, she willed herself to remember more pleasant times...

The warm day had been just right for cycling that spring when Cilla was seventeen. As she coasted down the Surrey hills with the sun in her face, the wind had caught her hair and stretched it out behind her. The smell of wildflowers filled her nostrils and she breathed deeply.

Ted whizzed by, turning to laugh at her. His dark eyes twinkled. "Come on. You're slow, even going downhill." He pumped the pedals and left her drifting with gravity. Somewhere behind her, her two brothers goaded the other girls on. Nigel's girlfriend was tubby and kept stopping to catch her breath. Trevor had brought along a thirteen-year-old classmate whose bicycle was too large for her. She stood in her pedals, valiantly pumping in an effort to keep up, but her bird-like legs soon tired.

At the bottom of the hill Ted leaned against a wooden fence in the shade of a large tree. "At last. I thought you'd stopped to rest." He grinned as Cilla braked, coming to a halt beside him.

"Don't be so cheeky." She looked back up the hill. "I wonder where the others are. Should we go back and look for them?"

"You're joking! Back up that hill! Of course not. They'll catch up."

But minutes later, the others were still not in sight. "Come on," Ted said.

"Where to?"

"Down there." He pointed across the patch of bright bluebells where a small brook gurgled its way over rocks and through the bracken. "We can sit on the bank and wait."

"What about the bikes?"

"Leave them. They'll be all right. The others'll see them and know where we are." He climbed the stile and, taking her hand, helped her over it.

Cilla sat down beside the stream and took off her shoes and socks. Her hot feet tingled as she dangled them in the icy water. Ted sat beside her and peeled off his shoes and socks.

"I wish you didn't have to be back in Portsmouth tomorrow. Your leave went by so quickly this time," she said.

"Yeah, I could do with another two weeks. It's been fun, but duty calls." He grinned at her.

"Ted Evans, I do believe you aren't really sorry to be returning to your ship." Cilla pursed her lips and studied him for a moment. "Ted, do you think there'll be a war? My dad says that man in Germany is wicked."

"I don't know. I heard some of the blokes on my ship talking about it. They seemed to think there'll be a war in Europe, at least. Perhaps Britain won't get into it."

"But if we do, you'll be in the thick of it, won't you?"

"I'm in the navy. If Britain goes to war, of course I'll be in it."

"But you're only eighteen."

He hadn't responded, but flicked his toe in the water, sending droplets on her.

She squealed and, scooping water onto her foot, sloshed it at him.

He jumped into the brook and began kicking the icy water at her.

Cilla slid down the bracken to join him and soon they were drenching each other, laughing. Squealing, Cilla turned and scrambled up the bank, but Ted grabbed her around the waist and together they fell, breathless and laughing. He moved his grip to her shoulders, pinning her to the grassy bank, and fell across her.

Suddenly, Ted grew very quiet. Slowly he released his grip, but his hands didn't move from her shoulders. He gazed so deeply at her that Cilla could see the golden flecks in his brown eyes.

Her laughter faded as a strange sensation came over her. Her heart pounded. Deep inside her, muscles she didn't know she had moved.

Ted's lips came softly to cover hers, and while the kiss lingered, she looped her arms around his neck. He ended the kiss. "Cor, Cilla," he breathed against her lips. Hungrily he kissed her again, hard and demanding. A moment later the touch of his tongue on her lips confirmed that this was a different Ted—

Ted with some newfound knowledge and experience.

She felt him tremble as he pressed himself against her. Her insides were on fire, and she was vaguely aware that some of her shirt buttons were open. He cupped her eager breast, and the muscles in her groin contracted again.

He released her lips and looked down at her. Stroking her hair, he studied her face as if he'd never seen it before. "You're beautiful, Cilla."

Beautiful! He'd said she was beautiful. The look on his face as it travelled lower was one she'd never seen in all the years she'd known him. How feminine she felt...how powerful.

Then gently, ever so gently, his fingertips traced the outline of her nipple straining inside her bra, and a little sound rose in her throat.

"Hey! Where are you two?" Nigel called from the road.

Ted jumped back from Cilla, breathing heavily.

"Cilla! Ted!" Her brother's voice persisted.

"Coming!" She jumped to her feet, buttoning her wet shirt and tucking it into the waistband of her shorts.

Ted rested his head on his bent knees and, without looking at her, said, "You go on. I'll catch up." His voice was husky.

Cilla snatched up her shoes and socks and picked her way through the bluebells. She ran up the incline just as Nigel was climbing over the stile.

"Where were you?" A frown of suspicion furrowed his brow. "Where's Ted?"

"He's coming." Her cheeks burned. She sat down to pull on her socks and shoes, wondering if her brother could hear her thundering heart, or if he had noticed the shirt button she'd forgotten to fasten.

After that day nothing remained the same between Cilla and Ted. She'd been frightened by the power of her own instincts, and when he was home, he seemed to avoid situations where they'd be alone...

Off and on, as she dozed throughout the endless night in the lifeboat, Cilla's thoughts were never far from Ted. She tried to remember when she had begun to seek opportunities to be alone with him, only to have her efforts thwarted by her brothers. That wasn't quite true, either. She remembered the last night Ted was home. The perfect evening—and she'd fought with him over the very plight she was in now. For the first time since the sinking, she allowed herself some self-pity. It wasn't fair that things should have turned out like this. Why hadn't she listened to Ted? He'd told her something like this could happen, but she'd been intent on proving her independence. She should have stayed home and married Ted on his next leave. She'd probably die in this bloody storm—in this bloody boat. She lowered her head, tucking her chin into the collar of her coat, and quietly sobbed for what might have been.

CHAPTER FOURTEEN

Dark clouds scudded across the sky. Black sledgehammer waves pummelled the raft, repeatedly drenching Ted and his two companions. Exhausted by the relentless punishment and in danger of being washed off the raft, the sailors hooked their cramped legs together.

Martin and Shaw dozed while Ted kept watch, just in case. In case of what? In case the Royal Navy came? In case the cursed ocean stopped heaving? Humph! That wasn't bloody likely. He tried to imagine the sensation of being warm, but his teeth chattered and he shivered. The rum was gone.

A short distance from the raft, a lifeboat swamped to her gunwales and kept afloat only by her buoyancy tanks sat low in the water. Just the tips of the bow and stern showed above the waves. Her passengers, up to their necks in water, gave the illusions of sitting unsupported in the sea. It reminded Ted of the picture in a nursery rhyme book he'd had as a child, and he had the insane urge to sing out "Rub a dub-dub, three men in a tub."

"Sod this!" Johnny Martin straightened up. "If we don't get picked up soon, we've had it. You realise that, don't you? We can't last another night on this bastard of a raft."

"Wha'd you mean? We don't have much choice." Ted eyed the big sailor.

Martin laughed sardonically. "Oh, yes we do! We could just drop over the side...put an end to all this. Unless the flamin' Navy comes before night. Either way the odds are about the same." He slumped back.

Ted turned to Rob Shaw to gauge his reaction to Martin's suggestion, and what he saw in the young sailor's red-rimmed eyes made his skin crawl with fear.

"I'm with Johnny." Rob's voice was dull and flat. "I'm too bleedin' cold to care anymore. If a ship doesn't come before dark, I'm going over the side."

Ted wasn't ready to give up, but he couldn't make it alone. Somehow he had to goad Shaw and Martin into hanging on. Cold and depleted down to the very centre of his soul, he closed his eyes to clear his mind and struggled to marshal some reasonable arguments to use.

"You pair of bloody fools. You've both got so much to live for—and we aren't dead yet." He sounded much more cheerful than he felt, but the shrieking wind knew—and mocked him. He groaned and clutched his midriff as his stomach cramped on the poisonous oil. "Johnny, wh...what about your wife?" He gasped while the pain subsided. "How...will she manage without you? And what about your girl, Rob? You can't give up. Think what you'll miss..."

"Shut up, Ted! Can't you see we've had it? We're done for. We can't last more than a few more hours." Shaw huddled with his back to the breaking waves.

"Well, I'm not giving up. My girl's out there somewhere, in one of those boats." He swept his arm in the direction of the lifeboats still bobbing up and down in the heaving waves. "And I intend to marry her as soon as I can."

The raft lifted on the crests, and Ted's body rose with it. Then as the vessel toppled back into the trough, he was momentarily suspended in mid-air. Gravity reasserted, smashing him back down with a thud, and forcing his breath to escape in noisy grunts.

At mid-day they ate tinned salmon, but with nothing to wash down the hard biscuits, they'd thrown them into the sea in disgust.

Now thirst was robbing Ted of any reasonable thoughts, and the salt water searing his blistered and bleeding hands drove him almost out of his mind. His resolve began to wane, and he raged against the malevolent storm. He mentally shook himself. He must not let the elements triumph in this battle for their lives. Perhaps if he could keep the other two occupied, they wouldn't think about taking the easy way out.

"At least let's get something to eat," Ted yelled above the banshee screech of the wind.

"Sod off, Evans! Don't come the Cheerful Charlie bit with me." Martin's black eyebrows came together in a deep scowl.

Ted studied Martin, measuring his capacity for anger at this stage. Was it enough to keep him alive? He braced himself and rummaged in the food locker. "Oh, my God! How did I miss this." He held up a tin of peaches.

"Open it, for Christ's sake!" Martin lunged at the locker. "Where's the opener?"

Ted felt a glimmer of hope.

Carefully, so that the bucking raft would not deny him even one drop of the sweet, cool peach juice, Ted sipped his share from a sardine tin. The nectar trickled over his tongue and down his raw throat, buoying his spirits. He watched his companions licking the peach juice, hoping to see a sign of some resolve to stay alive...Was it there?

Fingers of orange light from the setting sun broke through the clouds and danced on the white-capped waves. Ted blinked against the searing reflection and counted the other lifeboats. Some of them bobbed about empty, as did four nearby rafts, so he concentrated on the boats that still showed evidence of life. Even in its groggy state, his half-frozen brain knew it was especially important not to lose touch with those boats. He cursed the raft having no torch-light and prayed that the other boats would again flash theirs through the night.

He shifted his gaze to the Northeast, to a tiny speck at the edge of the horizon. Several times during the day an argument had erupted when a seabird or a smudge of cloud had masqueraded as a phantom ship. But this speck grew steadily larger. He squinted, hardly able to breathe as a ship with a funnel took shape before his anxious eyes.

"Look behind you, there's a destroyer." His leaden arms and legs stubbornly refused to move, but his heart thumped.

Martin and Shaw in unison glared at him. "Is this another of your bleedin'...?" Martin mumbled.

"No! Look for yourself. What do you think?" Ted didn't trust his own eyes anymore. "Go on, have a look."

With surprising agility, Martin sprang to his feet. Shaw clambered up and began to wave and yell in a raspy voice.

Only then, when Ted was sure he wasn't imagining it, did he haul himself to his feet and wave both hands. No sound escaped his raw, tortured throat as tears coursed down his cheeks.

People prostrate in the other lifeboats lifted themselves and croaked cheers. The grey warship raced toward them with her sirens hooting and twin rooster-tails of wake spewing behind her.

She swooped past the life-raft and sent a swell that made it difficult to stand, but Ted wanted to keep waving, just in case the ship hadn't seen the raft—or would leave without them!

He thought he would burst with relief and joy. He suddenly felt a great love for his companions. Slipping and staggering on the slick surface of the raft, they hugged and embraced each other, laughing hysterically.

Battling the fierce waves, the destroyer lowered a longboat, and the sailors steered from lifeboat to lifeboat. Ted's heart ached to see the pathetic little forms, too weak to stand, being carried to the deck of the rescue ship. Dear God! The children were half-naked, and the Lascars weren't wearing much either! How had they survived the storm?

Ted willed the rescuers to hurry. It seemed to take ages to transfer the children out of the lifeboat to the longboat, fight their way to the destroyer, and carry each child up the netting. A couple of women managed to climb to the deck unassisted. Others needed help. Ted scanned the survivors, looking to find Cilla among them. Perhaps she was in one of the far boats.

Soon the warship turned stern-on to the raft and edged toward it, churning up the waves and covering the three men with spume and spindrift.

Liquid poured from the ship's deck and coated the water around the raft. Martin looked up, glowering at the sailors peering over the decks of the ship. "Watch it! You clumsy bastards. What're trying to do to us?"

"It's oil," Ted said, relieved that the waves calmed almost immediately.

A rope snaked from the deck and smacked Shaw in the face, then jumped tantalisingly just out of his grasp. "I can't catch. Oh... oh!" he croaked.

The sailors on the deck retrieved the line and threw it again. Tumbling over Shaw in his eagerness, Ted caught the rope and hung on as the raft inched closer to the hull of the big ship and the net was within his grasp. His legs shook and buckled as he hauled himself upward.

A sailor with a jolly round face hefted them one after the other onto the deck. "All aboard for the skylark," he yelled.

"Thanks, mate." Ted grasped the sailor's hand, reluctant to let go for fear he and the ship were mirages, but the solid deck seemed real enough. In his imagination the raft still bucked him, and he lost his balance and staggered.

"Cor blimey! Drunk again, eh?" The sailor grabbed Ted's elbow and steadied him.

A tot of rum was shoved into his palsied hand, and he downed the liquid in one searing gulp. Someone threw a blanket over his sodden clothes and led him to the galley. The aroma of rich beef broth and fresh bread greeted his starved senses. His mouth watered, but his stiff dry lips refused to open. He forced out his tongue and ran it over the cracked surface, tasting a mixture of blood and salt. With trembling hands he dipped the crusty bread into the dish and sucked the soup. It burned his mouth, but he relished the taste and the sensation of it trickling down his parched throat. He ate a second bowl of soup and loaded his tea with extra milk to cool it.

A *HMS Tornado* crewman offered Ted the use of his shaving gear and a change of clothes. "You can catch a kip in my hammock too, if you'd like," said the young sailor.

"Thanks for the shave and clothes, mate. Maybe I'll take you up on the hammock later. Right now I have to find someone. Do you know where the civilian survivors are?"

"Some of the kids are down in the engine room and boiler room, thawing out. Some have been taken to the sick-bay."

Ted's legs still felt rubbery as he set out to search the ship for Cilla.

He found a group of exhausted children huddled in blankets in the boiler room, sipping what smelled like cocoa. Their drawn faces and hair were caked with white salt crystals, and their haunted eyes followed Ted as he crouched beside a freckle-faced little boy of about eight or nine. His skin was chalk-white, and his teeth chattered continually although the room was hot.

"I...say. I...say, thanks for rescuing us."

Ted smiled at him and gently placed his hand on the boy's stiff hair. "I didn't rescue you. I was out there with you."

"Oh." The boy stared at Ted.

Ted raised his voice so that all the children could hear him. "I'm looking for Miss Thornton. Have any of you seen her since you came aboard?"

A boy of about fourteen who appeared to be all arms and legs spoke up. "She weren't wif us."

"Do you know who she is?" Ted wondered if perhaps these boys didn't know the women escorts.

"Yeah, but I ain't seen 'er. Sorry."

In the far corner a girl waved her hand, attracting Ted's attention. Her carrot-red hair was frosted white with crusted salt. "I know Miss Thornton, but I haven't seen her since her lifeboat went off on its own. It never stayed with the rest of us," she slurred through raw, cracked lips.

"You mean her lifeboat wasn't out there when we were rescued?" He swallowed his gorge. This was a possibility he hadn't anticipated.

The girl nodded, staring at Ted.

"Thanks." A knot formed in the pit of his stomach as he turned away. *Where was Cilla?*

He found more children thawing in the engine room, and yelling to be heard above the noise, he questioned them. In response he received blank looks and shaken heads.

He searched the companionways, where children slept two to a hammock, but Cilla was not there. He questioned everyone he saw. Frantically, he asked the names of the adults in the cabins and of those who were in the sick bay. Cilla was nowhere on the ship.

Tears of frustration stung his eyes as wearily he climbed into a hammock. Every joint in his body ached, and his eyelids refused to stay open any longer, but his brain whirled with questions. Where was Cilla? Had another ship rescued her, or was she still out there somewhere? He shuddered. He'd doubted he could last two nights on the open sea. Her first consideration would be for the children in her care, not for herself. Would her dedication to the kids be enough to keep her alive? Suddenly, inexplicably, he felt her presence. He knew it wasn't tangible, but he reached out his hand into the darkness, trying to touch the deep love she was sending to him.

He concentrated on sending her his thoughts, and wherever she was, he knew she was drawing strength from his love. Cilla, Cilla, I love you.

CHAPTER FIFTEEN

Ted waited impatiently on the deck of *HMS Tornado* for permission to disembark. He was anxious to get ashore and telephone his mother. She might have news of Cilla. She could even be home by now! He placed his hand over his hammering heart. The emotional upheaval since the sinking, and worrying about Cilla, was beginning to take a toll. He sometimes found breathing difficult, and his hands shook.

A convoy of ambulances leaving the Greenock dock with survivors from the *Punjohpur* reminded Ted of those who hadn't survived. He closed his eyes and pinched the bridge of his nose, but the ghastly scenes, forever chiselled in his memory, remained vivid. Images of children valiantly struggling to keep their heads out of the oil-coated water refused to go away. His mind pictured the little bodies tossed like rag dolls in the waves around the raft. It wrenched at his insides.

He'd never forget the destroyer steaming for home under a brilliant sky with the three small shapes draped in Union Jacks laid out side by side on the deck. The three young children having survived the torpedoing and that dreadful day and night in an open lifeboat, only to die after being rescued.

He sucked in a breath and blew it out hard, remembering. The *Tornado's* crew, solemn and moist-eyed, lined up in ramrod silence on her quarter-deck. Young, smooth-cheeked sailors attending their first full naval funeral. Old salts whose weather-burnished faces reflected disbelief that even callous war could be so pitiless. The captain's voice cracking with emotion as he read the burial service, and the anguished weeping of survivors as the three little bodies were lowered into the sea.

"Evans!"

Ted blinked the tears from his eyes and turned to the officer addressing him. "Sir?"

"Here's your voucher to get rekitted." He handed Ted several papers. "Here's your travel voucher and a forty-eight-hour pass. Report to Naval Headquarters building." He pointed to a grey stone structure guarded by sailors with rifles and fixed bayonets. "They'll issue you a new pay-book and an advance and tell you where to pick up new uniforms."

Without a hat, he couldn't salute, but he stood at attention until the officer departed, then he stuffed the papers in the pocket of his borrowed jacket and ran down the gangplank, taking giant strides.

He licked his lips, tasting the smear of salve as he dialled the phone. Impatient, he fidgeted, listening for the familiar voice on the other end. *Come on Mum, hurry up and answer the bloody phone.*

Ted didn't remember his father, and his mother, a nurse, had had to work to support herself and Ted, so he'd spent a great deal of time at the Thorntons'. Cilla's father had been like the one he never had. A smile turned up the corners of Ted's mouth as he remembered when Cilla had been about four and asked, "Why does Ted go to Auntie Mary's every night?" She'd thought he was another brother.

"Hello." The voice sounded flat.

"Hello, Mum."

"Oh, Ted. I'm so glad to hear from you. Where are you? I thought you were at sea." Her voice quavered.

"I was, Mum. I got in this morning. Mum, is Cilla at home?"

His mother hiccupped a sob. "Oh, Ted. No… Oh, dear. You don't know, do you? She was going to Canada. And, Oh…Ted, Cilla's ship was sunk."

"I know, Mum. We were on the same ship. Has she been rescued yet?"

His mother gasped. "You were torpedoed, too? Oh, Ted…what happened? Are you all right, son?"

"Yes, Mum. I'm fine. What about Cilla? Have you talked to the Thorntons? Have they heard if Cilla's safe?"

"I don't…don't understand. Isn't she with you?"

"No. She wasn't picked up with us. Have the Thorntons heard anything?"

"What does that mean, Ted? Where is she?" Her voice sounded heavy with concern.

He sucked in his breath to steady himself. Oh, God! He wished she'd stop asking questions he couldn't answer. "It means I don't know where she is, Mum. That's what I'm trying to find out. What have the Thorntons been told?" He hadn't meant to use such an exasperated tone of voice to his mother.

She didn't seem to notice. "They got a letter this morning saying that the ship was sunk, but nothing more. Oh, Ted! Thank God I didn't know you were involved. Are you hurt, son?" Her voice was shrill with concern.

"No, Mum. I'm all right, but I'd better phone Uncle Dan and Aunt Maude.

I'm coming home as soon as I get kitted out again. See you tonight." He hung up the phone. Squaring his shoulders, he took several deep breaths while he rearranged his jumbled thoughts, then dialled the phone, still wondering what to say to Cilla's parents.

"Hello." Tension vibrated through Mr. Thornton's voice. In the background Ted could hear a woman keening.

"Hello, Uncle Dan. It's Ted."

A gasp. "Oh, Ted! Is that really you, lad? Have...you heard...Did you hear about Cilla?"

"Yes, Uncle Dan, I know. I was on the ship with Cilla."

"You were!? She's with you, then?" The joy and relief in his voice hit Ted like a hammer blow. "Maude...it's Ted and Cilla..."

"No...! Uncle Dan. No...! Cilla isn't with me," he yelled over Dan Thornton's exuberant announcement. "Her lifeboat hasn't been found yet."

"Oh," was all her father said.

"I'm sorry...I didn't mean to get your hopes up." He coughed to hide the catch in his voice. "How is Auntie Maude doing?"

"Not very well, Ted. It's the not knowing what's happened to Priscilla, you see. If we knew she was...if we knew for certain..." He cleared his throat. "Poor Maude. Whenever she closes her eyes, she imagines she sees Cilla bounced about in a lifeboat. She can't seem to stop crying." He sounded on the verge of tears himself.

"You mustn't give up hope. There's always a chance. When I last saw her she was in a lifeboat with some British officers. They'll take good care of her." He knew that was true. The mariners would give their own lives to save the women and children. But he also knew the lifeboat was overcrowded and that the storm had continued even after he was rescued. He shuddered, remembering the howling wind and the towering waves. He squeezed his eyes shut and fought a momentary doubt. *Stop it! She's alive. She's alive. Keep believing that.*

"Where are you, Ted? Can you tell me what happened?"

"I'm in Scotland. I'll be home tonight. I'll come and see you then."

"Good lad."

An hour later Ted was on his way home. Home to what? Cilla wasn't there. She'd always been there before. He didn't relish the task ahead of him, but somehow he had to convince her parents to stop grieving. His love for her gave him special insight, but would they believe that?

His new shoes hurt his toes. The skin on his feet was raw from being wet so long on the raft. Having to run to catch the fast train to London hadn't helped. He had the rare good fortune to get a seat in a compartment. He tossed his kitbag full of new clothes up on the luggage rack, leaned back against the upholstered headrest, and closed his eyes.

Remembering Cilla on the deck of the *Punjohpur* in the gale brought a smile to his thoughts. She'd been so defensive about that bloody Yank kissing her, and Ted had been so jealous he couldn't bring himself to tell her he knew she hadn't expected or even wanted that kiss.

Then he'd tried to out-scream the wind. It was hardly the time or the place, but he wished they'd had more time that night.

He smiled inside envisioning Cilla's parents' reaction when he formally asked her father's permission to marry her.

As the train chuffed into Victoria Station, his thoughts took on a more sombre note. Unless Cilla's parents believed in his intuition, they'd think he'd lost his mind. His heart told him. He could feel it. She was alive. He just had to find a way to convince her parents that he was right.

CHAPTER SIXTEEN

The new day dawned so like the previous day, and the day before it, that Cilla couldn't tell the difference between them. The lifeboat still heaved and pitched as it had for days and nights without let-up. In the growing light she prayed as she counted the bruised and exhausted children. The twelve had survived another cold and sea-battered night.

"Listen, everybody," Darroch croaked over the wind. "Our biggest concern now is fresh water. We still have a good supply, and if we ration it we can make it last until we reach Ireland. So, instead of water twice a day, we will have it only in the evening."

Cilla was already very thirsty, and the thought of having to wait until dusk for the meagre drink added fire to her parched throat. She licked her cracked lips and tasted salt. "How long before we make land?" she asked.

"I'm not sure, but we'll make it before we run out of water. Don't you worry. We just have to be frugal with what we have."

Ramboon, the wiry little Asian, narrowed his eyes while he listened to Darroch. He often told the other Indians what the Europeans were saying. As they listened to his latest translation, the Asians' eyes widened. Jabbering and obviously agitated, they pointed at the children.

"What's the matter wi' ye?" Darroch jumped to his feet, towering above the smaller men.

"Sah. The men are concerned that they will not receive a fair share of the water, sah." He spoke in a soft sing-song tone while his head bobbed from side to side. "Perhaps the children will be given extra water," Ramboon wheedled. He sat looking up at Darroch with a wide smile, but his demeanour was insolent.

"That's ridiculous. Everyone gets an equal share of two ounces per day. And tell your men not to drink the seawater. Do you understand? They'll get sick."

The Lascars prayed several times a day, beginning each prayer session by washing themselves with seawater. They scooped it into their ears and mouths, and didn't seem to spit it all out.

Ramboon drew himself up and regarded Darroch with an air of defiance. "Sah, in our own country we are used to drinking foul water. The sea will not harm us, if Allah wills it."

The Asians eyed the children warily and regarded Cilla with flagrant black eyes as she worked four buttons off her coat. "Millie would you give me your buttons, please?"

"I'd gladly give you the shirt off my back, Cilla, but what do you want the buttons for?"

"I read about it once. A group of people, lost in the desert without water, survived this way." She passed one button to each child. "Suck on this, it will help to make saliva."

"Of course! What a great idea." Millie turned to Clint. "Come on, Yank, give us your buttons."

"What, all of 'em?"

"Well, not the ones off your fly!"

Clint smiled for the first time since they had climbed aboard the lifeboat. Seasickness and the elements had taken a heavy toll on him. He appeared gaunt and pale, but he ripped the buttons from his shirt without a word of complaint.

Cilla didn't ask the Lascars for their shirt buttons. They had little as it was to keep their clothes fastened, but the British sailors gave up what buttons they could spare, and soon Cilla had enough for each child and adult to have one.

Millie lifted Kitty's foot and gently massaged it.

Tears filled the little girl's eyes and a cry hovered just behind the clamped mouth.

"I'm sorry if this hurts you, Kitty," Millie patted the little foot with the corner of her wool coat. "Cilla, the children are showing signs of trench-foot," Millie said.

"Trench-foot! Isn't that what cows get?"

"No, silly! It's a disease caused by this." She pointed to several pairs of bare feet soaking in the water on the bottom of the boat. "Soldiers in the First World War named it. They spent days at a time standing in frozen, muddy trenches. These children need to get their circulation moving. And somehow we have to try and keep their feet dry."

Cilla frowned. Keep dry! First they needed to *get* dry! She reached for Ruby's hand to comfort her. The child's fingers were stiff, but no more so than Cilla's own. Frozen blood caked her shredded flesh.

How could she and Millie warm children who wore only nightclothes and a lifejacket? They didn't even have shoes.

"Millie, what can we do?"

"All right children, listen." Millie's dry raspy voice crackled with concern. "I want you all to shake your hands—hard, and rub them together until they tingle and feel warm. Dry your feet on our coats, then massage each toe and around your heel." The children began to follow her directions. "That's right. Good! Now, try to keep them up, out of the bottom of the boat."

The miserable day turned into another miserable night.

Cilla was aroused from her shallow sleep by children's complaints.

"Go away. There isn't room for you. Ow! You trod on my hand," Brian yelled.

Black silhouettes bumped against Cilla. "What's going on?"

"It's the Indians, Miss Cilla. They're trying to get in our shelter."

"What's all the commotion?" Darroch yelled from the stern.

Cilla told him.

"You bastards," he roared. "Get back where you belong." A sliver of moon peeked around a dark cloud and glinted on Darroch's gun. The Lascars grumbled and slithered away to huddle in their wet blankets on the floor of the boat and under the thwarts.

After breakfast, Darroch picked his way from stern to bow, carefully stepping over the Lascars packed tightly in the bottom of the boat. "I'd like a wee word, ladies."

Cilla and Millie scrunched to give him a corner to sit on.

The First Officer unconsciously patted his pockets. "Damn, I miss m' pipe," he said as he squeezed between the two women. He narrowed his eyes and jerked his head at the Asians. "I've concerns about yon Lascars."

Cilla glanced at the pitiful brown-skinned men, dejected and shivering in the bottom of the boat. They no longer baled, and as the days dragged on and their energies flagged, the Asians had grown more surly and mutinous, refusing to take a turn on the handles unless Ramboon gave the order.

"It won't take much to send yon heathens over the edge." Darroch sat with his back to the Asians and kept his voice at a level barely audible over the howl of the wind. "They've given themselves up to the will of Allah. If He deems it, they will be rescued, if not, He will take them. But until then, they want to be sure they are receiving their fair share of the water."

"But they are." Cilla had seen the purser carefully measuring out the water so that no one had even a drop more than the others.

"Aye, but they don't understand it. In their culture men come before all others. Male children are above women, and wee girls are at the bottom of the chain. They don't understand why these bairns are sheltered and they're not. The only thing that keeps them in check is my revolver. If they thought I wouldn't shoot them, they'd not hesitate to throw the children, and you two lasses, over the side." He jerked his thumb at the fitful waves.

It had not escaped the Europeans' notice that the Asians outnumbered them. Cilla thanked God once again for Darroch. Without him they would all probably have perished long before now.

"You must at all costs keep your eyes on the bairns. And whatever you do, don't let the Lascars think for even one minute that you doubt our rescue." Darroch's bright blue eyes had lost their sparkle, and he wore a constant, worried frown as he chewed his lip where his pipe used to rest.

Cilla tried to encourage the children to talk of rescue, but she kept her own nagging doubts to herself. When her spirits sagged and she didn't think she would ever get warm again, she imagined sitting by a roaring fire. Her fantasies were not very successful. She moved painfully. She would never complain out loud in front of the stoic children, but there wasn't a muscle in her body that didn't hurt from being cramped. Her hands were shreds of bleeding flesh and her eyes burned. Her throat was so dry and swollen; she could no longer swallow even her own saliva. If they weren't rescued soon, they would all die of dehydration. The children had rarely cried or complained, but it was obvious, since the water ration cut, they suffered the most. There was hardly any call for the bucket now with so little to eliminate.

Ruby withdrew a little more each day, until she stopped talking about Freddie altogether. Kitty no longer declared "the Royal Navy ain't going to le' us dahn. Me mum said if we was to get sunk, the Navy'd save us." She remained the most cheerful of the girls, but talk of rescue seemed like a waste of spittle.

Just before dusk the purser passed out the day's water ration. "Anyone for a biscuit? We have plenty." Nobody took him up on the offer.

"When I get back home, I'm going to have the biggest plate of fish and chips you ever saw." Brian ran his tongue over his dry salt-caked lips.

"I'm going to have me mum do a loverly roast beef and Yorkshire pud." Paula's mouth worked and her eyes glazed as if seeing the meal in her mind's eye. "Lots of loverly brown gravy all over it."

"What's your favourite meal, Ruby?" Cilla asked. She was becoming increasingly worried about the little Cockney.

"I don't 'ave one," she mumbled through swollen, cracked lips.

Kitty rubbed her tummy. "I've got a favourite. Bangers and mash, floatin' in puddles of thick brahn gravy."

Whether from hunger or talk of home, the children's spirits flagged, and they fell into silence.

By nightfall the storm grew to an ugly, menacing foe. The lifeboat rode the waves like a roller-coaster. One minute Cilla felt herself buoyed to the summit of a precipice, dizzy and terrified, and the next facing a wall of black water lipped in foam that avalanched over the lifeboat from two directions.

"We'll have to ride this one out at anchor," Darroch yelled at Sutherland.

The sailors manoeuvred the stern of the lifeboat into the waves and threw the canvas-covered frame out to float, dragging against the wind.

During the night, the air grew cold and the rain turned to sleet.

The reluctant dawn found the battered lifeboat encircled by an unbroken horizon. Rain had frozen on the gunwales, and Cilla's fingers bled as she chipped the ice off and sucked it. The tantalising drops of liquid left her desperate for more.

Brian gave a sudden shout. "A ship! Look over there."

"Hey, yeah. It's coming this way." Clint stood up.

Visibility was good. A small cargo vessel, about four miles off, headed straight toward the lifeboat.

Cilla's stomach knotted with excitement. The children waved and cheered with raspy, dry voices. The Lascars chatted, suddenly animated, and Clint and the British officers took down the awning, preparing to be taken aboard the rescue ship.

The steamer stopped and turned broadside on to the lifeboat, but then, incredibly, she slew around and sailed away. If the ship's crew hadn't seen them, surely they could hear the hoarse shouts and anguished wails. The sailors cursed, and the children screamed as loudly as their arid throats allowed, waving and jumping up and down on the locker until the ship receded over the horizon.

Cilla stared for a long time at the empty sea.

Paula sniffled.

"Maybe it wasn't a ship after all," Brian said at last.

"Don't be so daft. 'Course it was a ship!" Kitty snapped.

Devoid of emotion, Cilla's body seemed light and hollow. She couldn't even find words to comfort the children. Everyone fell strangely silent. For many hours the only sound was the wind howling through the canvas.

At dusk the purser passed cans of condensed milk with two holes punched in the top.

"Where's the water ration?" Brian asked.

The purser glanced first at Darroch, then at the Lascars. "I...I'm sorry. The water is finished."

Clint glared at Darroch. "You son-of-a-bitch!"

"You said we'd get to Ireland before the water ran out," Brian said through a sob.

Ramboon muttered to the Lascars and immediately the clamour of jabbering voices brought Darroch to his feet, waving his revolver.

Darroch yelled. The Asians shrieked. Clint swore. Finally, when it was obvious nothing could be changed, everyone settled back down in their seats.

Without complaining, the children sipped their condensed milk.

Cilla sucked the thick liquid and rolled it around the inside of her mouth. It coated and soothed as it slipped down her parched throat, but in the end it only enhanced her maddening thirst.

"I know. How about some more about the witch of Buckinghamshire?" Millie smiled through cracked lips.

Cilla marvelled at the nurse. Good old Millie to the rescue with another of her stories. *How does she do it?*

"Now. Where were we?" Millie made herself as comfortable as the conditions allowed.

"I know! I know! The witch had just taken the hurt cat home," Paula said and wiped her nose on the back of her hand.

"No! The cat had just told the witch about the cruel man and..." Ruby interjected.

"And...and...the witch was going to put a curse on the man, and..." Bobby's words fell over each other.

Several times Cilla had thought the story had ended, but each time the children flagged, Millie came up with a new episode, and Cilla's respect and gratitude for the nurse grew.

CHAPTER SEVENTEEN

The train station, a scene of organised chaos, swarmed in a sea of military uniforms. Some people rushed up the platform; others forced a path in the opposite direction.

Soldiers dressed in khaki distinguished from each other only by their regimental shoulder flashes and hat badges. Women in auxiliary-service uniform or Land Army hob-nail boots. Sailors in uniforms of many different nationalities bumped into RAF with shoulder flashes of Canada and the European nations who struggled under Nazi occupation.

The few civilians stuck out amid the mass of uniforms, and a woman with honey-blonde hair—hardly unusual in England—had been enough to make Ted's stomach tighten with thoughts of Cilla.

He readjusted his kitbag to a more comfortable position on his shoulder and forged a path through the throng toward the gate leading to platform number seven.

A young boy carrying an armload of newspapers shouted to be heard above the din. "Paper, paper. See what 'idler's done now. Paper, sailor?" he addressed Ted as he jostled his way through.

Ted fumbled in the pocket of his bellbottoms and pulled out a coin, tossing it to the lad and snatching the newspaper without stopping. "Cheers, mate," he called over his shoulder.

His kitbag bounced painfully against his neck as he picked up his pace in response to the train conductor's whistle. Passing through the gate, he paused just long enough to get his ticket punched, then ran down the platform as fast as the heavy kitbag bumping on his shoulder allowed.

The train huffed and began to slowly pull forward. He grabbed the door handle, opened it, and tossing his bag into the train corridor, hauled himself in after it.

It was as crowded as Ted expected. These days, there wasn't a train travelling through Britain that wasn't jam-packed with members of the forces. He climbed over an RAF Corporal and tripped over a Scottish soldier before he found a vacant spot in the corridor. He pushed his kitbag as close to the window as he could, leaving just enough room for someone to squeeze past. He collapsed onto the canvas bag, gasping for breath. The air hung heavy with the inevitable blue haze of cigarette smoke, which he knew from past experience would become increasingly thicker along the journey.

After a few minutes, when his breathing slowed, he opened the newspaper, and the headline danced before his disbelieving eyes:

213 CHILDREN DIE AS HUNS SINK LINER IN STORM

A giant fist punched Ted in the belly, and his heart turned to ice as he scanned the rest of the story.

Two hundred and thirteen out of a party of 241 children being evacuated to Canada died along with fifteen of their escorts.

So it was official. The Press had the story. His throat burned and hot tears blurred his vision, but not his memories of the dead children. The newspaper report ended by saying that it had been six days since the liner sank, and the search for more survivors had been called off.

They're wrong! Cilla is still out there somewhere!

Warmth! Cilla stirred, aware of a gentle rocking motion. The raging storm had at last exhausted itself. She blinked at the brilliant sunshine splintering against her eyes and lifted her face to bask in its healing rays. She tried to smile, but her cracked lips were too painful to move. Then a dreadful thought struck! What if it was a dream or a mirage? She held her breath, fearful that if anyone spoke, it would destroy the calm.

The purser broke the spell. "What a beautiful morning," he croaked.

Cilla cringed, half-expecting the waves to batter the hull of the lifeboat again. She breathed.

For the first time in seven nights and six days, the purser was able to walk the length of the lifeboat without being thrown off his feet. "I have a special treat for breakfast," he said as he passed the used sardine tins.

"Cor, blimey. It really is a treat!" Kitty said.

Cilla carefully accepted her tin from the purser and peered into it. Tears blurred the vision of two peach slices floating in a mouthful of juice. Her taste buds ached with anticipation. She worked one cool peach slice around in her mouth before biting into it. Sweet juice trickled down her throat. She forced herself to stop and think about the sensation before she put the second slice in her mouth. Then she licked every last drop of juice from her salty fingers.

The peaches had a miraculous effect. Spirits rose, and for the first time in days, the children actually laughed.

Bobby finished his peaches and climbed onto the locker. He flexed his back, then peered at the sea and pointed. "Hey! Look at that. What're they?"

"They're whales," said Darroch, shading his eyes.

The pod cruised nearby. In ones and twos they breached the surface, shooting noisy jets of water high into the air. Leaping above the water, they threw themselves headfirst back into the sea. Their flukes, extended like enormous butterfly wings, created swells that gently rocked the lifeboat.

Suddenly, on some silent signal, the great beasts turned toward the lifeboat.

"Aghh!" A Lascar, perched on a thwart, shrieked. He jumped from his seat as if it were on fire. His eyes were wide with fear. He shrieked, pointing at the approaching whales. Screaming unintelligible words, his companions fought each other for a handle of the boats propelling gear. The lifeboat began to tip and sway violently.

"Sit down, you stupid bastards. You'll capsize us," Clint yelled, clinging to the gunwale.

The terror-stricken Asians pumped the boat out of the path of the whales with more energy than they had shown in a week. Just as suddenly as they turned toward the lifeboat, the whales changed direction and swam away.

The children snickered first. The snickers turned to giggles. Cilla picked it up, feeling weightless. Then Millie giggled. One by one the British crew and Clint joined in until all the Europeans were falling about with laughter.

The Lascars' scowls slowly turned to embarrassed grins, then chuckles, until everyone in the lifeboat teetered on the verge of hysteria.

The last great tail disappeared over the horizon.

Throughout the morning, between talk of the whales, the children mimicked the Asians. With gales of laughter, they re-enacted the Indians nimbly hopping to their feet and propelling the lifeboat out of the path of the whales.

In the mid-afternoon a seagull circled the lifeboat. Cilla craned her neck and watched the soaring bird, envying its freedom.

"Here. If you aren't going to eat these, give them to the gulls." The purser handed out some of the hard biscuits, but the mood turned sombre and the children stuffed them into their life jackets.

Kitty held hers out to Cilla. "Would you mind this for me, please?" Cilla put it in her coat pocket with the others that the children had asked to have saved.

Several more gulls swooped over the lifeboat, but they left without being fed.

"Where'd they come from, sir? Are we near land?" Brian asked.

"Aye. Close." Darroch squinted off across the placid sea. "I reckon we've reached the sea-lanes."

The children cheered. The Lascars jabbered and gestured, and fighting tears, Cilla hugged Millie.

Then over Millie's shoulder she blinked at the shape on the horizon. Cilla pointed. "Look! A ship!"

Sutherland balanced himself on the gunwale and, clinging to the mast for support, craned his neck. "It's more than just a ship." He grinned. "It's a whole bloody convoy of them heading straight for us!" He let out a whoop.

The children clambered onto the locker, and the Lascars climbed on the thwarts. There was no doubt this time as the great fleet expanded on the horizon.

"All right," Darroch yelled. Everyone sit down. Let's do it right this time." He looked about the lifeboat. "We need something to run up the mast as a flag."

"Here!" Cilla held out Jill's little nightgown. It had been too small for any of the other children to wear.

Sutherland ran the little lace-trimmed nightie up the mast and Cilla watched it fluttering against the blue sky. Please God, let them see it.

"Now. Get the flare ready." Darroch's hands trembled as he prepared the signal flare. "Wait'll they get closer. Wait! Mustn't waste them." He talked softly to himself.

Cilla fixed her eyes on the First Officer, silently urging him to hurry.

"Now!" Darroch sent the flare arcing across the sky.

The lifeboat passengers held their collective breath. Nobody made a sound. All eyes were on the ships.

Cilla thought first one had changed direction, then perhaps it was another. Silent seconds passed before she accepted that nothing had changed and panic set in. The ships maintained their course. Tears burned the back of her eyes, and she swallowed hard. She couldn't stand it if the ships passed them without seeing the flare. Damn that Darroch—he'd set off the flare too soon.

"Sod it." Darroch's hands shook as he fumbled with the second flare. *Would he never set it off? The ships would be long gone before he got the bloody flare lit.*

At long last. The flare shot up and arced across the sky before it descended into the ocean leaving only a plume of smoke. Everyone turned to stare again at the ships.

One large ship on the outside column almost imperceptibly changed course, and a light began to flash from her.

"They've seen us!" Sutherland yelled.

"Thank God," Cilla sobbed.

Just before midnight, Ted pulled the hood of his duffel coat over his head and felt his way along the darkened ship's deck. He stopped outside the radio room and scanned the cloudless sky hung with bright stars. The wind howled through the mast and rigging while the timbers moaned in complaint. Lit by a sliver of moon, white-capped waves crashed against *HMS Incomparable's* hull as she raced across the Atlantic. The warship, released from convoy, was making her way to a rendezvous on the other side of the world.

Ted opened the radio-room door and, driven by a gust of wind, slipped through the blackout curtain into the blinding light.

A young sailor wearing earphones sat before the wireless, twiddling with the dial. He looked up, scowling as the papers beside him fluttered. Then, seeing Ted, he smiled and pushed the headset from his ears. "Wha'cher, Evans. You got the watch?"

"Hi yer, Sparks. Yeah, 'till four bells. It's another bloody cold night." He rubbed his gloved hands together.

"Never mind. Not too many more. It's going to be lovely and warm in Australia. And we'll be back in whites before you can say Bob's yer uncle." The young radio operator leaned back, balancing his chair on the two rear legs and clasped his hands behind his head.

Ted smiled at his shipmate and imagined the warm weather they were heading into. "Anything I should know about?"

"No. Jerry must be taking a kip. At least we haven't heard he's about."

"Right. I'd best be off then. Peel will do his nut if I'm late." He grabbed a clipboard from a nail on the wall beside the radio table and scribbled his name. He checked the time and scribbled again. "See yer."

"Oh, Ted." The chair rocked onto all four legs again, and the wireless operator riffled through several sheets of paper. He pulled one out of the pile. "You were on the *Punjohpur*, weren't you?"

Ted's belly flip-flopped at the mention of the sunken ship. "Yeah. Why?"

"I intercepted a message tonight..." He ran a finger over the paper. "From *HMS Mantolin*. She picked up survivors from the *Punjohpur*." The sailor studied the message again. "A lifeboat with a bunch of kids aboard."

"Strewth!" Ted felt the blood rush to his head, and he could hardly catch his breath. "Anybody else? Any adults? Women?"

"Yeah. A couple of women. British officers and Asian sailors. Christ! Can you imagine what they've been through? It's been a week or more, hasn't it?"

"Where...where are they taking them? Are they...on their way back to England?"

The young sailor frowned at Ted and shook his head. "No. The *Mantolin's* in convoy. She's carrying troops to Singapore. Flippin' hell, Ted! You look as white as a ghost. You all right, mate? Do you think you might know some of the survivors?"

"Maybe." He was staring at the radio, but his mind reeled with the possibility that Cilla might—No! Not might be—Cilla was safe! He felt it. He couldn't explain it, even to himself, but he knew.

He blinked and focused on the present. "Was there any mention of...here let me see the message." He grabbed the paper. "Was there a response to this?"

"Yeah." The radio operator fumbled through the stack of messages and thrust one at Ted. "Here."

Ted's heart played a tattoo inside his chest as he read the instructions to the *Mantolin* regarding the survivors they had on board. "They're to proceed to Australia."

"You okay, Ted?"

"Yeah." He slowly laid the paper on the desk, feeling his mouth turning up in a grin. "I'd better get on watch. Thanks, Sparks." He reached out and shook the surprised young sailor's hand.

CHAPTER EIGHTEEN

Cilla stood in the middle of the cabin, shaking uncontrollably. She knew she had been aboard the *Mantolin* for some time, but how she got to the cabin or what she was doing there seemed beyond her immediate comprehension. A pair of blue-striped pyjamas lay, neatly folded, on the bunk within her reach. She lifted her right arm and studied her stiff sleeve. If she could remember how to get undressed, she could have a bath and put the pyjamas on. Why was this so difficult?

She fumbled with the bottom of her jumper, and her fingers brushed the gritty fastener on her slacks. She ran her fingertips over it again, unable to identify it. Was it salt? Perhaps it was rust? If the fastener had rusted she could never undo it, and she'd never be able to have a bath.

She snivelled, raising her hands in a defeated gesture, but of their own volition, they collapsed against her sides. Tears chased down her cheeks. A sharp rapping invaded her fuzzy thoughts. The sound was familiar—a tapping. She concentrated, trying to focus, and at last recognised that someone was outside the cabin, knocking.

The door inched open. A middle-aged man, very small, with sun-baked skin and bright eyes like two ripe blackberries, peered in. "Hello. How are you doing, miss?"

Cilla burst into tears.

"Oh, Miss. Whatever is the matter? Don't cry. You're safe now." He stepped into the cabin and closed the door.

"I don't know." She stood with arms akimbo staring at the floor. "I feel all funny..."

"That's not surprising after what you've been through."

"I want to take a bath, but I can't get this off." She plucked at her clothing with stiff fingertips and swayed toward him.

He took her in his arms and gently patted her back.

"I can't get undressed," Cilla sobbed against his shoulder. Her body jerked as she gulped air.

"Look, Miss. My name's Harding. Bert Harding. I'm the steward. How about if I give you a hand?"

Cilla nodded her head, and Bert led her to the bunk.

"Sit down, Miss. What's your name?"

She slumped down. "I...I'm...my name's Cilla." Suddenly she recoiled. "No! Don't touch me." She shoved at his hands working on her clothing.

"Look, Cilla. I've got a daughter about your age. How old are you? Nineteen? Twenty?"

"I'm twenty-two."

"There aren't any women on board to help you. There's only the lady that came aboard with you, and she's in as bad a shape as you are. If you won't let me help you, shall I get the doctor?"

Cilla nodded. Her head swam. She thought she'd been strong and alert when she first came on board. She'd laughed and joked with the sailors while she drank tea and ate soft bread and butter. What had happened since then? She touched her hair. It felt hard and sticky.

Bert came from the bathroom with a wet cloth and gently wiped her face. "The doctor is very busy at the moment. Some of the children are in a bad way, and most of the Asian seamen are in comas. Rest here until he can come." He turned to leave.

"Bert," Cilla sniffled. "Will you help me? Please."

"Of course I will." He returned to the bathroom and turned on the water in the tub.

"Now then," he said, coming back to her. "Let's get you out of these clothes."

He pulled a sheet from the bed and draped it around her. She was hardly aware that he had removed the salt-laden underwear she'd worn for over a week. His hand under her elbow steadied her as he led her, draped in the sheet, the few paces to the bathroom.

"Step in," he urged as he removed the sheet.

She lowered herself into the luke-warm water and yelped. Small pustules peppered her thighs where the constant dousing with seawater had eaten at her skin.

Bert filled a jug and poured the water over Cilla's head, washing the salt from her hair. The briny water cascading down her shoulders stung like fire. She sucked in her breath and cried out.

"I'm sorry. I know that must be painful." Bert towelled her hair. "Now. That's got the worst off. Tomorrow you can have a proper bath and wash your hair. I'll bring you some shampoo, shall I?" He wrapped a big soft flannel sheet around her and helped her to the bunk. Only then did she remember to ask about the others.

"Do you know how the children are? What about my friend, Millie? Is she all right?"

"The children are making a wonderful recovery, and your friend will be fine as soon as she gets some sleep. And that's what you need."

"How is Ted? Is Ted all right?"

She didn't remember Bert tucking her into bed, nor did she hear him say, "Everyone's all right. They're all safe. Don't you worry."

She awoke later with a start, disoriented, into total darkness. Her heart pounded and she swallowed a cold lump of terror. *Where was she?* Panic clutched at her stomach. *A ship. She was on a ship.*

Her throat was dry. She remembered a jug of water on the table beside her. It was there when she fell asleep. Was it still there?

Panic gripped her. *What if she'd only imagined it?* She fumbled with the light switch, and the room suddenly blazed. Blinking to adjust her vision to the light, she was overjoyed to find the jug just where she remembered it. Her hands shook as she slopped water into a glass and gulped it. She wiped her wet chin with the back of her hand, then switched off the light and fell back, exhausted.

A tapping woke her. She opened her eyes and stared around her. The knocking persisted.

Bert's face appeared around the cabin door. "Good morning, Cilla. How are you feeling today?" He strode the few steps from the doorway to the table beside her bed and set down a tray.

Cilla eyed the spread. A boiled egg, cereal with milk, fresh snow-white bread, butter, a dish of honey and a pot of tea. "Is this all for me?" Tears welled in her eyes.

"Yes. You get outside that lot and I'll bring the children to see you."

"Bert. When will we get home? Which port are we going to? Liverpool?"

"Oh, no, my dear. Not home. We're on our way to Australia."

"Australia! I thought we'd be taken back to England."

"Well, it's like this, you see. This is a troop ship. Got 1,200 soldiers on board, bound for Singapore. We have to stay with the convoy, so you'll be coming with us."

"My mum and dad won't know. They must be frantic with worry by now." She stared at the breakfast, her appetite waning. How would she know if Ted had been rescued? Was he safe or still out on the sea?

"Now, don't you worry, Cilla." Bert patted her hand. "The captain sent a cable to the Admiralty last night. I'm sure your mum and dad are celebrating your rescue right now."

"Have there been any other survivors from my ship?"

"Oh my, yes. Most of them were picked up the day after your ship sank. They're safely back in England now." He busied himself filling her jug with fresh water. "All right. Come on, let's see you do the cook proud. Eat up."

Her mouth hurt. She cut off the top of the egg and dipped a piece of soft bread into the golden yolk—soldier-boys, her mother used to call them. She finished the egg and ate the rest of the bread with honey. She only tasted the cereal because Bert insisted, but she'd really had more food than her shrunken stomach could tolerate.

True to his word, Bert had brought her a bottle of shampoo and a bar of Yardley's lavender soap. He ran a warm bath, and Cilla luxuriated in it, adding more warm water as it cooled.

An hour later, she put on clean pyjamas and towelled her freshly shampooed hair. She stared at herself in the mirror. Her hair shone, but her eyes were dull with dark smudges beneath them. The deep cracks in her lips were red with blood, and her wind-burned skin was hot and dry.

Loud drumming, as if several sets of knuckles beat a tattoo on the cabin door, startled her. "Come in," she called.

Two scrubbed and laughing boys and eight shiny-eyed, giggling girls stood around Cilla's bed. Their wind-chafed faces were white with calamine lotion, and their swollen and cracked lips sported a thick film of salve. The sailors had outfitted them in long sweaters that hung to their knees. Where the sweater ended, long woolly socks began and covered their legs and feet. The heels of the socks jutted out like rooster spurs, halfway up the back of their legs.

"Coo! Ain't it smashing, Miss Cilla? We ain't going 'ome after all." Kitty's eyes sparkled. They'd begun to call her Miss Cilla in the lifeboat, and Millie had earned the title Auntie.

"Yeah. An we ain't going to Canada neither," Bobby chimed in.

Cilla looked from one smiling child to another. It was hard to believe that they were the same children who had sat dejected in that damned lifeboat, watching the cargo ship disappear. They had made a miraculous recovery. "Where's Ruby? And Brian? They aren't here."

"No, Miss. They have to stay in the hospital. Brian's feet are really bad, and Ruby won't get up."

"Oh, Miss Cilla. Did you hear? One of them Asians died last night."

"No. I hadn't heard. Poor man." To have suffered all that time in the lifeboat and then to have died on the rescue ship. She bit her lip.

"Yeah, and you know wha'? After the doctor bandaged them Asians' feet all up, they went on deck and pulled off the bandages and made a fire out of 'em."

"What?"

"Yeah, an' they sat around warming their feet next to the fire."

"Yeah, an' the sailors put the fire out, an' you should have heard the captain yelling."

"And he didn't 'alf give them Lascars what for."

The children all talked at once. "Yeah. He put extra men on look-out in case a German U-boat or a raider saw the fire." Bobby's eyes were wide.

When Cilla could get a word in, she asked, "Have you seen Auntie Millie?"

"She's still in her bed, too. But she was laughing and joking wif us, so I 'spect she'll be orrigh'"

For ten minutes, each child tried to outdo the other, telling Cilla about the new friends they had made among the soldiers, but eventually they grew restless and eager to be off exploring.

"Cheerio. See you later." How wonderful it was to see them all looking well and happy again.

She couldn't bear to think about the children who hadn't survived. The helpless ones she'd seen swallowed by the towering waves. And the young bodies she'd help put into the sea from the lifeboat. Those memories would live with her every day of her life. At that moment she hated the Germans with more venom than she'd ever have thought she was capable.

She lay back on her bunk, thinking about Ted. During all the miserable days in the lifeboat, she'd forced her last sight of him, exhausted and covered with oil, out of her thoughts. She hadn't wanted to think he might have drowned, only that he was safe in England. The possibility that she might never see him again was not an option she would accept.

She stared up at the ceiling, seeing only his dark, shining eyes and devilish grin. That was the vision she'd keep of him; not of him dragging himself, blue with cold, through the fierce Atlantic.

Tears of rage and regret sprang into her eyes and spilled over. What a fool she was to have played 'little Miss Iron-drawers' and kept him at arm's length.

She'd had great plans for their meeting in her cabin. Millie had convinced her not to be such a prude, and she'd been eager to prove it to Ted.

Her tears flowed freely down her cheeks and soaked into her pillow as she silently railed at the Nazis. They'd deprived her of the chance to show Ted just how much she loved him. *But never again!*

CHAPTER NINETEEN

27 September 1940
Dear Mum and Dad,

I've been assured that you know I'm safe, and I expect by now you know where I am and where I'm going, but I don't think I'm supposed to mention it.

I've been told that most of the survivors were picked up more than a week ago, so I expect that Ted has answered most of your questions by now. When I get home, I'll tell you all about my adventure.

Physically I'm very well, but emotionally I'm still a wreck, having trouble sleeping and dealing with the memories of all those who did not survive.

I've thought so much about you both. Right now I'd give a lot to be able to curl up next to Dad and have a nice cuddle, like I did when I was a little girl.

Give my love to everyone—Nigel, Trevor, Auntie Mary and Ted— especially Ted. Tell him I haven't forgotten our last conversation. He'll understand.

"Get out! Ge' ou' and leave me alone." Ruby drew further into the blankets.

Cilla stared at the little girl, confused by the unexpected outburst. "Ruby, whatever is the matter?" She reached to stroke the child's black hair.

"Go away! It's all your fawt." Raw hatred filled her black eyes as she jumped out of the bunk and pummelled Cilla.

"What's my fault? What have I done?" Cilla tried to still the flying fists.

"It's your fawt about Freddie. If you'd let 'im stay wif me when I asted yer, he would have been wif us in the lifeboat, and he wouldn't be dead." She sank back and turned her head into the pillow.

"Oh, Ruby." Cilla tried to wrap her arms around the angry child, but Ruby stiffened her body, rejecting Cilla's attempts to hug her. Cilla's heart ached to see the little girl so despondent. "I'm so sorry, Ruby. But you don't know Freddie wasn't picked up with the others."

"He's dead. I know he is. An' it's all because of you. I hate you!"

Tears burned Cilla's eyes, and she turned away, totally dejected.

Cilla made her way slowly along the corridor, deep in thought. She knew exactly what Ruby was feeling. The burning need to blame someone and to vent her anger and frustration at the guilty left a permanent knot in her stomach. She felt that same hollowness, as though her body was a big void, but her brain still thought up terrible punishments for those responsible for sinking the *Punjohpur* and causing so many deaths. She didn't think she could ever recover from the loss of Pamela Merryman, little Jill, Mary in her old battered hat, and Jocelyn. The children and the Lascars who'd died in the lifeboat. Perhaps Freddie. She'd seen the doctor's dead body in the water. She'd also seen two of the schoolteachers, and the Salvation Army major and his wife. It was easy to understand Ruby's need to place the blame for the loss of her brother. What Cilla couldn't understand was why Ruby was so sure Freddie had perished. At first, in the lifeboat, she had clung to the thought that Freddie was alive. She told Millie that when she got back to England, she would never "smack his ears, ever again." Perhaps the same instinct assuring Cilla that Ted was alive had told Ruby that her little brother was dead.

Cilla climbed to the deck and leaned over the railing, watching but not really seeing the foam-lipped swell lifting from the hull of the ship as she sliced through the calm sea.

Millie lounged in a deck chair, dressed identically to Cilla in a cotton work shirt and trousers that Bert had borrowed from the young sailors. With the legs and sleeves rolled up and a length of rope holding the waist, they fit reasonably well. Millie had tied the tail of her shirt in a knot under her breasts, allowing the sun to shine on her exposed midriff.

"Hello. You look comfortable." Cilla slumped into a deck-chair beside her friend, feeling the sun-warmed air brushing her cheeks.

Millie shaded her eyes against the bright sunshine and squinted at Cilla. "Yes. Isn't this bliss? Pure bliss?" Millie stretched her arms over her head. "My husband would have loved this. We always dreamed of taking a sea voyage."

Cilla turned to Millie, surprised. "You've never spoken of your husband before."

"I'm a widow," Millie said in a flat voice. "Roger was a spitfire pilot. He was killed in the summer."

"Oh, Millie. I'm so sorry. Why didn't you tell me?" Cilla placed her hand on her friend's arm.

"Well, the opportunity didn't come up. You and I didn't really know each other before we were torpedoed, and the lifeboat hardly seemed the place to talk about it. Though I must admit, I thought a lot about Roger then. He was shot down over the English Channel and was never found." A sombre expression crossed Millie's normally cheerful face.

"How did you cope with your grief? You seem so well-adjusted."

"I volunteered with CORB thinking it would help me deal with it. And it did. There's nothing like being torpedoed and spending a week in a lifeboat to make one forget any other troubles," she said with a bitter smile.

Cilla was silent for a moment. "Millie. I've been to see Ruby. She's convinced that Freddie is dead, and blames me. She's very angry with me and won't let me near her. Do you think you could try and comfort her?"

"Of course, though I doubt she'll be any more receptive to me while she's still so angry. When she finally accepts Freddie's death and grieves, she'll need comfort. Then she'll recover." Millie frowned, looking sidelong at Cilla. "Um...and I've been watching you. You've got a lot of rage bottled up, don't you? It's time you faced reality and grieved too."

Cilla looked down at her hands resting in her lap. "Yes, I'm angry, but I'm trying to deal with the loss of our friends and the children. What I can't deal with is Ruby saying she hates me."

"Cilla. It's not the children or the escorts that I'm talking about. It's Ted."

Cilla's head snapped up. A terrible icy grip of fear clutched at her belly, and she sucked in a gasp. She'd convinced herself her intuition was right— that Ted had survived. But had she been deliberately avoiding the thought? Her confidence returned and she grinned at Millie. "No! Ted didn't drown. He is young and strong and was wearing a life jacket. Bert said the other survivors were picked up the day after the sinking, and I'm sure Ted was with them. Besides, I have this feeling right here." She placed her fist in her midriff. "I just know he survived."

Millie stood up and unknotted her shirt. "All right, Cilla. Have it your way. I think I'll go and have a talk with Ruby." She tucked her shirt-tail into her waistband and went below.

Cilla leaned back against the canvas chair and closed her eyes. Well, Millie was right about one thing. She was bloody well filled with rage.

Her cheeks burned with it. She gritted her teeth, fighting the urge to let the anger out in a scream. But she couldn't quite put her finger on what was making her so bloody cheesed off. Visions of Ted struggling in the waves filled her thoughts, and suddenly she knew that her fury was at herself. She turned her thoughts to his last night at home when he'd reminded her that they were no longer children. Everything had been so right, but she'd spoilt it. *Daft cow*! She railed at herself. Stupid and juvenile. She'd acted more like a flippin' schoolgirl than a schoolteacher.

She squeezed her eyes shut and silently renewed her vow that she'd never miss an opportunity again.

During their childhood, it had always been the four of them—Ted, Cilla and her two brothers. The boys never discouraged her from joining in their activities, but to do so, she'd had to endure their incessant teasing. Then, when she was on the brink of tears, it was always Ted who called a halt to the needling. "It's all right, Cilla. We were just playing. Please don't cry." She'd blink away the tears and look up to see his brown eyes twinkling at her. Then he'd drape his arm around her shoulder and everything would be fine again.

The memories came flooding back—back to being fourteen with puckered lips and eyes clamped shut. A kiss that was nothing like the annual childish brushing of lips under the mistletoe at Christmas.

On a late summer afternoon, when seeking some relief from the blazing summer sun, the four friends had rambled through the cool woods. The boys poked and punched one another along the way, trying to force each other off the path. Nigel and Trevor got farther and farther ahead. Suddenly Ted clasped Cilla's hand. He tapped his finger against his lips indicating she shouldn't speak, then her pulled her off the path. Crouched low, they crashed through the trees in their version of Fox and Hounds. Behind them they heard the familiar "Tally-ho," the signal that the brothers had missed them and were in pursuit.

Dragging Cilla behind him, Ted raced out of the trees and into the open field. He pulled her down beside him into the tall summer grass. Hidden among the golden stalks, they gasped for breath, giggled and listened for sounds of the hunters. Flicking a big fat fly from his forehead, Ted beckoned for her to follow. On hands and knees they crawled to the edge of the meadow, then broke for cover into the dense brush.

On their knees, facing each other with hands propped on thighs, they sucked in lungsful of air and stifled giggles. "Ssh...listen," Cilla said and cocked her head, but she heard only their own laboured breathing.

She turned back to face Ted, and met his nut-brown eyes, wide and full of wonder. She held her breath as their fingertips touched, and holding her hands, he leaned toward her. She knew what he meant to do and thought she would burst from the sheer thrill of it.

He tilted his head ever so slightly, and their tightly-pursed lips met. When the halting kiss ended, they each let out a long breath and sat back, gazing at the other. Ted licked his lips, and his Adam's apple rose and fell as he swallowed.

Her mouth felt as if it were filled with cotton. She ran her tongue over her lips.

A small, strangled sound escaped from Ted. He dropped her hands and grasped her shoulders, pulling her to him. This time his lips were relaxed and moist. The kiss lingered. He took one hand from her shoulder and slid it down over her throat, down, down until his knuckles brushed her budding breast, and she thought she would die from the exquisite sensation.

Twigs crackled under someone's footstep. Hastily they pulled apart, and a moment later Trevor pounced on Ted's back.

"Found you, little foxes!"

Walking back across the field, through the woods and home again, she kept her eyes averted, watching her feet, and knew he wasn't looking at her, either.

It was never the same after that. Something had forever changed, and a few days later Ted had left to become a naval apprentice.

When he did come home for holidays, Nigel and Trevor monopolised him, and for the first time, she found herself excluded from their conversations.

Cilla sighed. Fate—or her brothers' untimely intervention—had been against them from the start.

Ted hadn't completed his apprenticeship when the bike-ride episode happened, but it was clear to Cilla then that he'd been getting some other sort of training. How had he learned to kiss like that? The memory brought a stab of jealousy.

Cilla Thornton, you're a silly sod! She got up out of the deck chair and walked slowly to the railing. Mesmerised by the tiny white-lipped waves formed when the keel sliced through the water, she watched the wake for a long time. Her stomach ached with the effort of keeping her emotions trapped inside.

CHAPTER TWENTY

28 September 1940

By the time we reach somewhere to post this, it will be novel length.

Don't know exactly where we are, but it's getting hotter.

I must tell you about some the people who are with me.

Millicent Parkin, who was my cabin mate, has been a wonderful friend. She's a nurse and was absolutely marvellous with the children in the lifeboat, telling them stories and giving us all encouragement. I don't think I would have made it this far without her, and even now she watches over me.

I can't praise our British officers enough. I'll tell you all about them when I get home.

I also need to tell you about the children. One of the fifteen girls for whom I was responsible died during the attack, and three others died in the lifeboat. One who survived, Ruby, blames me for the loss of her younger brother. She had asked me to let Freddie stay in her cabin, but the assignments were made—boys with boys and girls with girls. Had he been with Ruby, he might have survived. Poor, dear little Ruby. She told Millie that she can never go home again because her mother will never forgive her for losing Freddie. I feel responsible, but I don't see how I could have done anything differently.

Was it only ten days ago? In the lifeboat, I thought I was going mad—perhaps I was a little. Now I wonder if I will ever be completely sane again.

You know me—I've always accepted people for who they are, but now I have this dreadful hatred of the Germans. Millie's husband was a fighter pilot, killed during the summer air battles—how can she forgive them? I'll never forgive, but God help me, I wish I could forget the image of the dead children.

Sorry if I sound morbid and depressed. I wish I could talk to you, Dad.

I'll write more later when I'm not so emotional.

29 September 1940

I'm still feeling a bit unsettled today. The children worry me. They were so exuberant the first few days after the rescue. Now they seem deeply depressed. I expect we all are.

Brian is fourteen, the eldest of the three boys with us. Bobby is seven. Nine girls survived. Paula is a quiet ten-year-old, and Kitty is a street-wise nine-year-old from the East End of London. Each of them has sores in their mouths so that they can't eat. Ruby has no appetite. The doctor says it is a delayed reaction to all that they have endured and only time can heal them. I hope that is true for all of us and that time will heal me.

More later.

From the fantail, Cilla watched the soldiers exercising on the deck below, as they did every morning. Captain St. John had asked that Cilla and Millie keep to the fantail when they were on deck and stay in their cabins after dark. The captain's face flushed, embarrassed, and said the army officers made the request.

Cilla had snickered. "I wonder what they're afraid of? Do you suppose they think we'll seduce their men?"

"What, all of them?" Millie broke out in gales of laughter. "Anyway, after the confines of a lifeboat, this space feels as big·as a ballroom." She danced a few waltz steps around the deck.

The soldiers, dressed only in shorts and plimsolls, jogged around the deck. Their bare torsos glistened with sweat in the blazing sun.

Cilla's gaze came to rest on one young man as he did jumping jacks. His dark hair and chiselled, hard-boned face mirrored the strength and grace of his body.

He wasn't Ted, and she knew he wasn't Ted, but his raw maleness reminded her of him. Quite suddenly, a desperate sadness overwhelmed her. Unbidden, fat tears spilled out of her eyes and down her cheeks. She sucked in a loud sob.

Millie turned at the sound, a look of concern clouding her face. "Oh, Cilla!" She put her arm around Cilla's shoulders and led her to their deck-chairs hidden against the bulkhead.

Millie held her in her arms and rocked her back and forth. "Go ahead and cry," she whispered over Cilla's great racking sobs. "I'll stay here with you. It's good to cry. It's all right, you need to grieve."

After several minutes, Cilla reached in the pocket of her sailor trousers and pulled out a handkerchief—a present from Bert. She wiped her eyes and blew her nose. "Thank you, Millie. I feel better now."

"Good. I'll go and see if Bert can rustle us up a cup of tea." Millie got up and left the deck.

Cilla sucked in a deep breath. Millie had been right, of course. She needed to get that out of her system. Her own emotions aside, she still had a responsibility to the children.

A hand rested gently on her shoulder. "Hi."

"Hello, Clint." She couldn't look at him. Her eyes felt like red-hot coals, and she imagined her face was still swollen from crying.

"Millie told me I'd find you here."

She stared out to sea. "I don't feel like making small-talk, Clint."

"Cilla. I owe you an apology for my behaviour just before the ship went down. That wasn't really me. It was the booze. I can't believe that I attacked you like that. I'm sorry." He placed his hands on her shoulders and turned her to face him.

She kept her head lowered and dabbed her eyes.

"Can we be friends again? What can I do to make it up to you...short of spending another week in a lifeboat, that is?"

She smiled and raised her face. In the sunlight his thick hair gleamed gold. He was wearing a sailor's work pants and shirt with the sleeves rolled up above his elbows, exposing strong forearms covered with silky blonde hair. His skin had bronzed, and Cilla decided he had far more than his fair share of sex appeal, not to mention self-confidence.

"That's all in the past. Let's forget it." Without warning, tears spilled over again.

Clint drew her close to him, speaking softly into her ear.

"Ah, Cilla, sweetheart." Taking her chin between his thumb and forefinger, he raised her face and kissed her lips.

She shivered in the warm sunshine as a cold finger of apprehension touched her spine. She pushed herself free of him. "Don't do that, Clint."

"Okay, okay. I understand." With a restless movement of his shoulders, he moved away from her. "It's too soon. There's plenty of time for us."

"Time has nothing to do with it. I'm not interested in you." It was all she could do to keep from laughing out loud at the look of disbelief on his handsome face.

His mouth dropped open and he scowled at her. "You don't mean that. I know different."

"Yes, I do mean it." She doubted any woman had ever rejected him before.

Disbelief gave way to a casual laugh, as if he saw the joke she surely had intended. "You'll feel better in a few days. You're still carrying a torch for that Limey sailor, aren't you? Once you put him out of your mind, we can get to know each other better."

She clenched her fists and fought to hold back her tears. "You arrogant swine. There's no point in us getting to know each other better. I don't want to. Tell that to your over-confident ego."

A dazzling smile lit his face. "You'll come around before we reach Cape Town." He raised one hand in a cavalier salute. "See ya, sweetheart."

Dumbfounded, she fought an angry retort as she watched him saunter away.

30 September 1940

You wouldn't believe how hot it is. And if it's possible, the closer we get to Africa, the hotter it gets.

It feels so good to able to write to you, Mum and Dad. It helps me to get control of my emotions. I'm still a wreck as far as that goes, but being able to tell you my concerns is a help and a comfort.

Ruby had hysterics last night. She screamed for Freddie. I've been so worried about her, but she seems better for finally letting go. It will take a long time for all the children to fully recover.

It's a shame that they missed the fun and celebration for the soldiers and young sailors who crossed the equator for the first time. Neptune, King of the Sea, and Thetis, his Queen, held court. I wish Millie and I could have taken part, but we didn't have any suitable clothes to wear to be dunked in the water. Clint, our handsome American travelling companion, took part. Clint Jennison is an actor. He's smashing—and he knows it! On the surface he's charming, but underneath he's cold and selfish, incapable of any real feelings. Millie can't stand him, and Bert goes out of his way to avoid contact with him.

Bert—I haven't told you about Bert Harding, have I? He's our steward—a lovely little man who cared for me and gave me my first bath when I first came aboard. Don't worry, Mum, he treats me like the daughter he has at home. Anyway, Bert says it's all right to mention the ship and places we've been, because by the time this letter reaches you, we'll be long gone. Any spy reading this won't know where the ship is at that particular time. Does that make sense to you?

2 October 1940
We are anchored off the coast of Sierra Leone. Hot! I had no idea anything could be so hot.

The mail was taken off the ship this morning, so my last letter is on its way to you.

This morning, dozens of canoes filled with small, very black men from Freetown surrounded our ship. The fresh fruit they brought looked wonderful, but of course we have no money to buy any. The soldiers (you must have gathered by now that I'm aboard a troop ship) bought fruit and tossed coins in payment. Most of the money fell into the sea, and the natives dove for it. The water is so clear and blue. The children were delighted with the display and, in lieu of coins, threw bottle caps. Much to the dismay of the black men who went in after them. On reaching the surface, the natives shook their fists at the children. It was very naughty, but a lot of fun for all of us.

Bert says we'll reach Cape Town within the next few days. The children will leave the ship there. It will be a relief, although I shall miss them. They are all badly in need of medical treatment. Millie, Clint and I are to travel on. I'll post this letter when we get to our next stop. Who knows, I may be home before it reaches you. Can't wait to see you.

P.S. 5 October 1940. We arrived at Cape Town early this morning to find Table Mountain covered with its legendary cloth of white cloud. What a sight! It took almost two hours to dock, and as we passed several other ships from our convoy, the soldiers and sailors cheered us. I wasn't sure why until Bert told me they were showing their pride in the children, Millie and me for our bravery. I'd hardly call what we did brave—it was self-preservation! Anyway, my emotions got the best of me, as you know they always do.

Native soldiers stand guard at the dock gates, and the harbour is crowded with ships of every size and type.

A CORB bloke paid us this morning. Can you imagine we are to be paid only for the contracted amount, £5? Had we been going to Australia to begin with, we would have received the handsome sum of £20. Well, £5 is more than I had yesterday.

Three women from a local service organisation came aboard when we docked and brought clothes for us and the children. Millie and I were at last able to get out of the trousers and shirts we borrowed from the sailors. It feels strange to wear a frock again – but so much cooler.

Much love, Cilla.

CHAPTER TWENTY-ONE

The cabins hummed with excitement. The generous people of Cape Town had sent huge boxes of new clothes. The children, only half-dressed, ran around like puppies chasing their tails. They squealed with delight as they pulled each new item of clothing from the boxes, then squabbled over who was to get which items.

"Let's leave them to it," Millie said, and Cilla agreed. The children weren't being greedy, just excited and overwhelmed.

Paula was still crying. She'd cried since the ship docked. Millie did her best to find out why, but Paula couldn't tell her. It was all very vague; something about whether the families who had volunteered to foster the children for the duration of the war would like them. With the rest of the children so wound up, Cilla decided to just leave Paula alone and concentrate on getting the others ready to leave.

Mr. Watson, the CORB representative, waited patiently on deck to introduce the evacuees to the families who had volunteered to foster them for the duration of the war.

Kitty squirmed while Cilla brushed her hair and tied the bow at the back of her dress. Millie practically sat on the boys to hold them still while she slicked down their hair.

Paula cried while she dressed in slow motion.

In the midst of the chaos, Cilla looked up to find the *Punjophur's* First Officer watching from the doorway of the girl's cabin. Tears brimmed in his bright blue eyes. Sutherland peered over Darroch's shoulder. He scrubbed at his teary red eyes while the purser dabbed at his eyes with a bright new handkerchief.

"We came to say our goodbyes and to wish ye all the very best," Darroch said. "It's been a pleasure to have known and served with all of you. You've all done Britain proud." He solemnly shook hands with the boys and kissed each girl on the cheek.

The children mumbled their parting words. Some bit their lips, others sniffled.

Millie and Cilla got special hugs and kisses. "You're grand lassies," Darroch said as he took his leave.

Sutherland and the purser were beyond words. They hugged each child before giving Millie and Cilla kisses on the cheek.

Cilla flicked the tears from her eyes. "I'll never again eat tinned peaches without thinking of you," she said to the purser.

He smiled and wiped his wet cheeks.

Up on deck, Cilla knelt in front of Bobby and straightened his tie. His lip trembled. If he cried, she knew she would not be able to control her own emotions.

"There. You look very smart." She smoothed his hair and stood up, biting her lip.

Several cars pulled up on the dock beside the ship and stopped, one behind the other. "Time to go, everyone," said Mr. Watson.

Swallowing the lump in her throat, Cilla hugged each child and kissed his or her cheek. All except Ruby, who turned away.

The two older boys exhibited a bit of bravado, making themselves as stiff as boards as Cilla and Millie attempted to hug them. A couple of the girls giggled self-consciously, pretending to be absorbed in the rickshaws lined up on the dock below.

Paula continued to cry.

Kitty had finally had enough. "For Gawd's sake, gew', shut yer gob!" she yelled at Paula, who cried even harder.

Seeing Ruby leave would be the most difficult. Cilla hated to let the little girl go with so much anger still directed at her. She understood it, but it hurt with an almost physical pain. "This looks to be a nice city, Ruby. I'm sure you'll be very happy living here," she said, casually trying to get some response.

Ruby suddenly turned and flung her arms around Cilla's waist. "Oh, Miss Cilla. I'm going t' miss yer." Burying her face against Cilla's ribs, she sucked in a loud sob.

Cilla stroked the shiny black hair with one hand and patted the child's back with the other. "I'll miss you too, Ruby." Tears pooled in her eyes. "Will you write to me?" The previous evening, she and Millie had each given the child her home address.

"'Course! But I don' write too good. Will you write back?"

"Absolutely. I'll tell you about the fog and the rain in England, and you can tell me about all the sunshine here." As she swept her hand to indicate Cape Town, someone grasped it. She turned as Kitty raised Cilla's hand to her cheek.

Cilla pulled Kitty to her and hugged her close. "You'll write to me too, won't you, Kitty?"

"Yes, Miss Cilla. But me an' Ruby'll have the same things to tell yer." They were to live with the same family on a farm just outside of Cape Town.

"That's all right. I'll want to hear it all. I know you'll have a wonderful life here. Be good girls and study hard in school." She squeezed the bony little shoulders, wishing she could think of something profound and lasting to say to them.

"How long do you fink we'll be 'ere, Miss Cilla? I mean how long before the war's over?"

"It can't last much longer, Kitty. Perhaps by Christmas. Six months at the outside." Cilla wished she believed that. The news from Britain wasn't good, but at least the threat of invasion seemed to have passed.

"Miss?" Ruby sniffed and wiped the back of her hand across her nose. Her dark eyes flooded with tears. "I'm sorry I was so awful to you, an' I'm sorry I said it was your fawt about Freddie. It weren't you, it was that bleedin' 'itler's fawt what made Freddie...an' your Ted die."

"Oh, Ruby..." Cilla ignored what she'd said about Ted, and crushed the little girl to her. Just knowing that Ruby no longer blamed her was like having an elephant removed from sitting on her chest.

"Come along, children." Mr. Watson tried herding them toward the gangplank.

"This is it, kids." Millie ran from one child to the next, giving each one last hug. She pulled out a bright new handkerchief and mopped her eyes.

"Goodbye, Auntie Millie. Goodbye, Miss Cilla." The children picked up their carrier bags and brown paper parcels of new clothes and started down the gangway.

Together, they'd been through the most difficult time some of them would ever know. A great new adventure, without the dangers, awaited them in their new environment, and they seemed eager to begin.

"Cheerio." The word stuck in Cilla's throat.

Ruby took a few steps, then turned back to Cilla. "Don't forget. You promised we'd meet again after the war."

Cilla swallowed and nodded. She touched her fingertips to her lips, sending one last kiss to the little girl who had become so dear to her. Unable to hold back the torrent of emotion any longer, Cilla sobbed.

As the children climbed into the waiting cars, Cilla and Millie, with arms around each other, slowly walked down to the dock.

The cars followed each other down the quay and through the gate to the street. Cilla waved for as long as she could see faces peering out of the back windows.

"Excuse me." The voice was calm and feminine.

Cilla's new lacy handkerchief was soaked and almost useless for absorbing any more tears, but she couldn't see through the watery veil. She wiped her eyes and turned to regard the soft-spoken woman. "Yes?"

"My sister and I wondered if we could show you around Cape Town?" She was well into her forties, solemn, tall and angular, giving the impression of aloofness. Cilla thought perhaps she was shy. She wore a flowered dress that hung from wide shoulders, sensible shoes, and a navy straw hat.

Physically, her sister was her total opposite: short, roly-poly with rosy cheeks and a bright smile. She, too, wore a flowered dress, but her straw hat had an enormous bunch of imitation cherries on one side, and a red ribbon fluttered at the back.

Cilla dabbed at the persistent pools in her eyes. "Oh, thank you very much. That's most kind of you."

Millie snuffled and stepped forward, smiling through her tears. "That's exactly what we need right now. We'd be delighted to accept."

"I understand there's a young man with you. Do you think he'd like to join us?" said the first woman.

Cilla looked about for the American. "I don't see Clint, and I'm afraid I have no idea where he might be."

"Well, that's all right, then. Perhaps he wouldn't enjoy accompanying four women after all."

Cilla and Millie looked at each other and grinned. *Clint not enjoy the company of four women!*

"Do introduce us, Pearl," the plump sister said. She fidgeted unable to wait for her sister. "I'm Opal Van Noor and this is my sister, Pearl Oberman." Her eyes twinkled, and seemingly without taking a breath, she continued. "You must have been through an dreadful ordeal, being torpedoed, and then those awful days in the lifeboat. We were delighted to hear about your rescue and what you did for those poor children and..."

"Opal, do stop nattering, dear. The young ladies won't want to spend the day with us if you keep on so."

"Oh, yes. Of course. I do tend to go on, I'm afraid." Opal touched her fingertips to her lips and, glancing first at Cilla, then Millie, shook her head as if chastising herself. "Do forgive me," she said.

Miss Pearl Oberman and Mrs. Opal Van Noor obviously loved their country and delighted in showing it off.

"We must go to the top of Table Mountain first," Opal said. "You'll get a wonderful view of the entire city from there."

As the cable-car rode to the top of Table Mountain, the city below grew smaller, while the vista grew wider and less defined. Beyond the buildings and the harbour where people no bigger than ants bustled back and forth along the docks, Table Bay sparkled in the sunlight.

At the top of the ride, Cilla stepped off the cable-car and caught her breath at the scene laid out below. White sandy beaches edging azure water contrasted with the dark green of the trees and patches of colourful flowers growing in every nook and cranny of the city. Lilliputian ships in battle grey sat in rows as if waiting for a young boy's hand to guide them from their berths. Above it all, the ever-present seagulls soared like tiny snowflakes against the brilliant sky.

Before the cable car even reached the bottom of the ride, Pearl had another plan. "How would you like to see the Rhodes Memorial?"

Cilla and Millie looked at each other and nodded. "Oh, yes, please."

Pearl drove at breakneck speed through breathtaking scenery, sending clouds of red dust behind the car. Suddenly she turned into a driveway with vast, grassy lawns and trees on either side and slammed on the breaks.

"This was Rhodes' home." Opal pointed to a beautiful house. "The Prime Minister lives here now, though."

They got out of the car and walked around the grounds, stopping when Pearl pointed far off in the distance. "From here you can see the Atlantic and Indian Oceans converge."

Suddenly, Opal squealed.

A small grey monkey sat on her shoulder and plucked at the cherries nestled on the brim of her hat. Startled by her scream, he grabbed a cherry and jumped to the ground, dragging the hat after him as he scooted up a nearby tree.

"My hat!.. My hat!" Opal's grey hair stood up on end, enhancing the look of shock on her round face.

"I'll get it." Millie ran toward the tree, but the monkey dropped to the ground, still holding the hat and pulled on the cherries.

"Come back, Mrs. Parkin. The monkeys are dangerous." Pearl clutched her handbag with one hand and her straw hat with the other.

Millie dropped to her knees and began to crawl toward the monkey, who seemed to ignore her while he chewed on a cherry. Millie crept steadily to him until he was just within her reach. She slowly stretched out her hand. The monkey made a flying leap onto a tree branch and plonked the hat on his own head, while Millie fell flat on her stomach.

Cilla tried to stifle her laughter, but it bubbled out while tears ran down her cheeks.

"Oh, dear. Oh, my," Opal snickered. Pearl threw back her head and joined Cilla in roaring laughter.

Cape Town at dusk turned into a city of lights. They twinkled up the sides of Table Mountain, and across Table Bay, ships and boats blazed with light. It had been more than a year since Cilla and Millie had seen city lights.

Voices carried on the hot night breeze grew louder as the two women approached the *Mantolin's* berth. Beneath a light at the foot of the gangplank, Clint stood waving his arms about and bellowing. He gestured in an apparent argument with a harried man.

Caught in the quayside lights, glistening sweat ran down the stranger's grim face. His white shirt was plastered to his back, and he gripped his briefcase so tightly his knuckles turned white.

Several people passing by stared at Clint, the centre of attention—and revelling in it. "I really don't give a good goddamn what my contract says. I have had it with torpedoes, lifeboats and being hassled by you CORB people, none of which my contract even mentioned. I had to be crazy to get involved. It's not my war."

"Mr. Jennison!" The stranger spoke in quiet, measured words. "If you break your contract, I'm afraid I have no authority to pay you."

"That's all that's bothering you? You've got to be kidding! £5 isn't even tip money. Hardly compensation for what I've been through. Keep it. Buy yourself a beer on me."

He turned, and seeing Cilla and Millie, his expression changed to a charming smile. "Hi, girls. Glad you got back in time for me to say goodbye. I got a ship home to the States."

Cilla's chin dropped. With an effort, she clamped her mouth shut and walked toward him so as not to have to shout. "What are you talking about?

I thought you'd been instructed to go on to Australia with Millie and me."

"Well, I don't care about prolonging my involvement in this goddam war. I've found a ship that will take me to Canada and from there I can easily get home."

The look on Millie's face expressed what she thought of Clint leaving. Good riddance!

"Well, goodbye, Clint. I hope you arrive home safely, this time." Millie said, and turning, started up the gangway.

Out of the corner of her eye Cilla saw the CORB man scurry away. "Best of luck, Clint," she said and extended her hand to him.

Clint just couldn't seem to resist just one last display of arrogance. "So long, Miss Thornton." He kissed the back of her hand, then executed the cavalier salute Cilla had seen before, wheeled and swaggered away.

CHAPTER TWENTY-TWO

October 1940
Dear Mum and Dad,

We left Cape Town this morning in the most oppressive heat. As beautiful as Cape Town is, with Table Mountain towering over it and the colourful flowers growing absolutely everywhere, summer here is too hot for me.

The cabin is stifling, so Millie and I spend a lot of time on deck. This morning we saw flying fishes clearing the waves almost at deck level. Later we watched a school of about fifty porpoises, looking like a pack of hounds, with their heads and arched backs skimming the water. I couldn't help thinking how much the children would have enjoyed it.

The ship seems cavernous without the children. I miss them so much, but I know they're safe now and will have a wonderful life.

Give my love to the boys when next you write to them. My love to Auntie Mary and to Ted when you see him.

I'll post this at our next stop, Bombay.

Love you, Cilla.

When *HMS Incomparable* sailed into Sydney harbour, the city was already agog with excitement. The United States Naval Squadron was about to pay the city a courtesy visit and the Australians were preparing a big celebration. Wherever the Union Jack and Australian flags flew, the American flag flew alongside.

The officials could call it a courtesy visit, but the crew of the *Incomparable* knew better. They'd brought a very important British Admiral and his staff to Australia just to meet with the American Rear-Admiral. Rumour had it that the meeting was to persuade the Americans to join Britain in what was fast becoming a world war.

Ted found the excitement infectious, but for reasons of his own. He might find Cilla already here! The very least he hoped was to find out for certain that she was one of the latest survivors of the *Punjohpur*. Just when excitement sent his expectations soaring to their highest peak, doubt invaded his thoughts and sent him into deep melancholy. He had only a couple of days before he'd sail back to Britain, and he still had to find out who the survivors were and when they'd reach Australia.

The *Incomparable's* complement, dressed in their tropical whites, stood at attention on the deck to welcome the American cruisers and destroyers. As the visiting ships passed the Heads, they fired huge jets of water in all directions, spraying the spectators on the surrounding cliffs. Car horns blared, and wild cheering returned the greeting. The fleet finally swung around the Point of Garden Island and into their berths at the famous Woolloomooloo docks.

Ted grabbed his leave pass, saluted the flag of the *Incomparable*, and raced down the gangplank.

The excitement in the city was at fever pitch. The shops and businesses had closed for the celebration. Laughing, cheering women hung out of windows and crowded the sills of every office building festooned with decorations and banners.

A band playing a Sousa march grew louder as it approached.

Children raced in and out of the crowds. Bottles of beer passed between people lined up on the curbs. Boys climbed lamp-posts for a better view and hauled the girls up after them.

"Here come the Gobs," yelled a girl with a raucous Australian accent. She was halfway up a lamppost, holding a large red hat on her blonde curls with one hand. Her other arm and her legs were around the pole, much to the appreciation of the males on the sidewalk below.

The band led about six hundred American officers and sailors in little white, pot-shaped hats. As the parade swung into view, the wildly cheering crowd rushed the marchers. Abandoning their discipline, the Americans waved to the crowd, shook hands, and returned the girls' generous kisses.

The Australians' festive spirit contrasted sharply with Ted's sombre, determined actions. He raced up one street and down another trying to find someone who could direct him to the nearest Red Cross office. He couldn't find one shop or office open. People on the street either didn't know or were in too jovial a mood to stop. Time was running out and he was growing desperate.

Frustrated and disappointed, he shunned the celebrations going on all over Sydney and reluctantly returned to the *Incomparable.*

The sailor standing guard of the near-empty ship peered slack-jawed at Ted as he casually climbed the gangplank.

"Hey, Evans! What the hell are y' doing back here? I hear there's free beer and booze flowing down the streets of Sydney, and the women are eager."

"Wha'cher, Smiley. Yeah, everybody seems to be having a good time. Too bad you have duty."

"Yeah." Smiley's voice drooped. "Just my luck to be stuck here tonight."

"Hey, listen, Smiley. I don't feel much like celebrating. How about if I take over your watch?"

"Are you joking?"

"No. I mean it. Give me a minute to change and sign in."

"Cheers, mate!"

"Oh, Smiley." Ted turned and grinned at the sailor. "Just remember—you owe me."

The party in Sydney turned wild. When it threatened to become a riot, the British sailors were confined to their ship. For three days Ted paced the decks and agonised over not being able to get ashore. Finally, the day before the *Incomparable* was to sail for home, the captain released his men for one last look at Sydney.

It was Ted's misfortune to be scheduled for duty.

He found Smiley dressed in a clean white uniform, tying his shoes.

"Hey, Smiley. You aren't planning on going into Sydney, are you, mate?"

The young sailor stood up and straightened his middy as he turned to Ted with a suspicious stare. "Yeah. What about it?"

"I think you know."

"No! Not today, Evans."

"Look. I just need a couple of hours. You don't have to take my duty all day. I'll be back as quick as I can, and then you can leave."

Reluctantly, Smiley agreed, and Ted fled to the city. This was his last chance to find out if Cilla had been rescued, and he didn't even know where to begin looking.

The streets still bore signs of the American Squadron's visit, but businesses had reopened, and Ted found the Red Cross office. A rather large, matronly woman, overflowing her tight uniform, listened sympathetically, then shook her head.

"I'm terribly sorry, but we don't have the names of any torpedoed survivors. We heard about the two women and a dozen or so children, of course. We think it was just wonderful that they survived for so long in an open lifeboat."

"Do you know when they are expected here in Sydney?"

"No. I'm sorry I can't help you there. It's hardly the sort of information the Red Cross office would have anyway."

Ted gave an exasperated sigh. "What about the children? Who will take charge of them?"

"Well, the children aren't aboard anymore. I was told that they were left in Cape Town with a representative of the Children's Overseas Reception Board."

"Oh, right. CORB. Of course, they would know, wouldn't they?" Ted suddenly felt hopeful. "Can you give me directions to the Australian CORB Office?"

"Certainly." The woman thumbed through a dog-eared telephone book. "Yes, here it is." She scribbled on a piece of paper and handed it to Ted.

He thanked her and hurried out onto the street. Breaking into a run, he charged through the crowds, causing the people to jump out of his way. The warm Australian spring day only added to Ted's excitement, and sweat trickled down his spine, plastering his white middy to his skin.

The CORB office turned out to be one smoke-filled room over a newsagent's shop. Through the haze, an elderly man with a cigarette clamped between his lips peered over the top of his spectacles. "Good'ay. What can I do for His Majesty's Navy?"

Ted explained, and the old man studied his face, hesitating before he answered. "Well, I'm not sure I ought to be telling you this, but...you don't look like a spy to me." His throaty chuckle became a hacking cough. He pulled the soggy fag end from his mouth and choked his way to the next sentence.

"The ship is expected here, but you're a couple of weeks too early." The old man put a fresh cigarette between his lips and lit it from the wet brown stub.

"A couple of weeks! Oh, sod it! I'll be back at sea by then." Ted rubbed his chin while he thought. "Can you tell me the names of the two women?"

The old man drew smoke into his lungs and coughed while he mashed the remnants of his coffin nail into the overflowing ashtray. He riffled through a pile of ash-covered papers on his ancient desk. "Yes. Here they are," he said and whipped out the sheet of paper with a triumphant smile.

Ted sucked in his breath and held it while the old man read the names.

"Mrs. Millicent Parkin and Miss Priscilla Thornton."

Ted thought his lungs would burst. "Oh, thank God," he breathed at last.

"It would seem that you know the ladies, then?" He grinned, exposing a set of nicotine-stained false teeth.

Words stuck in the back of Ted's throat. He was afraid if he tried to speak, he'd bawl. At last he swallowed and answered. "Yes…oh, Christ. I can't tell you how relieved I am."

"I can see that. Well, then, it's a pity you won't be here to meet them." The old man studied him intently. "You all right, mate?"

Ted gripped the edge of the cluttered desk and sucked in lungsful of smoke-filled air. "Yeah." He blew the word out. At last his heart quit trying to jump out of his chest and his breathing calmed. "Could I leave a message with you for Miss Thornton?"

Ted's hand trembled as he accepted the paper, pen and envelope from the old man and wrote: *Cilla, darling. Wish I could be here when you arrive. There's so much I want to say to you. I've seen your parents. Your brothers are fine. Can't wait till we meet again in good Old Blighty. All my love, Ted.* He carefully folded and sealed the envelope and wrote Cilla's name on the outside. "You will make sure she gets this, won't you?"

"Absolutely. I'll hand it to her myself." He took the envelope and, opening the drawer in front of him, forced it inside on top of more papers.

"Thank you...thanks very much." Ted shook the old man's hand and left the office in a state of uncertain euphoria. Knowing Cilla was alive overshadowed all fear he had that she wasn't likely to get his message. Even if the old bloke remembered it, he probably wouldn't be able to find it.

CHAPTER TWENTY-THREE

Bombay
12 October 1940
Dear Mum and Dad,

Our Lascar shipmates are home at last. As the ship got closer to the harbour, they became increasingly excited, jabbering and gesturing, and waiting on deck for the ship to dock, they could hardly contain themselves. They came to say goodbye to Millie and me, holding their hands together in front of them as if saying a prayer and bowing. They seem to have forgotten their animosity toward us in the lifeboat.

You would not believe how humid it was. The sea was so hot it actually steamed! The humidity didn't seem to affect the bare-foot natives carrying huge loads of cargo on their backs onto the ships, but it did tend to hold the smell of spices in the air.

Millie and I had a look around the city. For all she's endured, Millie is always such a happy person. She is so much fun and I really enjoy her company.

The streets of Bombay are extremely narrow and the houses so close. We could almost touch them from the window of the huge buses that careen through the streets. We wondered at the mortality rate of the rickshaw drivers and policemen who stand in the middle of the intersections and direct traffic. Of course, they are quite visible dressed in their bright blue jackets and shorts and yellow Tam-O'Shanters.

I'll never smell spices again without recalling this colourful city and its dreadful poverty.

Next stop Colombo!

Colombo, Ceylon
24 October 1940

Millie and I went ashore on small tenders. We only had a couple of hours on land and spent the time at the most beautiful zoo imaginable. Whipsnade has nothing on it.

Thank goodness we bought sunglasses in Cape Town. The sun is so brilliant here, it hurts the eyes, especially reflecting off the water. The humidity is oppressive, but without the humidity, the gorgeous tropical flowers wouldn't bloom everywhere in such profusion.

We're sailing again, and Bert said we've crossed the Equator for the third time.

I'll write more later and mail it before we leave Singapore.

Singapore
30 October 1940
Had our first sight of Singapore this evening. I don't know what I expected after reading that Singapore held one of the strongest military bases in the Far East. It is a low, oval-shaped island with green hills reminiscent of England but with palm trees. Ashore, we found it more cosmopolitan than previous cities we've visited, but with lots of Chinese and other Orientals riding about on bicycles or in rickshaws. I was surprised at how few white people we saw.

We returned to an almost empty ship. The troops have disembarked, and it's quite eerie to walk along corridors and not see another human being. All the ship's sounds seem magnified, and I swear I can hear the children laughing.

Ted flexed his aching back and readjusting his binoculars, settled down to scan the empty sea. After so many months of war, the pose was almost second nature to him, the difference being he wasn't bracing against the raging Atlantic.

As summer approaches the tropics, the hours just before dawn, when the night breezes cool the air, become the most pleasant. Soon the gentle lapping of the ocean against the hull had a lulling effect. Still alert to his surroundings, he no longer heard the pulse of the *Incomparable's* engines as she sped across the Pacific toward home.

When Ted first went to sea as a boy, the midnight to 04:00 watch had been a time for reflection on the older sailor's talk. He'd listened and learned, eager to put his newfound knowledge into practice when he reached the next port.

The stars hung low in the velvety sky like diamond fruit waiting to be plucked. His thoughts began to wander...

"Hello. Wake up, sleepy head." Cilla's voice reached him from the front door.

He'd been sitting on the edge of the bed, dressed only in his smalls, the dream of making love to her still vivid. "I'm awake," he mumbled and scrambled into his trousers.

Her fingernails played a short tattoo against the door, and she peeked in.

"Are you decent?" Her blue eyes sparkled mischievously.

"All the same if I'm not." He turned his back and finished buttoning his bellbottoms, then sat back down and pulled on his socks.

"My, my. Do you usually greet the morning so pleasantly?"

"Let me at least wake up. What do you want, anyway?"

"To tell you that Mum is making you breakfast. She thought since your mum had to go to work that you probably wouldn't get anything to eat."

"Mmm. Well, I'll just finish dressing." He reached for the big square collar of his uniform.

"Here, let me."

"No! Don't." He scowled at her as if she'd intended committing murder.

Suddenly her blue eyes clouded, and her lower lip trembled. "What'd I do?" her voice cracked.

"Cor, Cilla. I'm sorry." How could she know he was wound up tighter than a spring? He needed time, but she looked so hurt that he reached out and stroked her satin cheek with the back of his fingers. Their eyes met, hers still on the brink of tears, and held. He pulled her to him, aware of his heart hammering against her breasts.

Her lips parted as if to speak, but he lowered his head and caressed her lips with his.

She looped her arms around his neck and returned his kiss. Slowly he withdrew, ending the kiss with a soft tug on her lower lip.

Her cheeks glowed pink. Her lips were still wet from his kiss, and her eyes, no longer spilling with tears, sparkled.

He lowered his lips to hers again and moved his hand slowly up her side, then stopped at the curve of her breast. Momentarily she tensed, but she didn't resist.

Still holding her, he turned until the edge of the bed pressed against the back of her legs, then he lowered her. He slipped his hand down her thigh to the hem of her dress and began inching his fingers against her bare leg.

She turned her mouth from his kiss and grabbed his wrist in a vise-like grip, pulling it from under her skirt. "No, Ted."

"Ah, Cilla," he groaned and dropped his head onto her breast. He admired her restraint. One of them needed it.

While she caressed the back of his neck, his breathing evened and his heart slowed its wild thumping.

"Come on, Ted. Get up. Mum will wonder."

Ted reluctantly pulled his thoughts away from his longing for Cilla. He checked the luminous dial on his wrist. Fifteen minutes before 04:00, then the watch would change.

He continued to scan the calm Pacific Ocean for anything out of the ordinary. There were others on the deck keeping watch. Two wing lookouts kept watch, another signaller on the opposite side of the deck, and the Officer-of-the Watch on the bridge.

The stars faded and the sky had lightened just enough to distinguish it from the darker ocean. He swept his binoculars across the horizon and was startled to see three specks. He continued to study them until they became three ships.

"Officer-of-the-watch, sir," he called to the figure standing on the bridge above him.

"What is it, Signaller?" The voice sounded tired.

"Ahead, starboard. Three vessels, sir."

The sky was becoming lighter, and the officer bent forward, staring through his binoculars.

"Right you are, Signaller." He dropped the glasses to hang around his neck and sent an urgent message by voice-tube to the captain's cabin.

The look-outs kept an anxious watch on the approaching ships.

Within minutes, the captain raced along the deck, fastening his greatcoat, and climbed the ladder to the bridge. The legs of his striped pyjamas flapping against his ankles contrasted sharply with the gleam of his highly-polished shoes.

Ted adjusted the focus on his binoculars and studied the three ships, now quite visible.

The captain turned and shouted down the voice-tube, "Wireless Operator, send out this message. *Sighted suspicious vessels.*"

"Aye, aye, sir," answered the radio operator and immediately the Morse-code key began to chatter.

Suddenly, a great puff of smoke rose from the lead ship. The whine of a shell reached the crew on the bridge of the *Incomparable* before the salvo smashed into it, disintegrating the telegraph. Cables, the mast and radio antenna crashed to the deck, pinning one young sailor. His screams of agony disappeared in the deafening explosions as shells continued to pound the ship. A fire started below.

"Medic! Medic!" someone screamed.

Ted raced toward the trapped sailor, reaching him at the same time as several others. They each began to strain against the mast, but weren't making any headway.

"We're working against one another. All right. Together now! On three! One, two, three." With a mighty effort the sailors raised the wreckage and pulled their unconscious shipmate free.

Aware of his aching back and shoulder muscles, Ted made for his battle station on what remained of the bridge.

"Chief Officer?" the captain yelled. "Prepare the stern gun for action."

"Aye, aye, sir."

"Chief Radio Operator?"

"Sir?" the radioman yelled back.

"Did our signal get out?" Captain Scott asked as calmly as if inquiring about a cricket match score.

"No, sir. We're trying again with the emergency set."

"Good. Send, '*Being fired upon by three raiders*' and give our position, Chief."

"Aye, sir." Then, after just a brief pause, "Message sent, sir."

"Good man! Now destroy all code books."

"Yes, sir!"

"You! Evans." Captain Scott pointed. "Give them a hand burning the codes and messages."

Before Ted could acknowledge the captain's order, the skipper yelled, "Stop Engines."

The mate sprang to the telegraph and yanked the brass handle to 'STOP.'

Captain Scott snatched the voice-tube. "Chief Engineer!"

"Sir?"

"Stop engines. We can't outrun them."

"Aye, aye, sir."

Ted grabbed a code book from the pile beside the wireless operators and began ripping out pages, throwing them into the fires burning around the radio room.

By now the three ships had surrounded the *Incomparable*, and each shone a powerful searchlight on the stricken ship. Sailors in every stage of undress clambered from the sleeping quarters below and took up their battle stations.

The shelling suddenly stopped. Ted's ears vibrated from the silence. The phone beside him rang, and he grabbed it, listened briefly, and then turned to the captain. "Chief Officer says the gun is ready for action, sir."

"It seems futile to use force at this point," the captain muttered and took the phone from Ted's hand.

"Chief? This is the captain. Hold your fire. We got a wireless message away. If the shelling begins again, fire on them."

"Yes, sir. But sir, the searchlights make range-finding difficult."

"Almost impossible in the dawn light, I should imagine, Chief. Do the best you can. We'll fight to the death if we have to."

"Aye, aye, sir."

Ted rejoined the wireless operators working frantically to destroy anything they thought would be of use to the enemy, while other crew members heaved stores into the fires or over the side of the ship.

A boarding party of German sailors, bearded and dirty, clambered onto the deck of the *Incomparable*. Armed with knives, they rushed the British sailors in an attempt to stop them heaving the last of the stores over the side. The British crew succeeded and left little for the enemy to loot from the sinking ship. Then they began to taunt the Germans.

The officer in charge of the boarding party waved a revolver and stormed at the British officers and crew, yelling unintelligibly at them.

Ignoring the German officer, Captain Scott barked, "Abandon ship!" and the British crew prepared to obey his order. The bombardment had destroyed several of the lifeboats, but enough remained to carry the *Incomparable's* skeleton crew.

Ted perched on the gunwale to make room for a stretcher with a badly burned sailor. "I wonder if they'll take us on board or if they'll leave us in the lifeboats," he said to Smiley sitting next to him.

"The boarding party's leaving. We'll find out soon enough, now."

When the raging German officer and his men pulled away from the burning ship, the guns on the large raider began firing on the *Incomparable*. She continued to burn and explode, sending up fountains of sparks, but she refused to sink. Then as her crew watched, a torpedo struck her, breaking her back, and sent her to the bottom.

A German officer in a small motorboat ordered the lifeboats to a vessel flying the Rising Sun of Japan, with the name *Tokyo Maru* painted on her side.

Ted clambered up the netting thrown over the side of the ship and found himself surrounded by German sailors. He turned to Smiley, confused. "What the hell is this? Japan's supposed to be neutral!"

A German sailor rushed at Ted with a bayonet, screaming at him in German. Ted had no idea what he was saying, but to be on the safe side, the British sailors raised their hands. The German pointed with his bayonet, indicating the hold.

The British sailors raised the hatch and released a putrid stench of unwashed bodies and raw sewage. The German gestured and, one after the other, the prisoners slowly climbed down into a living hell.

CHAPTER TWENTY-FOUR

12 November 1940
Dear Mum and Dad,
It's going to be difficult to give up this lazy life.
I feel quite pampered—sailing around the tropics on what has turned out to be a luxury liner, visiting exotic places and being more than well-fed into the bargain. I wish I could bring you home some of this marvellous food and especially the fruit.
Later—
I take it all back about visiting exotic places. We arrived at Fremantle today. What a miserable place it is, too. All the shops had closed for some sort of holiday, but the dusty, uninteresting streets were full of people lolling about, seemingly oblivious to the millions of flies drawn by the millions of sheep. Millie and I beat a hasty retreat back the ship.

Melbourne
17ᵗʰ November 1940
Do you remember the old trolley trams that used to run around London? They have them in Melbourne. This is a beautiful city of fine buildings and wide streets. The shops are full of goods (not like poor old England), but they're quite expensive by our standards.
Our next stop is Sydney, and Millie and I are both excited. We wonder how long we will have to wait there for a ship to bring us home.

The tang of salty ocean air tasted pleasant and somehow different than the Atlantic. Cooled by the night, the *Mantolin's* metal railing chilled Cilla's forearms through the sleeves of her light jacket. She shivered, but not from cold. Excitement tingled her spine.

Next stop Sydney! The last stop on her journey before heading home.

Home. Was it really only two months since the sinking of the *Punjohpur*? So much had happened. She shuddered as the vision of the dead and dying children filled her mind.

Red-streaks splayed from the edge of the horizon into the violet sky. Little by little the sky lightened and like a huge ball of orange twine, the sun crept above the horizon.

"Hello. You couldn't sleep either?"

Cilla turned at the sound of the familiar voice. "Hello, Millie. No, I don't think I closed my eyes all night." She spoke just above a whisper so as not to disturb the tranquillity of the emerging day. "God really is in his heaven this morning. Have you ever seen such colour?"

Millie sucked in a deep breath. "Spectacular," she breathed.

The kaleidoscope continued, changing the colourless sea and paling sky, until they reached the colours that Cilla had always thought them to be.

The ship seemed to fly across the sparkling sea as if she knew her perilous journey was nearing its end. The Sydney Heads, rising a hundred feet or more into the perfect blue sky, seemed to part as the *Mantolin* glided between them into the harbour.

White yachts wove their way around the pretty bays. Red-tiled villas with lovely gardens sloped down to sandy beaches.

"Oh, Cilla, look!" Millie pointed at a bird circling the ship.

Sydney, Australia
20th November 1940
As we sailed into the harbour today at dawn, a strange bird circled the ship several times and finally landed on the mast. A ship's officer told us it was a Kookaburra and said it was most unusual to find one this far away from the jungle. It stayed, laughing and chuckling until we reached the wharf, then it flew off. Millie and I thought it a most auspicious beginning to the next step of our homecoming.

What a welcome we received! You'd have thought Millie and I had single-handedly ended the war. The people are wonderful and cannot seem to do enough for us. A committee of women came aboard with clothes—right down to underwear, stockings and shoes. We had several choices and ended up with some nice frocks to bring home with us.

We are going to the CORB office today to see when we'll get a ship home.

*I shan't write again because I'll beat another letter home—I can
hardly wait.*
    See you soon.
    Love you, Cilla.

Cilla grabbed Millie's arm and, ducking around a building, retreated from
the throng of newspaper reporters and photographers. As the last strains of
the welcoming bag-pipes faded in the distance, they jumped on a passing bus
heading for the downtown area of Sydney.

They'd been given directions, and with the help of a friendly bus passenger,
they left the bus outside a newsagents. Cilla dropped the letter to her parents
into a nearby post box and looked about her. "This can't be it, surely."

"It's the right address. Look, there's a sign." Millie pointed to the
inconspicuous lettering.

At the top of the rickety staircase a door stood half-open, and Cilla peered
in. The room reeked of cigarettes, and a blue haze of smoke whirled above
the stacks of file folders and papers covering a desk against the far wall.
Someone coughed and wheezed behind an open newspaper.

"Excuse me. We're looking for Mr. Mearson," Cilla said.

A man jumped to his feet, stuffing the newspaper down toward the floor.
He pulled a half-smoked cigarette from his mouth, scattering ash across the
papers on his desk.

"You've found him. That's me." He stubbed the soggy cigarette into an
overflowing ashtray. "What can I do for you ladies?"

"We're CORB staff. We were instructed to come here. I'm Priscilla
Thornton and this is Millicent Parkin."

He slipped a nicotine-stained nail beneath the flaps of a fresh cigarette
package. "Oh, oh, my!" A deep hacking cough stopped him. He pulled a
large handkerchief from his pocket and held it to his mouth. His face turned
bright red, and veins stood out on his forehead.

Millie started toward him, but he stopped coughing just then and gasped.
"Welcome. Welcome. I do apologise for not meeting the ship, but I didn't
think I'd catch up with you among the great crowd that was there to greet
you. I thought this would be better—to come at your leisure." He inserted a
cigarette between his lips and struck a match to it. Smoke wreathed his head.

"That's perfectly all right, but we're most anxious to know when we can
go home." Cilla didn't add how anxious they were to get out of the smoke-
filled room.

"Of course. Of course you are, and I have some good news." He began coughing again. "I've been able to make arrangements for you... to join... twenty other escorts and nurses returning to England," he spluttered between gasps and coughs. "A small steamer will take you as far as Singapore. There you'll meet a liner that will return you to England." The coughing resumed.

"Oh, that's wonderful. When do we leave?" Millie said.

"The 24th."

"Millie, that's only four days from now." Cilla hugged her friend. "Thank you so much, Mr. Mearson."

"Come back here tomorrow and I'll give you all the particulars."

Millie yanked open the door and Cilla sucked in a breath of smokeless air.

"Miss Thornton!"

Cilla turned. "Yes?"

"I almost forgot. I have a message for you." He grabbed his handkerchief again and coughed into it while he rummaged through his desk drawer.

"A message for me? Nobody knows me here."

"A British sailor was in here a couple of weeks ago looking for you..." He pulled out an envelope and handed it to her.

Cilla had only to glance at her name on the outside to know who had written it. Her heart thumped as she feverishly ripped open the envelope and read the message inside. Weak with relief, she steadied herself against the edge of the ash-strewn desk.

"Oh, thank God! Millie, it's from Ted."

CHAPTER TWENTY-FIVE

A deafening explosion catapulted Cilla to the floor. She landed hard on her hip and bumped her head on the leg of the bunk. Before she could get her bearings in the darkness, the cabin floor suddenly jolted. Terrified and bewildered, she scrambled to her feet and gripped the edge of her bed with both hands, memories of the torpedoing of the *Punjohpur* uppermost in her mind. *It can't be happening again!*

A tremendous roaring, then a long streak of sound like a bed sheet ripping. The *Rangoon Princess* shuddered.

The staccato of gunfire disintegrated the porthole and raked the cabin bulkheads. Instinctively Cilla threw her arms over her face and dropped to the floor. An awful stillness settled.

Groping for her clothing, she shook the fragments of glass from her shorts and shirt and slipped them on. Panic gripped her as she fumbled under her bunk for her shoes. It was so quiet she wondered if anyone else were even alive. She tipped her shoes over and heard the tinkle of more glass. Struggling into her life jacket, she jerked open the cabin door and stepped into a blanket of smoke-filled blackness. People, coughing and gagging, bumped into each other as they staggered along the corridor.

Flames glowing through the dense smoke cast an eerie light. Holding her arm in front of her eyes, Cilla groped her way to the next cabin and banged on the door.

"Millie," she yelled and yanked open the door. A blast of heat and suffocating smoke billowed out and caught her full in the face. She staggered back, choking. The cabin walls blazed all around Millie, still apparently asleep in her bunk.

"Get up, Millie. Come on. You can't stay here." Cilla yelled from the doorway. Millie moaned.

Cilla pulled her life jacket around her head and rushed in. Lit by flames, Millie's face shone ghostly white. Her eyes were wide and filled with terror. With each laboured breath, blood hissed and bubbled from a wound in her chest where a shard of glass protruded about five inches.

"Oh, God. No." Millie needed more help than Cilla could give her. She stuck her head out of the door and yelled into the corridor. "Help me, someone. Help, please."

Pat Sentry, one of the nurses, waved the smoke away from her face. "What's happening?" She coughed.

A thunderous roar followed by a tearing shriek, and the ship seemed to jump. "Damn. We're being shelled." Pat staggered into the wall.

"Pat, help me. Millie's been hurt." Cilla turned back to the burning cabin with Pat at her heels.

"Her lung's been punctured," said Pat, leaning over Millie's bleeding chest. "Let's get her out of here. Jean, give me a hand," she yelled, and Jean Morrison appeared at the cabin door. "Jean, we need to carry her in the sheet."

"Grab the sheet at her feet, Cilla," Jean said.

There was no easy or gentle way to move Millie, and she groaned.

Someone at the end of the corridor shone a torch-light. A male voice called out. "Follow me and I'll lead you to the deck." The half-dazed people needed no second bidding. Those with minor injuries helping the more badly wounded, formed a queue and trailed after the beam of light.

Cilla gripped the edges of the sheet in both hands and staggered through the smoke and debris. The procession suddenly halted, and she almost dropped her burden.

"What is it? What's wrong? Why are we stopped?" She gasped for breath, choking on the smoke.

"It's an inferno up there. We can't get through," someone at the head of the line answered.

"Turn around. Go back," the voice with the torch ordered.

It was impossible to turn Millie in the confined space. Cilla switched her grip on the sheet and reversed her direction. She had no idea where she was or where she was going. Fire burned ahead, glowing through the swirling smoke in front of her. Her throat burned and her eyes streamed.

A bright light shone through the haze, and a male voice ordered, "This way. Follow me."

Reaching the deck, they gently set Millie down, and Cilla collapsed, sucking in great gulps of fresh air. The silence was deafening now that the firing had stopped, and the ship's engines were quiet. Even the people moving about the deck seemed almost as if they were afraid to shatter the calm. The wounded, laid out in a row, made no sounds.

Dawn was just breaking on a dead-calm sea. Two hundred yards away, a sinister black ship flying the Nazi flag and wearing painted swastikas on her bow, rode at anchor. Close by, two more ships flying Nazi flags but with Japanese markings, trained blinding searchlights on the burning *Rangoon Princess*.

A German officer leading a boarding party clambered onto the deck. He waved his arms and yelled at the German sailors, who frantically tried to haul cargo out of the burning holds. The fire was so intense that they weren't able to salvage much.

"Abandon ship! Take to the lifeboats!" a British voice ordered, and the crew of the *Rangoon Princess* prepared to lower the lifeboats.

Millie had lost all colour in her face and appeared to be unconscious, but when a young sailor helped lift her into the lifeboat, her eyes suddenly flew open and she grimaced. Cilla settled on a thwart next to her and took Millie's hand.

The boat swung away from the ship's side and descended until it floated on the water, giving Cilla a pronounced sense of deja-vu.

The crew rowed swiftly toward the other lifeboats, congregating about fifty yards from the *Rangoon Princess*, and provided a perfect view of the stricken ship, ablaze fore and aft. Visible through the smoke and flames, a lifeboat with her side blown out by shell-fire still hung in position, and on the bridge a German sailor in a white uniform signalled to the Raider.

Cilla felt nauseous. How could this be happening? She was on her way home. She was on her way to Ted. And now this. She turned to the British officer sharing the thwart. "What are our chances of getting away?"

He shook his head. "Not very good, I'm afraid. Look at the guns turned on us. If we don't comply with their orders, they'll blow us out of the water."

The Pacific Ocean was not cold, but shock and the early-morning breeze chilled Cilla. "How are you doing, Millie?" She folded the edges of the sheet around her friend, all the time knowing that Millie could not answer.

Millie's face was colourless except for the flecks of blood around her mouth. Her wound appeared to have stopped bleeding, but she no longer made any sound. Cilla leaned close to her friend. "Millie," she whispered, "we're going to make it out of this. Please hang on. Don't die, Millie. Please don't leave me."

A fast boat manned by German sailors approached. It slowed beside the lifeboat, and a young Nazi officer stood up and touched his cap visor in salute. "You, go to black ship," he instructed the rowers of the lifeboat. Cilla sensed his urgency as he sped away to each of the other lifeboats in turn. He waved his arms and pointed, indicating which ship each lifeboat was to make for.

The Raider, looking very large and forbidding, towered over the little lifeboat.

"Up. Come up." The German sailor gestured from the deck above her.

Cilla started to climb the netting slung over the side.

"No. I can't go without Millie."

"Go on Miss. We'll bring the injured lady right behind you." Cilla hesitated, and the British officer nodded, encouraging her.

"Up! Up!" the German screamed at her.

She grasped the rough wet rope and hauled herself upwards. At the top, two Nazi sailors helped her onto the ship. Several wounded lay side by side on the deck.

The Germans lowered a stretcher over the side to the lifeboat. It reappeared with Millie, pale and unconscious, strapped to it.

Cilla pushed her way to Millie's side, but a Nazi sailor turned her away. "*Nein, Fraulein. Nein!*"

"Please, let me stay with her," she begged.

"*Nein!*" a German with black and broken teeth screamed at her, pushing her roughly toward a small iron ladder. Others from the *Rangoon Princess* were already climbing down to the ship's interior. Susan Sedgewick's leg was bleeding from a deep gash, and Phillipa Weston had trouble going backwards down the narrow ladder with her broken arm supported only by a makeshift sling.

At the bottom, an armed guard indicated with a jerk of his head that they should keep moving. Passing through a small, square galley, Cilla glimpsed a room to the left full of filthy, bearded men. In a room to the right, several people lay on mattresses on the floor. A corridor led into an irregular-shaped room about thirty feet long with a painted iron floor. In the middle stood two long trestle tables with fixed benches.

Cilla watched from just inside the door until Millie was lowered on the stretcher and carried into the room with the mattresses.

"Cilla. Are you all right? Your hands are bleeding." Maggie, a Scots woman of about forty-five returning from a successful trip transporting evacuees to New Zealand, took one of Cilla's hands in hers.

"I am?" Cilla studied her hands where dozens of slivers of flying glass had scored her skin. The cuts weren't deep, and she'd been so worried about

Millie that she hadn't felt them, but now they were beginning to sting.

"You'd better let Jean or Pat have a look at your hands. You've got glass sprinkled on your hair too. Come here and I'll pick it out."

Cilla sat down on one of the benches and looked about her new quarters while Maggie picked glass fragments out of her hair.

Susan Sedgewick limped into the room with her leg bandaged. Pip still wore her sling, but her arm was secured between two wooden splints.

Suddenly above, scurrying footsteps sounded, followed by the shriek of iron joists, then with a thud the doors closed.

"Well, I don't think we're going to Singapore to meet the liner," Pip said, giving the room a disgusted look. "I'm starved. All this early morning activity has given me an appetite. I wonder what sort of breakfast this luxury cruise ship has on the menu."

Cilla gave a bitter laugh. Below her feet, the ship's engine began to throb.

CHAPTER TWENTY-SIX

A young Nazi sailor in a dirty white uniform and a cap with long black ribbons hanging from the back sauntered into the room carrying a large enamel jug and a single tin mug. He looked the women over and, with a contemptuous sneer, dumped the jug on the table next to Cilla, slamming the mug down beside it, then swaggered away.

"What is it?" Maggie said.

Cilla peered into the jug and sniffed at the black liquid. "I think it's meant to be coffee." She splashed a little into the bottom of the mug and sniffed it again.

"Well, go on. Taste it," urged a woman across the table.

Cilla sipped the bitter brew and got a mouthful of grounds. She shuddered and passed the mug to the woman sitting next to her. "Try straining it through your teeth."

The sailor returned and plunked down a large baking tin full of thick black-bread sandwiches.

Hunger and curiosity drove Cilla to examine what oozed from between the slabs of coarse bread. She put the sandwich to her nose, detecting a peculiar smell before she nibbled the edge. "What is this awful stuff?"

"I'd say it's rancid lard," Maggie said, peering between the black bread slices.

Cilla wrinkled her nose and shook her head. "It's awful."

"You'd best try and eat it. I doubt the rest of the meals are any better. My name's Margery Dixter, by the way. We haven't met."

Cilla introduced herself and met Lucy Frye at the same time.

"Now what?" Cilla said, narrowing her eyes at the tall officer standing in the doorway. He tucked his hat under his arm, clicked his heels together and gave a stiff bow from the waist.

"Excuse me, ladies. I will now interview each prisoner individually. Please step this way." He pointed to a table at the far end of the room and, one by one, he interrogated the women.

When Cilla's turn came, he beckoned to her and indicated she should sit opposite him. With very deliberate movements he placed his hat on the table, removed a silver case from his jacket pocket and offered Cilla a cigarette. She shook her head.

His eyes never left her face as he placed a cigarette between his lips and carefully lit it with a fancy lighter. Cilla stared him down until he opened a notebook and pulled a pen from somewhere inside his coat.

"What is your name?" He tilted his head and blew a long plume of smoke.

Cilla bit her lip to keep from laughing at the dramatics. She told him her name and he wrote it in the notebook.

"Now. You will tell me what port you were bound for."

She figured he already knew so there was no harm in confirming it. "Singapore."

"For what purpose?"

"I was to catch another ship there to take me home to England."

He wanted to know if she had heard anything about German mine-laying. Had she heard about the German Raiders?

Cilla giggled. "No, but I heard about the British Navy sinking your invincible *Graf Spee.*"

The German's eyes narrowed, settling on hers in a withering gaze. Cilla stared back unblinking, until he seemed to catch himself and the corners of his mouth turned up in a smile. "Ah, yes. Well, that was a long time ago."

"Not so long ago that we British have forgotten how we sank the pride of the German Navy." She enjoyed his discomfort.

He consulted his notebook again and continued questioning her, asking what she was doing in Australia and which English ports were still in use.

"How would I know that?" She was getting a bit fed up with his stupid questions, but he persisted.

The cigarette still jutted from his square face, and he held his head thrust up to avoid getting smoke in his eyes.

Cilla watched, fascinated, as the long grey ash grew and drooped.

"What British port did you sail from? Aboard which ship?"

"The *Punjohpur* out of Liverpool."

"Was she armed? Did she carry guns?"

"No," Cilla lied. She had seen the big guns on the deck of the *Punjohpur,* but she wasn't going to tell this Nazi anything more than she figured he already knew.

"What date did you sail?"

"September 13th."

"What was her cargo?" He gave a smirk. "Troops?"

Cilla swallowed hard. What had the Germans heard? Some of the other CORB escorts had told her the ships they sailed on carried troops as well as the evacuees.

"No! Two hundred and forty-one children and twenty-two civilian escorts."

"To Australia?" His head shot up and he frowned at her.

"No. To Canada. We were torpedoed four days out."

"Ah, yes." He smirked.

Cilla was sure he knew all about the *Punjohpur* and her passengers. The supercilious bastard was just checking his information. She wished now that she had said they were going to Australia. That would have thrown a spanner in the works.

"Children and troops," he mumbled as he wrote.

"No! I told you, no troops. Are you trying to justify sinking a ship full of children?"

"I beg your pardon, Miss Thornton, but there was ample justification. There were Royal Naval personnel aboard. That ship was the convoy leader. Therefore, it stands to reason that the commodore's staff were members of the Royal Navy. The illustrious German Navy cannot be held accountable for the irresponsible British action of putting children on a warship."

Cilla bit back a retort.

Gravity finally won, and the ash bounced down the front of his coat. He flicked it away with an irritated gesture and stubbed out the cigarette under his foot.

"And what was the name of the ship that rescued you?"

"*Mantolin*"

"*HMS Mantolin.*" He repeated the name as he wrote it. He consulted his notes. "Hmm. Most of the *Punjohpur's* survivors returned to England. Why not you?"

"My lifeboat was separated from the others. We were picked up later than they were."

"How much later?" He regarded her with one eyebrow raised.

She dropped her head and mumbled, "Eight days."

He chuckled and scribbled in his notebook. "You have certainly seen your share of the war, haven't you, *fraulein*?" He checked his notes again. "The *Mantolin* took the children to Cape Town and then carried the troops on to Singapore? Is that right?"

That left Cilla speechless. The bloody Germans seemed to know where all the allied ships were at all times.

"And where is that ship now? Has she already left Australia?"

Ah, ha! They don't know everything. "I don't know where she is."

When the interrogation ended, a young sailor came around, yelling and gesturing to a bag he carried.

"What's his problem?" someone asked.

Suddenly he snatched up a handbag and jammed it into his bag.

"Oh my God! They're taking our valuables! No! You can't have that." Sylvia tried to yank her bag from the sailor's grip. "I was a first-class passenger. You can't take my jewellery."

Few had saved anything except what they wore, but Sylvia had managed to rescue a small suitcase containing her valuables. Now she was in a panic.

"Why are they doing this?" Her eyes widened and she visibly trembled. "They're going to kill us."

Lucy pulled off her wedding ring and slipped it into her palm. "I don't think so, or they would have left us on the *Princess.* Maybe they're taking us to an internment camp." The German rushed her and pried open her hand, forcing her to drop the ring into his bag.

He left with the bag of booty. Cilla slumped down onto a bench and stared blankly at the wall, wondering when she would see Ted or her parents again.

"Cilla!"

She roused herself and turned to see Pat Sentry and the German doctor staring at her.

"Yes. What is it? Is Millie all right?"

The doctor answered in a thick German accent. "We are doing the best for your friend. I have operated, but she is very ill."

"May I see her?"

"She is heavily sedated, and I regret to tell you I do not think she will recover." The doctor's eyes reflected genuine sorrow.

Two dirty, unshaven sailors staggered into the room under the weight of a big iron pot. They set it in the middle of the room, and one removed the lid.

"What is that? It looks revolting." Cilla grimaced. The fact that there weren't enough enamel plates to go round was not going to trouble her.

"You really should try to eat some of it, Cilla. As bad as it looks, it's all there is." Lucy Frye held her nose and spooned the green stew into her mouth. Cilla's stomach heaved, and she shook her head.

The sailors removed the iron pot of muck, and one returned with an arm-load of netting. He dumped it unceremoniously on one of the trestle tables.

"Now what?" Irritated by the day's events and so hungry her stomach growled, Cilla was in a black mood.

"Hey, I do believe they've brought us hammocks." Lucy untangled one from the pile and examined it.

"So!" The sailor opened a hammock and pointed to an iron bar about five feet or so from the floor. He reached up and attached first one end of the hammock, then the other to the bar, so that it hung about three above the floor. He studied it for a moment, then, seeming satisfied, left them to sling the rest of their beds.

"Right. Now that it's tied up there, how do you get into it?" Lucy said. She was large and one of the older prisoners.

"I don't think I can even try," said Pip, supporting her broken arm.

"I'll give it a go." Cilla gingerly sat in the middle of the net, then swung her legs up into it. Too late, she realised she'd disturbed the centre of gravity. The hammock turned turtle and she landed in a heap on the floor.

"Are you all right?" Margery helped Cilla to her feet, but Cilla was laughing so hard she couldn't straighten up.

Lucy raised a knee into the hammock. "Damn!" she yelled as she too crashed to the floor.

"Oh, blimey. What the hell are we doing?" Cilla grabbed her sides and roared with hysterical laughter until tears rolled down her cheeks.

In turn, those who felt capable attempted to master the hammock. A couple of them even made it, but the rest just joined Cilla in howling laughter.

"What is happening? Why do the Englisher ladies laugh so?" The doctor stood in the doorway, studying them quizzically. "I will send you something to do." With a scowling glance over his shoulder, he left.

Cilla picked up one of the blankets the sailor had brought and prepared to sleep on the floor. "Has anyone noticed that all the stuff they've brought to us is brand new?" She studied the tag on the blanket. "And everything seems to have Japanese markings. I wonder what their game is."

"Ssh, Cilla." Margery pointed to the ceiling, where obvious small microphones dangled on the end of cords.

Pip eyed them. "Well, then, I hope they're listening to this—Sod all you bloody Germans," she yelled.

A fierce looking sailor with a cutlass in his belt came into the room, counted the prisoners, and without a word, flicked a switch and plunged the room into darkness. The unmistakable sound of a key being turned sent a shiver up Cilla's spine. Locked in below water-level, it wasn't hard to imagine their chances if British ships attacked the Raider.

"Where do the stupid buggers think we're going?" Cilla jammed her life jacket under her head for a pillow and curled up in the blanket.

In the darkness, someone quietly cried. Overhead a guard tramped monotonously, and water lapped against the hull of the ship. Cilla bit back sobs and slept fitfully.

A bolt slammed, and with a sudden flourish the door flew open, flooding the room with bright, artificial light.

"What's going on?" a sleepy voice said.

"I think it must be morning."

"How the hell can you tell in this bloody black hole?"

One by one the women roused themselves.

The two sailors who had brought the green stew each carried a basin of water into the room. "This...one month," the sailor said and solemnly handed each woman a square of towel and a bit of soap.

"To last a month? Ye gods, they expect to keep us a month on this floating coffin." Sylvia stared at the sliver of soap.

"Ach, dinna fret. We'll all be dead of starvation long before this wee bit of soap is gone." Maggie splashed the cold water on her face.

The same two sailors brought in breakfast of sour black bread and coffee. Lunch was a watery soup.

Cilla thought if she didn't starve to death, she would certainly die of boredom.

"Miss Thornton." The doctor came up behind her and gently touched her arm.

Jean stood beside the doctor. One look at the sorrowful expression on their faces told her before they even spoke.

"Millie's gone," Jean said, wrapping her arm around Cilla's shoulder.

Cilla clapped her hand over her mouth to hold back an agonised scream of almost physical pain. No! Not Millie! It wasn't fair!

"I am profoundly sorry, Miss Thornton." The doctor turned away.

Cilla went to a corner of the room. Left alone, she buried her face in her hands and sobbed until she felt exhausted.

Later in the day, the interrogating officer returned, immaculately dressed and wearing gloves. He removed his cap and placed it under his arm, then, clicking his heels together, he bowed. "Ladies. The *Kapitan* has determined that it is safe to stop the ship now so that we may bury the dead. If you will follow me, please."

The fading daylight seemed so strong after being below that it was difficult to see at first.

The Raider had stopped, but two sailors stood at the look-out. In the distance lay the other two ships that had taken part in the attack on the *Rangoon Princess*.

At least a hundred sailors, smartly dressed in clean white uniforms and standing stiffly at attention, lined up in two rows, on one side of the deck. Black ribands, bearing the name *Krief-Marine* in gold letters, fluttered from their caps in the evening breeze. In front of them stood fifty or sixty officers, immaculate in dark uniforms and grey gloves. At right angles to the crew stood the filthy, gaunt male prisoners.

The officer who led them to the deck directed the women to sit in the chairs placed directly in front of the men.

The bier, covered by a red ensign, lay on a Union Jack. Overhead, the Swastika flag fluttered at half-mast.

"No," Cilla growled, and driven by anger at the sight of the ugly ensign, she started toward the flagstaff, determined to rip down the Swastika. Her best friend would not be buried under the enemy's flag.

"No, Cilla. Stop." Urgent whispers and firm hands restrained her.

"*Achtung!*" The German sailors stiffened to attention. The captain marched down the line of prisoners, stopped, swung to face them and gave the English salute.

"Sod you!" Cilla hissed.

The captain stepped up to the bier and began an oration in German that would have done Hitler proud.

Cilla lowered her head and tried to block out the raucous voice by focusing instead on Millie at her happiest. She remembered the fun they'd had just being tourists in the exotic cities of the Far East. She even managed an internal smile when she recalled Millie's efforts to retrieve Pearl Oberman's hat from the monkey.

At last the German harangue ended, and a British prisoner stepped forward. On the lapels of his shabby uniform he wore the insignia of a Navy chaplain. "Our German adversary has condemned Mrs. Millicent Parkin for taking upon herself the task of accompanying children through the dangers of war at sea. I would just like to point out that were it necessary, the whole nation of British women would not hesitate to do the same thing to protect our children from capture by an enemy."

A German officer stood behind the captain and whispered, obviously translating the chaplain's words. The captain's face became beetroot red, and he started forward, but stopped as the chaplain offered a short but poignant prayer.

Two German sailors—one with a concertina, the other a pipe—played a German military march. As the music ended, a rich baritone from among the prisoners started to sing "Eternal Father, Strong to Save..." Other voices, male and female joined in. *"Whose arm doth still the restless wave..."*

Cilla choked back a sob. She blinked away her tears and, determined not to let the Germans see her cry, added her voice in singing The Sailor's Hymn: *"Who bids the mighty ocean deep, its own appointed limits keep..."*

German sailors stepped to the bier...

"Oh hear us when we cry to Thee..." And Millie's body, neatly sown into a canvas shroud, was lowered into the fathomless Pacific. *"For those in peril on the sea."*

CHAPTER TWENTY-SEVEN

Cilla wiped the back of her hand across her damp forehead. The day had hardly begun, and already the air in the sparse sleeping quarters was stagnant and depressingly hot.

"I wish we could do more for Pat," she said, carefully wrapping a button from her blouse in a square of toilet paper.

"What is it they say about it not being the gift but the sentiment that counts?" Lucy added her gift to the little bundles already on the table. "Pat will be pleased that we even remembered."

"Did I hear my name mentioned?" Perspiration plastered Pat Sentry's hair to her neck, and her eyes drooped with fatigue.

"There's the birthday girl," Pip said.

Pat grinned. "How on earth did you know it was my birthday?"

They drowned out the question by singing "Happy Birthday," and Jean pushed a toilet paper bundle toward Pat. "Come on, Pat, hurry up and open your presents. I've got to get to the sick-bay," she said.

Pat chuckled as she peered at her gifts: a safety pin, a hairpin, Cilla's button and a piece of toffee in a brightly-coloured foil wrapper.

"Ah, ladies." The doctor stood in the doorway of the stifling room, smiling. "I heard your singing. Many happy returns of the day, Sister Sentry." He handed Pat a brand-new pack of playing cards. "I hope this will help you pass the time."

"Thank you, Doctor, but I sincerely hope I never have to spend another birthday in these conditions."

"Ah, yes." He nodded gravely. "I have given you ladies much thought and I wonder...you are always joking and laughing, don't English women ever cry?"

"Of course we do," Cilla said, "but how can we now? We have no handkerchiefs." She chuckled and the others laughed, enjoying the joke.

"Then I shall see that you get handkerchiefs." The doctor spun on his heel and left.

"I think we hurt his feelings," Maggie said.

"Naw, Germans don't have feelings." Pip made no bones about her hostility toward the enemy.

"Well, to be fair, he's treated us pretty well," said Pat. "He's an excellent doctor and has a very compassionate nature."

"That's true," Cilla said. "He really did his very best for Millie, and he certainly showed me compassion when Millie died."

"Well, I'll give him that. And he did his best with my arm." Pip begrudged the compliment. "But he's the exception."

Pat offered the doctor's gift. "Anyone care for a quiet game of cards?"

Margery reached for the pack. "Thanks."

"I'm going to get a kip so do make it a quiet game, won't you," Pat said.

They had just settled down to the first hand of rummy when the interrogation officer appeared in the doorway. "Ladies, you may go on deck for ten minutes' exercise."

As eager as schoolgirls on a day trip, the prisoners abandoned their card game and raced for the outdoors.

Momentarily blinded by the brilliant sunlight, Cilla filled her lungs with briny air and turned her perspiring face to catch the breeze. She opened her eyes and wafted her shirt to cool her body. "Pip! Do you see what I see?" She nodded her head toward the horizon. "Are those the same Japanese ships?"

"I don't know," said Pip. "They're too far away. I wonder what the *Schweinhunde* are up to now."

"What is that you keep saying? What does it mean?"

"What? You mean *Schweinhunde*? Pig-dog, I think. I read it in a book and it seemed appropriate here."

Cilla giggled. She liked her young friend with black, twinkling eyes. Her olive skin and jet black curls proved her Romany heritage, but her accent was pure London.

Boredom set into the routine as the temperature climbed and humidity became more oppressive. With nerves on edge, tempers seemed on the verge of erupting.

The appearance of the interrogating officer in the doorway came as a welcome diversion. He clicked his heels together and bowed slightly. His announcement was even more welcome.

"Ladies. This ship is not suitable for you. You will be moved to another ship in five minutes." He wheeled around and left.

"What's all this about then?" Lucy asked.

"Who cares, if it means a change of scenery." Pip was already on her feet and ready to go.

"Do you think they're going to take us to Germany?" Sylvia whined. She always whined and couldn't quite seem to grasp the fact that her first-class passenger status on the *Princess* gave her no special privileges on the prison ship. She was, quite literally, in the same boat as the CORB women.

"Wherever they take us, let's hope it's better than this old scow." Margery gave the room a disdainful look.

Having surrendered all their possessions, there wasn't a watch between them and no way to tell how long they waited before the officer returned.

"Ladies, you may bid the men prisoners farewell from their doorway. They are to remain on this ship."

The women crowded around the door and had a good look at the captives they had only glimpsed when they came aboard four days earlier. The men, some wearing remnants of naval uniforms, were all very thin with long hair and beards, and appeared to have been prisoners for some time. Despite their condition, they sounded surprisingly cheerful.

"Good luck, ladies."

"Best of luck to you."

"All the best."

The women said their goodbyes and blew kisses to the men.

By the time they reached the deck, the ship had stopped and the gangplank already lowered.

"They're not wasting any time, are they?" Cilla commented, and nobody disagreed.

Amid shouts they didn't understand, an armed guard herded the group into a motor launch, and almost before they were seated, it sped away across the sparkling water.

Under a cloudless blue sky, with the wind in her hair, Cilla found the ride exhilarating. Still, as the distance between the launch and the Japanese ship closed, Cilla wondered, not without some apprehension, what awaited.

The men in the putrid hold quieted when the ship's engines stopped. They listened without commenting to the heavy iron anchor rapidly scraping over the side and splashing into he sea.

"Now what?"

"Ssh! Listen."

Running feet. Yelling. The activity accelerated.

"It's not an attack."

"That sounds like the gangway going down."

"Wonder what's going on."

"Let's find out." The captives dashed for the lavatory, where a convenient knothole gave a view to the outside. For more than an hour they took turns.

"Come on, Smiley, give us a look," Ted urged, and Smiley reluctantly gave up his position at the spy hole. Ted lay flat on his stomach on the floor of the fetid lavatory and peered through the spy hole.

The ominous black Raider lay at anchor about two hundred yards away. An armed officer was leading a group of women down the gangplank into the launch. Ted could hear the launch engine revving up, and suddenly it roared away from the side of the black ship.

"That's long enough, Ted. It's my turn now." Sparks began to tug at Ted's dirty shirt.

Ted shrugged him off. "Wait...wait...wait. God almighty!"

The wind had caught Cilla's honey-blonde hair and slicked it straight back from her face. She flicked a strand from her mouth, and as the launch closed the distance between the ships, she turned and looked up almost as though she could see him through the hull.

The launch slowed, but it was difficult to tell whether it was coming to the *Tokyo Maru* or passing on to the other ship that lay beyond.

"Come on, Ted. You've had more than your turn, and others are waiting for a look."

"Just a minute more." Ted kept his eye up to the hole.

"No. Give it up!"

Just then the launch came into view loaded with RAF personnel. Ted realised they had come from the *Tokyo Maru* and were transferring to the Raider. That could only mean Cilla had been brought to this ship. His heart pounded against the floor of the lavatory.

"Sod it all, Evans. Let someone else have a look."

Ted moved away from the hole, breathing heavily.

German sailors leaned over the railing of the *Tokyo Maru*, watching the women waiting below in the launch. The motor boat eased up to the gangway, and the German guard leapt deftly onto the platform.

Cilla hesitated. The guard's feat was not as easy as he made it look. Carefully gauging the rise and fall of the little boat on the swells, she took a flying leap and landed in a flurry. Two German sailors helped her on deck, then herded her behind a roped-off area.

Long before they reached the deck, Cilla heard the group of boisterous RAF personnel who had been on the *Rangoon Princess.* Seeing the women again, they whistled and blew kisses. The Germans tried but had to give up keeping them from clasping the women's hands as they climbed down into the now-vacant launch. When the boat revved its motor, they were still calling out words of encouragement and waving.

"Good luck to you," Cilla called back and waved as the launch sped the unfortunate prisoners to join those already on board the German Raider.

Next, the officers of the *Rangoon Princess,* still smartly dressed in their uniforms and wearing their life jackets, came up on deck. The Germans didn't even try to prevent them from grasping the women's hands. The captain's eyes glistened with tears as he folded Cilla's hand in his. "God bless you. God bless you all," he said. As each officer filed past, he gave the very British thumbs-up.

It was all Cilla could do to hold back the tears, but she refused to use the handkerchief that the doctor had given her. She swallowed the lump in her throat and waved as the launch carried the officers, not to the Raider, but to the other Japanese ship.

The Germans seemed to be in a hurry to get the transfers over with and to get underway again. Within minutes of the last prisoner leaving, the ship's engines began to throb, vibrating the deck.

"Ladies will please to follow me." A wiry young officer with thin blonde hair and pale eyes led them forward to the lower deck. He stepped back, and with a smirk on his face, gestured through a heavy iron door to a room lit only by a bare light bulb hanging from the ceiling. A dozen or so straw mattresses strewn on the floor were visible through the gloom. There were no portholes or any means of ventilation.

"Are we required to stay in this room?" Lucy had drawn herself up to her full height, towering over the German.

The smirk left his face, and instead he glowered. "No. You may go freely to the deck," he said.

"Good. Let's not hang about here," Pip said. With her uninjured arm, she grabbed Cilla's hand. "Come on deck."

Cilla leaned her forearms on the railing and sighed as the sun sank like a ball of fire into the ocean. "Pip, imagine what people paid to sail these waters before the war."

The sound of a gong startled her. "What's that?"

Pip laughed. "I do believe it's a dinner gong."

"What?! Calling us to dinner on a prison ship?" Cilla giggled, finding the notion impossible to believe, but she and Pip went inside, just in case.

The dining room had several round tables each set for six people.

Four women, one holding a baby, sat at one of the tables. They broke out in smiles as the prisoners from the *Rangoon Princess* entered the dining room.

"So you're the reason they locked us in!" A large, broad-faced woman greeted the newcomers in a pure Australian accent. "Hello, I'm Gwen. Where'd you come from?"

Under the supercilious gaze of the Nazi guards, the women exchanged names and stories of how they came to be prisoners of the Germans hiding behind the Japanese flag.

The Australians had been returning to their homes on the islands around Australia after Christmas shopping on the mainland.

"Rotten blighters! We were only on a little island steamer. They could tell we weren't a warship. And what did they get for their trouble? Women and kids, that's what!" Gwen glared at the guards.

There was evidence everywhere that the *Tokyo Maru* had, under another name, once been a small luxury liner of the Hamburg-America Line. A portrait of Hindenburg hung at one end of the dining room, and at the other a portrait of Hitler with roving eyes. Cilla poked Pip and nodded at the eyes that followed no matter where she sat.

"*Schweinhunde*," Pip mumbled and deliberately plonked down with her back to Hitler.

At each of the six places around the table sat an elegant blue and white china plate with a gold band around the edge. It seemed out of place and far too refined for the three huge black-bread sandwiches piled on it.

Gingerly, Cilla lifted the corner of one sandwich. Inside was a chunk of cheese. She hungrily bit into the second sandwich containing a slice of German sausage, and her jaw snapped. "Oh, crickey! What's in here?" She rubbed her cheek.

"We should have warned you," Gwen said. "Don't try and eat it if you have dentures or a bridge." She leaned back and roared with laughter. The German head steward glared at her. Cilla wasn't sure if he understood what Gwen was saying, but he obviously got the meaning.

"Do you have this often, then?" Cilla asked.

"Every day at this time. One cheese, one rock hard sausage and one jam."

"Jam!" Cilla separated the slices of the last sandwich to discover a smear of something that could have been marmalade.

"Good evening, English ladies. I am *Kapitan* Hilldebrandt."

The captain, cigar in hand, stood in the doorway. He was about sixty with sparse, greying hair and a barrel chest.

"I hope you will be comfortable while you are guests aboard my ship. I am sorry if you find it a little crowded, but we will do our best for you."

"Guests!?" Cilla said in a loud whisper.

"The quarters you have been shown are not suitable for ladies," the captain continued. "If you will find it more comfortable you may sleep in the lounge or share the cabins."

The main room had no ventilation, and the cabin portholes were blacked out and locked at night.

Cilla and Pip elected to sleep on the floor of the lounge, where the hot night air circulated a little more freely.

The morning dawned as hot and heavy as ever. A sailor brought a bucket of fresh water and set it in the middle of the floor. Cilla could hardly believe the luck. Fresh water! She put her hands in, preparing the splash some on her face.

"Oiy! oiy!" Gwen's voice boomed. "That's our drinking water."

"What?!"

"That bucket of water is all we get between us."

"Sorry," Cilla said, embarrassed by her gaffe. She licked the water from her hands and jumped as the breakfast gong sounded.

On the posh china plate sat a mound of dirty-looking rice with black shrivelled things in it. The question was, were the maggots still alive? They didn't appear to be moving, so Cilla tentatively pushed them aside and spooned some rice into her mouth. It was only palatable by having been boiled in salty seawater. Beside her plate were two slices of black bread and a spoonful of jam. She smeared the jam on one piece, but the other had green mould on the underside, and she pushed it away.

"Here, if you're not going to eat that, give it to me." Gwen reached across the table and swooped up the mouldy bread.

The big-boned woman was starving. Cilla was half Gwen's size, and she too was constantly hungry—but not quite into eating maggots and mould—yet.

179

CHAPTER TWENTY-EIGHT

Each morning, in batches of about thirty at a time, the male prisoners came on deck for ten minutes of exercise. Not all of them got to enjoy the fresh air every day, so when Ted's turn came, he eagerly scanned the empty upper deck for Cilla.

After ten minutes, the women had still not appeared, and Ted returned to the hold bitterly disappointed. To see her was becoming an obsession with him. Just to glimpse those wonderful blue eyes—or to see her smile. To know she was actually on the ship and not be able to hold her or even see her was more punishment than spending his days in the foul hold. He fantasised about her reaction when she looked over the railing and saw him for the first time.

One of the *Incomparable* engine-room mechanics was badly burned in the attack almost three weeks earlier. Ted had been to visit him in the hospital a few times.

Rumour had it that two female nurses had come aboard and were now taking turns in the hospital, helping the doctor. Ted contrived to get their help and went to visit.

"Wha'cher, Jock." Ted tried to sound cheerful and encouraging. The general consensus among the prisoners was that the doctor was a good bloke, but Jock's burns were not healing well. "How're you doing?"

"Hello, Ted. Not so bad." The Scotsman certainly didn't sound as if he felt well. "Did you know we've got a couple of pretty nursing sisters to take care of us now?"

"Yeah. Lucky old sod, you are. Where are they anyway?"

"Sister Pat's around here somewhere. I think she went to try and get us some extra water from the galley. Those bloody Germans are keeping it all for themselves."

"I don't know about that, Jock. I think they're rationed, too."

Suddenly, alarm bells rang. Running footfalls and the sound of the guns being uncovered signalled another impending attack.   A German officer running past stopped when he saw Ted and began yelling partly in English but mostly in German. Ted didn't have to understand what he was saying.

"All right, all right. Don't get your knickers in a twist. I'm going," he grumbled at the German. "See you later, Jock," he said to his friend.

Locked in beneath the hospital and the women's room, Ted knew he didn't stand a chance, but having Cilla aboard added a new dimension to his concern, should the hunter become the quarry.

Cilla covered her ears with her hands to block out the roar of the guns on the deck above. The muffled explosion of the torpedo hitting the *Punjohpur* and the thunderous shells smashing into the *Rangoon Princess* were still fresh in her mind. She consoled herself with the thought that Ted was probably back in England by now.

The attack stopped, but it was several hours before the doors were suddenly flung open.

"Ladies will please go to the dining room for their evening meal," Herr Swartz addressed them in perfect English.

Four strange women and two children sat at the table where Cilla and Pip usually ate. The little girl was about two and the boy about eight or nine.

"Hello." Cilla pulled up a chair and looked into the terrified eyes of the little boy. He was soaking wet and shivering. "Where did you come from?"

"Oh, thank God! You speak English." The one who spoke snuggled the little girl as if to comfort herself more than the child. "Our boat was attacked this afternoon. We were going home for Christmas." She began to whimper into the child's hair. "My husband is on the island and won't know what has happened to us."

Cilla patted her arm. "I'm sorry."

"What's going on? Is this really a Japanese ship?" Another of the newcomers was as confused as the rest when they came aboard.

"No," Pip said. "They're sodding Germans hiding behind the Japanese flag."

"Has Japan entered the war, then?"

"It was still neutral when we were taken down," said Pip.

"This poor little bugger's been separated from his mother." The woman indicated the frightened boy.

"Oh!...I thought you were his mother." Cilla reached for the boy but he stood stiff and unyielding.

"No. Callous bastards. Before he could get into the launch with her, they took off. She's not on this ship."

"How did he get so wet?"

"He got soaked by the back wash." She suddenly started and her eyes widened. "God almighty, what have we got here?"

A steward came to the table carrying two small enamel mugs and placed one in front of each of child.

The woman who had been speaking immediately clamped her lips shut and glared up at the man.

Cilla chuckled. "It's all right. This is Charlie. He's English. One of us, from the ship we were on." She smiled at him. "Hello, Charlie."

"Hello all. Some milk for the kiddies." He indicated the mugs, and bending over the table, he whispered, "I'll try for a bit of tinned fruit for the little 'uns later." He glanced around at the German guards, then winked.

"Oh, thank you. I won't tell you what I was thinking about you." She smiled for the first time.

"We know. All the newcomers think our stewards are bloody Germans." Pip held her sandwich to her nose and sniffed at it.

Cilla peeled off the boy's wet jumper and encouraged him to drink his milk.

While they ate their black-bread washed down with unsweetened black tea, the women exchanged stories of their capture. The new Australian prisoners had been aboard a small steamer returning to their island homes after a visit to the mainland. Two of the women were especially anxious and fearful for their husbands, who'd been taken below to join the rest of the men.

"We're planters, not combatants," said one on the verge of tears.

Cilla shrugged. "We're teachers and nurses," she said.

Ted sat beside his friend's bed. The Scotsman appeared to be in much less pain than when Ted had last seen him. "You look good today, Jock. Feeling better, are you?"

"Yeah. The doctor's a good bloke, but he has too many patients and not enough medicines. Since those nurses came on board, my burns are healing nicely."

"What's this then, a visitor?"

Ted spun around. It had been some weeks since he'd heard a female voice, and he immediately thought of Cilla.

Pat Sentry stood at the foot of Jock's bed holding a hypodermic.

"This is Ted Evans. Off the same ship, we are. This is Sister Pat, Ted."

Ted stood and held out his hand to Pat. "Sister, do you know Priscilla Thornton? I think she may have come aboard with you."

A sudden bellow startled the three of them. "What are you doing here again?" the German officer yelled at Ted. "You cannot roam the ship as you please. Get below!"

Ted looked pleadingly at Pat Sentry before he scooted out of the door.

A second later his head reappeared. "Sister! Tell Cilla I love her." He vanished again before the German reached him.

Ted returned to the steaming room that reeked of fear and unwashed bodies and wondered if he would ever be able to tell Cilla that himself.

Later, Jean Morrison took over the hospital duty, and Pat Sentry returned to the main room.

"Cilla. I have a message for you."

"A message? For me? Who from?"

"A British matelot by the name of Ted Evans."

Cilla's legs failed her just then, and she plonked down hard on a rickety metal chair.

"What? Where did you get the message?"

"From him. He's here, on this ship. Cilla, he wanted me to tell you he loves you."

Words failed Cilla. Her emotions were in turmoil and she broke into tears.

The days that followed seemed endless. Every day she waited for the prisoners to be brought on deck. And every day since she'd got his message, she'd returned below, disappointed.

Pat and Jean carried messages back and forth between them, and Cilla even had messages from Ted yelled to her from other male prisoners. Cilla and Ted were the source of many conversations. Even the Germans seemed amused by it.

Knowing he was in the hold just below the lounge where she slept, and not having actually seen him, was sheer torture. Every day she waited on deck, but his turn for a gulp of fresh air never seemed to come.

As she stood on deck at her daily vigil, anxiously watching the closed doors of the hold, she began to wonder if it had all been a mistake or a cruel joke.

The doors to the hold flew open and as each prisoner stepped onto the deck, blinking in the brilliant sunlight, she searched his face. Their dirty hair hung over the collars of their filthy shirts, and full beards hid their features.

Then she saw him. As soon as his head appeared from the hold, he shaded his eyes and began scanning the deck above him. He was very thin and his clothes were in tatters, but she would have known those brown eyes anywhere.

"Ted! Ted! Over here, darling." Cilla teetered on her tip-toes, leaning far over the railing. She could hardly see him through her tears of joy.

"Cilla! Cilla! Oh, blimey! It's really you." Below Cilla's outstretched hand a mushroom-shaped bitt protruded about three feet from the deck. Ted leaped onto the it and, straining, could barely touch her fingertips.

"*Nein*!" a German guard yelled. He raised the rifle with the butt poised to strike.

"Ted!" Cilla screamed.

Jumping from the bitt, Ted deflected the blow with one arm.

"Ted! Look out!"

The guard raised the rifle again and would have struck Ted on the head, but an officer stepped in and grabbed the gun stock.

He yelled at Ted and, gesturing, ordered him to the other side of the deck. Then all the prisoners were forced back down into the hold.

Cocky and defiant, he hung back to the last. "I love you, Cilla," he yelled. "They can't take that away from us." He grinned and blew her a kiss.

She smiled and waved to him. "I'll love you forever," she yelled as he disappeared from her view back into the hold.

A monsoon struck and buffeted the *Tokyo Maru*. Above the scream of the wind, her timbers creaked and her engines groaned in protest at the lashing waves. Locked in her hold, the seasick prisoners retched and prayed.

"Well, there is one advantage to all this," Cilla said to Pip, "these German ships aren't able to attack in this weather."

Several times in the days before the storm, a flustered Herr Swartz had pleaded, "Will the ladies please go to their cabins at once?"

The women, locked in with the portholes shut tight, listened to the guns roaring on the deck above. Each new attack on the unarmed steamers brought more men, women and children captives. The holds were becoming jammed. Cilla thought the ship would break apart from the sheer numbers in her hold before the monsoon blew itself out. Pip had another concern.

"Cilla. We know there aren't enough lifeboats for all of us. What do you think our chances are?" She seemed uncharacteristically despondent.

A mighty wave lashed the ship, and the deck suddenly rose, then dropped, heaving Cilla's stomach with it.

"Truthfully? Not good if we start to break up."

The storm finally blew itself out three days later, and Pip cheered up.

"Listen, Cilla. I've been thinking. These sodding Germans have it too easy. Let's have a bit of fun." Pip's eyes sparkled.

She laid out her simple plan, and Cilla roared with laughter. "However did you come to be a seavacuee escort?"

"Well, I was thinking of joining the Navy and reckoned I ought to find out if I really liked the sea before I joined the WRNS, but I've changed my mind after this lot. I think I may try the Air Force. How do you think I'd look in a WAAF uniform?" She tossed her dark hair and grinned at Cilla.

That evening when the German guard came to count the prisoners prior to shutting them in, Pip slipped behind the door. "*Eins, zwei, drei...*" The guard counted the heads, consulted his list and began again. "*Eins, zwei, drei, veer...*" His jaw dropped while his brow knitted together in a deep frown. He turned and flew out the door as Pip stepped from behind it, grinning.

"What are you doing? You're going to get us all in trouble, Phillipa." Sylvia wrung her hands.

The guard reappeared with Herr Swartz, who quickly counted his prisoners and, satisfied, spoke gruffly to the young sailor. The guard scowled and shook his head once before flicking out the light. The room exploded into laughter.

"I don't think that was a very good idea, Phillipa." Sylvia worried constantly about what terrible plans the Germans had in store for them. In any case, she trod very carefully around them. "If you torment them, they'll throw us all into the sea."

"Oh, shut yer gob, you old bat. Don't be such a spoil-sport. Everyone but you got a bit of a laugh," Pip said.

The next night, Pip brought Cilla into another scheme. "It's easy. You stand on one side of the room and I'll stand on the other. While Jerry's counting, you take a step, in any direction, but make a move. That will catch his eye, and he'll look in your direction and lose count. Then I'll distract him. It will drive him insane!"

"That's brilliant!" Cilla howled with laughter, envisioning the prank.

Sylvia crept close, trying to hear their plans. "What are you two up to now? Another harebrained scheme to get us all in trouble? I tell you, they'll ship us all to Germany and put us in a brothel. You won't think that's so funny."

"Is that a bit of wishful thinking, Sylvia?" Pip grinned. "You mention it so often I think you wish you would end up in a German brothel."

"Oh, you young girls. You have no idea what danger you put us all into with your stupid games."

"Put a sock in it, Sylvia. Nobody's been in any trouble for having a bit of a lark yet."

Cilla pulled Pip away from the distraught Sylvia. "I must say, there's never a dull moment with you around, Pip." Cilla hesitated. "I have a plan of my own. It doesn't involve you, but I'd like to hear what you think of it."

"Fire away. I'm all ears. Anything to keep the *Schweinhunde* on their toes."

"Pat, what's the schedule like in the hospital ward?"

"Why? What do you want to know for?" Pat squinted at Cilla.

"She was just wondering if there might be a chance to go with you one of these nights." Pip spoke in a very low voice.

"What!?"

"Ssh! Don't let on to anybody else, especially that paranoid Sylvia."

"What's this all about?"

"I've come up with a plan to see Ted, but it needs your co-operation."

"Out with it, then. How can I help?"

"I need you to get a message to Ted to be in the hospital ward, perhaps tomorrow night. He could go and visit his friend, and I'll find a way to be there too. I don't want to get you in any trouble. But, oh, Pat, I've just got to see him if only for a few minutes."

"What do you want me to do?"

"Just get the message to Ted to be there."

"What time?"

"That depends on when the doctor leaves."

"He goes for dinner about six and usually comes back to check on the patients, but he's almost always gone for the night by seven-thirty."

"That doesn't give you much time." Pip ran her fingers through her hair, a habit she had when she was thinking. "How about this. Pat tells Ted to visit his friend as near seven-thirty as he can. Then the doctor will be out of the way. You'll go with Pat when she goes on duty. She can make up some excuse about giving you some training or something."

"Hey, wait a minute! The doctor trusts me. I don't want to jeopardise that."

"Pat's right, Pip. The less I have to involve her, the better. I just have to figure out a way to get past the guard here. Coming back doesn't matter. I will have seen Ted by then."

"All right! All right!" Pip's dark curls bounced up and down with the exited nods of her head. "How about this. I distract Dieter; he's always making eyes at me. You slip past him, and Bob's yer uncle! What do you say?" She had the most devilish eyes, and they sparkled as she laid out her plan to Cilla. She was quite right about Dieter being attracted to her, but she had made it a point not to have anything to do with the Germans.

"Won't he think it funny that you suddenly start paying attention to him?" If anyone was to get into trouble over this, Cilla wanted it to be her and not her friends.

"Naw. I'll make it worth his while, and you can slip back in here before he locks up at eight."

"That's a terrible risk for you, Pip."

"That's what friends are for, isn't it?" She put her arm around Cilla shoulders and gave it a squeeze. "I'll give him the glad-eye tonight, just to try it out." She winked and sashayed away, exaggerating the sway of her hips.

"Don't look so worried, Cilla. She's enjoying this," Pat said with a reassuring smile.

CHAPTER TWENTY-NINE

"Something is definitely different." Cilla cocked her head and listened for any sound that might give her a clue as to why the ship had stopped.

The guards, scrubbed and dressed in clean white uniforms and scurrying around with anxious expressions, only added to the mystery.

"Hey, Dieter, *was ist los?*" Pip tried out her few words of German. "What's all the excitement about?" She'd made it a point to win his trust and get very chummy with him the previous evening. Now, the young guard rewarded her friendship with a warm smile.

"Ladies, please to tidy up sleeping quarters. *Schnel*...er, fast." He flapped his arms to emphasise the need for speed. "Important visitor comes."

The Commodore came aboard with his staff about an hour after breakfast. He was big, both tall and heavy-set. His white uniform was immaculate, and around his fat clean-shaven neck, he wore not one, but two Iron Crosses.

"Now there's what I'd call a real *Schweinhunde*." Pip wrinkled her turned-up nose and examined him as though he smelled bad.

Following at a respectful distance, the captain and Herr Swartz showed off the prisoners to their fat, bombastic commanding officer.

"*Guten morgen*, Englisher ladies." The corners of the Commodore's mouth turned up, but the smile didn't register in his pale blue eyes.

"Good morning, sir," Sylvia piped up.

"Shut-up, Sylvia." Pip raised her elbow and jabbed Sylvia in the ribs.

The commodore showed no indication that he had heard the rebuff but turned to the children, patting them on the head and murmuring in German.

Some of the children warily tolerated his attention, but others flew to their mothers and hid behind their skirts, peering out with registered distrust.

Dieter stood stiffly at attention by the door, and when the Commodore turned and mumbled something to him, he drew himself up even more.

"*Ja wohl,*" he said and took off running. He returned with several chocolate bars and, bowing, handed them to the Commodore, who carefully broke each into equal pieces and solemnly presented one piece to each child.

He turned sharply, almost knocking the little captain over, and spoke sharply to him.

"Ladies, the Commodore says you may go on deck, immediately. Will the nursing sisters please accompany the Commodore while he visits the wounded?"

"Let's get out of here and find some *fresh* air." Pip wrinkled her nose toward the Commodore and tugged at Cilla's arm.

The air on deck was hot and humid, but still preferable to the stifling lounge below.

Cilla blinked at the brittle sunlight. "Pip," she hissed. "Look!" She gestured with her head at the other two ships alongside.

A young sailor with a rifle stepped forward. "Ladies must stay on this side." He indicated the deck farthest from the Raider.

"What are the *Schweinhunde* up to now?" Pip craned to see the black ship.

German sailors, glancing furtively at the women prisoners, yelled to one another. Their guttural shouts carried across the decks as they scurried back and forth between the three ships, carrying supplies and hooking up oil and water hoses.

"Hey, Pip. Look, there's an island." The sight of green trees and shrubs after nothing but endless sea for almost four weeks brought melancholy tears to Cilla's eyes. Life aboard the prison ship had become hard work. Dirt and heat were constant companions, and the need for water was almost as acute as it had been in the lifeboat. At times she doubted she could go on, except for Ted being aboard. She was certain, though, that his living conditions were even worse than her own.

"Do you see any signs of life?" Pip shaded her eyes from the sun's brilliance and scanned the shoreline.

Cilla stood on her tip-toes and craned her neck for a better view of the little island. "If there are natives living there, I expect they've gone into hiding." She lowered her heels and regarded the dark-haired girl beside her. "Pip, do you ever think you'd like to end all this?"

"Don't talk so daft. I wouldn't give these bastards the satisfaction of having one less prisoner to feed. You'd better forget talking like that too, or I'll get a message to Ted."

Cilla felt her mouth turn up in a smile. If she had to endure captivity, she was glad she had Pip as a companion. In the weeks they'd been captives together, Cilla had thought often thought how much Millie would have enjoyed the fun-loving Pip. "I wonder if there's any fresh fruit growing there." Cilla licked her lips.

"Hmm...what I wouldn't give for something besides maggoty rice and sour bread." Pip's eyes had almost glazed over.

Cilla chuckled. "You had something different for dinner last night, don't you remember?"

"Remember? How can I ever forget that disgusting sour macaroni? Ugh!"

They stayed on deck, but after an hour it became clear the male prisoners would not be out that day.

Instead, the Commodore and his entourage appeared and stood on the deck just below Cilla and Pip. The fat Commodore's jowls wobbled as he talked earnestly into the captain's face. Cilla actually pitied the captain, who wore a worried frown and fidgeted from one foot to the other.

"If I were to spit from here, I could hit the top of that fat bastard's hat." A wide grin lit Pip's face, and her black eyes danced mischievously.

"Don't you dare," Cilla hissed, but the vision made her chuckle.

The captain and Herr Swartz hoisted stiff-arm Nazi salutes, which the commodore returned with an affected flip of his hand, reminiscent of Hitler.

Soon after the Commodore and his retinue returned to the *Manyo Maru,* the wounded were brought up on deck. German sailors rigged the stretchers and slung them over to the Commodore's ship.

"There's Jean Morrison. Hey, Jean. What's up?" Cilla leaned over the railing and yelled.

Jean shaded her eyes and squinted. "There's a proper hospital on that ship. I've been looking for you, Pip. You're going over for the doctor to have a look at that arm."

"Like hell, I am." Pip still kept her arm in a sling, and although she didn't complain, it was obviously painful.

"They'll reset it and you'll be much more comfortable," said Jean.

"Go on, Pip. You're not hurting them, only yourself by refusing," Cilla put her arm around Pip's shoulder.

She hesitated a moment longer. "Oh, all right. I'll go. I might be able to find out something useful over there."

After about an hour Pip returned wearing a new cast and a clean sling. "Here, you won't believe the way those prisoners are treated on that ship. They loll about in deck chairs sipping out of real glasses," she said. "And they're clean and don't look as if they've missed many meals, either."

"Aren't they all our officers?"

"Yes. Mostly navy and merchant marine, but I got a glimpse of at least one RAF uniform and an army officer."

"Well, there you are then," Gwen said. "They're insurance against the day when the German officer's turn comes to be prisoners. The British officers will remember how well they were cared for and return the favour."

"Well, I don't think the sailors on this ship eat any better than we do." Cilla pursed her lips and thought of the meagre portions of bad food they had to eat. "So, that must mean all the good food and water goes to the Commodore's ship, and I don't begrudge our own officers."

"Excuse me, ladies." Herr Swartz tapped on the door and came into the room with an armload of old sheets and deposited them on the table.

"What's this then." Gwen poked the bundle and carefully lifted one corner.

"For ladies to make new clothes." Herr Swartz made the announcement with a rare smile.

"Clothes? What are we to cut and sew them with?"

The smile slipped off the German's face. He'd obviously not thought how they were to make them. "I will get needles and thread for you."

Most of them desperately needed clothes. Cilla's shorts were filthy and torn. She'd ripped a strip off the bottom of her shirt to tie back her hair. Her only underwear, stiff from many washes in sea water, was in tatters. But she was no worse off than most of the other escorts and nurses. Only Sylvia, whose cabin aboard the *Rangoon Princess* had not caught fire, had managed to salvage most of her belongings. She even had a hair brush and comb, but she wouldn't share anything.

"What day is it, Pip?" Cilla asked.

"Day? I haven't the foggiest. Can't tell the difference between them any more."

"I don't really mean day. I mean date. It must be almost Christmas."

"Ask that soppy Sylvia. She's got a calendar, I've seen it."

Cilla tried to put the days in their right order in her mind, but eventually she had to ask Sylvia.

"My dear, it's December 20th." Sylvia's tone suggested it was common knowledge.

"I was pretty close. Hey, Pip. Christmas is in five days. Do you think we'll have ham or goose for Christmas dinner?"

"Put a sock in it! You're making my mouth water." Pip smacked her lips. Food had become a constant source of conversation.

While she bantered with Pip, Cilla splashed some of her drinking water onto her face. She pulled the community comb, almost toothless after so much use, through her hair.

"How do I look, Pip? She pirouetted in her new shorts and halter top made from the sheets. "I'm ready to see Ted."

Before Pip could answer, Jean Morrison returning from her duty in the hospital, interrupted. "Ah, Cilla. There you are. Pat said to tell you it's off for tonight."

"Oh, no." She felt sick with frustration. "Why?"

"Because the ships are staying at anchor, so the schedule is out of whack. The commodore's visit has put the doctor under a great deal of strain, and Pat thinks he'll hang about the wards keeping an eye on the patients tonight."

"Bugger!" Cilla swallowed her disappointment. "Thanks for letting me know, Jean."

"Cheer up. You can try again as soon as we set sail."

"Pat told you my plan then?"

"Yes. Don't worry, it's safe with me." Jean spoke secretively. She gathered Cilla in her arms and hugged her.

The *Toyko Maru* started her engine. It coughed and spluttered, turned over briefly, thumped a few times, and died.

"Did you hear that? I wonder what's wrong with the engine?"

"Sounds a bit dickey to me," Pip said.

The engine restarted, and clattering like a child beating a spoon on a tin washtub, the ship limped out of the lagoon.

The Raider and the commodore's ship disappeared over the horizon, but toward evening they reappeared.

"Hey, look. Something's up." Cilla pointed to the signals flashing from one ship to the other. "I wish Ted could see this. He'd be able to read it."

"I think this old bucket must be done for. I wonder what they'll do with us."

"They could transfer us to those other ships, but I'll bet they're as overcrowded as we are."

"Hey, maybe Sylvia will get her wish." Pip laughed at her own joke.

The *Tokyo Maru* continued ploughing her noisy way back and forth within sight of several islands. Speculation and rumour, each more depressing than the last, swept through the ship. The latest and most common was that the Germans were waiting for another ship to come and take all the prisoners to

Japan.

The official announcement, when it came, put an end to the rumours, and the prisoner's fate was something none of them had anticipated.

CHAPTER THIRTY

The three ships, anchored side-by-side off a small island, flaunted Swastikas on their bow and on flags fluttering from their masts. They made no pretence of being Japanese.

Cilla turned her back to them and leaned on the deck railing, biting her lip to hold back the tears. She hardly noticed the beauty of the sun disappearing in a fiery ball over a placid lagoon. She should be ecstatic. Instead, her emotions were in real turmoil.

All the women, children and wounded men were to be released on the island the next day.

The captain had refused to say what would happen to the remaining captives. Charlie, the English steward, said the Nazis had cut their own rations of rotten food, and water was a distinct luxury, so they could hardly keep the prisoners much longer on the vermin-infested ships. It seemed likely they would be taken to Germany and imprisoned for the duration of the war—and who knew how long that would be.

In all the weeks on the ship, Cilla had seen Ted just for those few minutes on the deck, and after tomorrow there wouldn't even be that possibility. God alone knew when they'd ever see each other again.

She opened her eyes and sucked in a deep breath of frustration. She was very close to tears again.

"There you are, Cilla. Come on below. The supreme *Schweinhunde* wants to give us his final words of good riddance." Cilla blinked the tears from her eyes and, without commenting, followed Pip.

The air on the deck was heavy, but down below it was almost thick enough to cut with a knife. In the stifling lounge, lethargic women with sweat-damp hair bickered at one another, and mothers with frayed nerves fretted at their children, whimpering from dehydration.

The Commodore followed by his retinue, breezed in and stood at the head of the room with a Cheshire-cat grin plastered across his fat jowls.

"Ah, ladies. Good evening. As Herr Swartz has already informed you,

you will be taken ashore tomorrow. I just wanted to tell you that a British planter and his wife live on the island. Indeed, it is British territory, but it was not always so. Before the Great War it was held by Germany, and I had the pleasure of spending some time there, so I can assure you that you will be quite all right." He glanced around before continuing. "Now. You will be given sufficient food for two or three days, and there is plenty of fresh water on the island, and fruit grows in abundance."

An excited whisper like a breeze through the palm trees Cilla had seen growing on the island grew to loud exclamations. "Fresh water!"

"Fresh fruit!"

The commodore raised his hand for silence before he continued. "Unfortunately, we cannot spare any utensils for your use."

"What?" Pip jumped to her feet and struck a defiant pose. "How the hell are we supposed to eat?"

The commodore gestured, and several of his staff started toward her.

Cilla quickly yanked Pip back down.

The commander shook out a large white handkerchief and wiped the sweat from his forehead before he spoke again. "You will have to manage for plates, but your British men have been told of your plight and have made wooden spoons for you."

Gwen stood up. "Three cheers for the men!" She led the cheer. "Hip-hip hooray!"

"Hip-hip hooray," the women yelled. "Hip-hip hooray!"

The commodore gathered his fat lips into a tight little wad, his face slowly turning from beet-red to purple. Sweat dripped off the end of his bulbous nose.

"Sit down. If you wish me to continue, you will be silent. I will not tolerate any further outbursts." He drew himself up and planted his large square hands on his hips, reminiscent of Mussolini, and glared at the crowd of bedraggled women and children. "A party of men prisoners will be sent ashore to help you get settled."

Cilla perked up, but one woman couldn't contain her excitement. "Will our husbands be among them?"

"That is not for me to say. In any case, they will return to the ship before we sail."

The woman who had asked the question began to cry.

Gwen drew herself up to her full height and struck a mutinous pose. "These women's husbands are non-combatants. By what right do you keep them captive?" Her rich Aussie accent punctuated every word. "Or for that matter, why did you take us prisoner? We've never been given a satisfactory explanation."

The Commodore gave Gwen a withering glare and continued with his directions for their release as if the interruption were nothing more than a minor annoyance.

"The Nursing Sisters will be responsible for the care of the wounded," the commander said, "and I must extract a promise from you that you will not try to make contact with anyone on the mainland for forty-eight hours. Now, I wish you good luck and hope that your troubles will soon be over. Cheerio." He stomped out.

The women began an excited buzz of questions, comments and speculation to one another.

"Ladies, please to remain." Herr Swartz, showing signs of acute stress, spoke in a tired voice. "Before you leave the ship tomorrow, your luggage will be searched. You must not take any item with you that belongs to the Government of the Third Reich." He then beckoned to a sailor, who brought him a bag. From it he pulled out the passports, money and jewellery taken from the prisoners on the first day. He spread them across the table at the head of the room. "You may come up and claim your valuables."

Sylvia reacted with a little shriek and darted up to the table.

Cilla turned to Pip and laughed at the irony. "What luggage?" They stood in all that they possessed. In the struggle with Clint Jennison the night the *Punjohpur* was torpedoed, Cilla had lost her only piece of jewellery: a gold locket given to her by her parents. The seawater had ruined her watch.

The night was interminable. Only the children, exhausted by the stifling heat, slept. Too agitated to sleep, Cilla dozed, listening to the other women excitedly recalling every word spoken by the fat Commodore. Some tried to read more into his words than he'd actually said. Others argued and added their own theories.

Dawn came at last. The prisoners gathered their meagre belongings for inspection, then trooped to the dining room for the last breakfast of maggoty rice boiled in sea water.

Cilla stirred her ration of one teaspoon of jam into hers, held her nose and swallowed it as quickly as she could.

As soon as the doors were unlocked, everyone made a dash on deck. The *Tokyo Maru* was anchored just off the end of the island near a boat house and jetty.

A boarding party of about thirty German sailors armed with knives, and two officers armed with revolvers, clambered into a launch and sped away toward the island.

"Hey, look! People! There in the trees!" Pip pointed to native men, bare above the waist, and women in brightly-coloured dresses. Curious children ventured out into the open. As the launch neared the jetty, the native people turned and ran away through the trees.

All morning the launch roared back and forth between the ships and the island, carrying Germans and stores. There seemed to be a festive air about the whole operation. Several sailors fished off the jetty, and their loud laughter carried on the breeze back to the ship.

"Ladies, please go now to lunch." Herr Swartz seemed very pleased with himself. "Afterwards you will return to your quarters for inspection and instructions for disembarking."

"I don't think I can face another black-bread sandwich." Pip wrinkled her nose in a look of disgust.

"Perhaps as a farewell gesture, they'll give us something different. Come on, at least let's get our ration of water. I'm parched," Cilla said.

The heat and humidity had long since turned the bread bright green, but the starving captives no longer refused to eat it. They had the same mouldy bread sandwiches for their last meal aboard, and to wash it down, unsweetened tea.

Cilla could hardly wait to sink her teeth into whatever grew on the island.

On deck, the heat and humidity were almost unbearable, and the anxious women, strung along the railing of the upper deck, stared at the closed doors of the hold below.

"It must be nothing short of hell down there," one of the women observed. She tugged at the child clinging to her legs. "Stop fidgeting, watch for Daddy." The boy climbed the rungs and hung precariously over the railing. His mother hauled him back down "You'll be the death of me yet," she scolded.

The women had debated how the Germans would choose the men to accompany them ashore. Each expressed hope that her man would be among the lucky ones. Cilla had her own ideas. She didn't think luck would have anything to do with the Germans' selections. The men would probably be conscripted from among the latest captives since they'd be the healthiest and strongest. Ted had been a prisoner for many weeks so she doubted he'd be among the chosen, but she still hoped

Suddenly, in a flurry of activity, the hold doors opened. A German sailor armed with a rifle led six prisoners on to the deck. Behind them, four more prisoners carrying a stretcher between them climbed out. They were all young like Ted, but, as Cilla had anticipated, they were in comparative good health. The women shouted and blew kisses. The men grinned and waved, giving the women the thumbs-up.

Cilla hugged her midriff in an effort to calm her excitement and anticipation as she craned her neck to see the next stretcher brought on deck. Ted was not one of the bearers.

Another stretcher followed. One woman let out a squeal, "There's my husband." She climbed the rungs of the railing waving and yelling, "Bob, Bob. Up here."

"'Ello, love," he called out, and as the stretcher was placed on the deck, a German guard grabbed him and forced him back into hold below. The woman burst into tears.

Another small group of men clambered onto the deck from the hold. A child called, "Daddy. Hello, Daddy."

A male prisoner, tan, strong and healthy with touches of grey at his temples, responded with a wave and a kiss blown off the end of his fingers. A German guard immediately grabbed him, but the man broke loose. In two strides he was propelling himself over the side of the ship. The water splashed and a gunshot rang out.

It was as if the entire ship had drawn its collective breath, except for the screech of a child and a woman keening.

More men climbed from the hold. The woman standing next to Cilla let out a gasp and clamped her hand over her mouth as if to stifle the greeting on the edge of her lips. "There's Tom, my husband," she said in a loud whisper.

"Ssh," someone said. "Looks like the rotten bastards aren't letting the men with families leave the ship."

A third stretcher was hoisted up, and there was Ted! He wasn't helping to carry the stretcher but hovered at the side of it, wiping the man's forehead and straightening the sheet that covered him. He squeezed the man's arm almost as if it were some sort of signal.

Cilla sucked in a loud breath and gripped Pip's arm. "What on earth is he doing?" she whispered. Her stomach churned. He obviously didn't belong there, and armed German sailors seemed very interested in each stretcher being carried to the small boat.

Fingers of fear climbed Cilla's spine. "Pip, he's trying to escape! Oh,

God. Please don't let them catch him. They'll shoot him, too."

"Careful, Cil. Don't let on. Don't draw attention to him." Pip squeezed Cilla's hand.

She held her breath as the stretcher lowered into the launch. Ted never lifted his face, but she could see that although he still had a beard, it was neatly trimmed. His long hair curled softly around his ears. He sat very still, leaning slightly forward, casting a shadow across the man on the stretcher as the launch sped away to the island.

Intense heat saturated the air. Ted leaned across Jock, shielding him from the blinding sun. He knew the man must be suffering and wished he could give him a sip of water, but he dared not move for fear of bringing attention to himself. He looked down at Jock's sweating face, and his friend slowly dropped one eyelid in a conspirital wink.

When the launch reached the jetty, Ted helped to carry Jock into the trees, where the temperature seemed a little cooler. Overhead wild parakeets fluttered and squawked with alarm at the sudden human invasion.

"Go when you the chance, lad," Jock whispered.

"Not 'til I get you some water." Ted turned to the German guard leaning against a tree in the shade.

"Water?" He gestured to the stretchers, but the German only shrugged his shoulders.

"Bastard." Ted looked around helplessly. They were on the edge of a clearing, and the only water he could see was the ocean in front of him.

A clattering, growing louder, came from the rough path that led out of the thick grove of trees down to the shore. An old lorry, grinding its gears, bounced into the clearing and shuddered to a halt. A white man and woman climbed out.

"Hello! Welcome to Remaru Island. I'm Cal Mercer and this is my wife, Caroline." He was tall, well-bronzed and about forty or a few years older—it was hard to tell under his big, floppy hat. He wore sturdy boots and khaki shorts.

His attractive wife, a few years younger than Cal, had a huge, friendly smile. Her sun-bleached hair wisped from under a straw hat, and she too wore shorts. Her slim brown legs drew admiration from foe as well as friend.

She ignored the Germans and extended her hand to the Britons and Australians. "Lovely to meet you all," she said. She turned to the men on the stretchers. "I expect you'd like some water, wouldn't you.

"There's a little stream just through the trees behind you," she said to Ted. "I'm sorry, I didn't think to bring anything to carry water in."

"Not to worry," said Ted. "Come on, you lot, let's have your tins." He collected the cigarette tins and cups and started though the trees, then stopped as the first lifeboat full of women and children arrived at the jetty. Cilla wasn't among the passengers, but he recognised Jean Morrison and Pat Sentry and offered a silent prayer of thanksgiving that the nurses had arrived to take over the wounded.

The air was much cooler near the stream. Ted drank his fill of the cool water, then stuck his head in it. It ran through his beard and cooled his chest. He quickly filled the cups and tins while he looked about him, taking note of the tall trees and thick underbrush. Knowing the direction of the stream would be useful when he made his escape.

As he passed the guard, the German grabbed one of the cups and downed the contents in one gulp. "'Ere, you get your own bloody water." Angry and frustrated, Ted wrenched the empty cup from the enemy seaman. His immediate reaction was to smash his fist into the German's face, but that would only draw attention to himself. He returned to the stream and refilled the cup.

Ted lifted Jock's head and brought the cup to the Scotsman's lips. "All right, mate?"

Jock gulped the water before answering. "Oh, aye." He licked his lips. "I di'na remember when water tasted so good." He cast his eyes about and whispered, "Ted, di'na fret yersel' about me anymore. Do ye ken the nurses have arrived?"

"Yes, they're down at the jetty," Ted said.

"I'll turn the lorry around and back it up. You can put the stretchers in the back," Cal Mercer said to the work crew.

"I don't think so." Ted pointed to the old green lorry, now full of laughing Germans.

"Bugger 'em! Well, all right. I'll drive them to my place and come back for the wounded. It might be better to let them rest here anyway. Come on, Caroline."

The German guard pulled himself away from the tree and, using his rifle, indicated that the work party should get into the lorry.

"We can't leave these blokes all by themselves," said a big Aussie.

"They'll be all right," Ted said. "The nurses are here." He grinned at Pat and Jean, just making their way to the clearing. "Hello, girls! Is Cilla with

200

you?"

"No, Romeo. She'll be along, don't worry." Pat grinned at him.

"Pat, thanks again for the trim." He fingered his beard.

"Sorry it couldn't be a real shave, but Cilla won't mind."

Jean looked past him. "Watch your back, Ted. Jerry's behind you," she said.

The old lorry spluttered to life and began a slow roll out of the clearing.

"*Schnel! Schnel!*" the German yelled in alarm. He poked Ted in the ribs with the barrel of his gun.

"All right, I'm going. See you later, Jock. Cheerio, girls," Ted yelled as he clambered over the tailgate.

The road was no more than a cart-track full of ruts and rocks. Great clouds of red dust churned by the wheels of the lorry choked the men wedged against the tailgate.

Ted coughed and covered his eyes and nose, but as the truck made its slow, bone-jarring way, he became aware of a tantalising smell. It wafted down the dusty road until his taste buds ached. "Umm...smells like steak." He spoke to nobody in particular, but around him, men licked their lips and swallowed their Adam's apple.

The truck ground to a noisy halt in front of a large wooden structure perched on pilings, well above the ground. The roof of plaited palm-fronds extended to shade the wide veranda.

Cal Mercer climbed down from the cab and ambled to the back of the lorry. "This is my place," he said, gesturing with a nod of his head to indicate the building.

A hundred feet or more beyond the house, beneath a covered shed, several dark-skinned men were cooking over an open grill. Nearby, an enormous pot steamed over an open fire.

"Gawd! Look at the size of that pot. Looks like the pictures you see cannibals cooking people in." Ted stared at the fierce-looking black men.

"You aren't far wrong there," said the planter, unfastening the tailgate. "These people used to be cannibals before the missionaries came. They occasionally resort to the practice, but haven't since I've lived here."

"Thank God! I thought you were going to tell us that smell was human." Ted laughed with feigned relief.

The Germans elbowed their way past the prisoners and hit the ground running to the sandy beach nearby. They tore off their uniforms and jumped into the turquoise water.

"I'll go back for the stretchers and nippers now," said Cal Mercer. He climbed back into the cab of the lorry, and enveloped in a cloud of dust, the truck bounced off down the cart-track.

Caroline Mercer planted her hands on her hips and addressed the work crew. "Right, where shall we begin? The Germans said we should expect about sixty women and children and seven wounded. Let's see now." She frowned and pursed her lips. "The women and children can sleep in the dining room and lounge in our house. It's quite large, but I'll need you to help take the furniture out. We can use the hut, too." She pointed to a small building about fifty yards from the main house. "I think the wounded men will be quite comfortable there, but it needs a bit of a clean." She smiled at Ted and handed him a broom and a stack of woven palm mats. "That can be your job. The rest of you can come with me."

Ted took the broom to the hut. Woven palm-frond walls stopped about eighteen inches from the roof, allowing the hot air to escape from beneath its thatched roof. A deep layer of sand covered the floor of the hut, and the walls and ceiling were havens for spiders, ants and some crawly things Ted had never seen before. He swept the room, literally from top to bottom, and covered the floor with the palm mats. He checked his work, then, pleased with his efforts, he stood the broom outside. The smell of grilling meat from the cookhouse wafted to him. Ignoring it would take some willpower. He listened. Yelling and laughing from the beach seemed to indicate that the Germans still frolicked in the water. Close by he could hear the occasional laughter of the work crew. The rest of the compound was quiet, and nobody was in sight. He'd never have a better chance.

One quick look toward the Germans on the beach, then, crouching low, he ran for the trees. The jungle swallowed him—but not quite fast enough.

CHAPTER THIRTY-ONE

"Halt! Halt!"

Ted didn't stop to see who was yelling or whether the alarm was directed at him. He may have been seen, but he wasn't going to make it easy for them to catch him. He crouched, bent almost double to make as small a target as possible, and with no longer any need for silence, he crashed through the tangle of vines and trees. Weeks of starvation and inactivity on the prison ship had taken their toll and slowed him, but he consoled himself with the knowledge that his pursuers were in no better physical shape than he.

The crack of gunfire sent his adrenaline pumping. With a loud snap, the bullet imbedded itself in a tree directly in front of his face. Bark showered him, prickling his skin and stinging his eyes. It flew into his open mouth and fell into his beard. The thought flashed through his mind that the shooter was an excellent marksman, but he had no intention of waiting around to congratulate him.

Overhead, thousands of parakeets took to the sky, screeching. Ducking and weaving, Ted ran through the underbrush, pausing only when a deep gorge stopped him. A stream reflected in a glimmer of sunlight far below. To his left, the sound of cascading water drew him onward. Dragging gulps of air into his starved lungs, he scrambled up a steep incline toward the source of the stream. He had no idea what he'd do when he reached the waterfall. He had no plan; only the human need for self-preservation drove him to keep moving. Budgerigars rose from the trees like great green clouds, marking his progress with their flapping wings and raucous squawks.

Pain wracked his chest. He had to find a place to hide and catch his breath. Just ahead, a green, leafy mound about five feet high and with branches dragging the ground seemed to offer a haven. Trembling with exertion, he carefully lifted the fronds and crawled inside, collapsing to his knees. His pulse pounded in his head. He sucked air in great shuddering gasps as he carefully rearranged the branches of his hideaway.

He thumped down on the hard-packed ground and drew his knees up to his chin, making his long body as compact as possible. The birds quieted as they resettled into the tops of the trees.

A sudden guttural shout in the distance sent the birds soaring again, screeching frantically.

Minutes passed. Inside the bower, the trapped, dank air hung wet and heavy. Outside grew very quiet. Ted strained his ears to catch any tell-tale sounds of his pursuers, but even the parakeets had quieted once more. He silently drew the muggy air deep into his lungs and, on the verge of exhaling, heard a stealthy footfall. A shadow blocked the sun through the fronds. And incredibly, poking under his hide, not six inches from his thigh, was the toe of a dirty boot.

Hardly daring to breathe, he waited for the man to discover him. He tensed, ready to spring. One thing was certain—he wasn't going back to that bloody ship without a fight.

By late afternoon, only the women from the *Rangoon Princess* still waited on the landing area for the returning lorry.

The air was heavy and still, too draining even for the birds and insects. Cilla stretched out in the shade of a tree. "I wonder if these people ever get used to the humidity," she mumbled through a yawn.

Pip propped against the tree trunk, ignored the statement. "You look bloody awful, Cilla. Do I look as thin and dirty as you?"

Cilla shrugged. "If that's your idea of a compliment, thanks. And by way of returning it, you look an absolute fright, but who's to notice? Besides, it's too hot to care."

"Still, I'm not complaining, mind." Pip closed her eyes. "I'm off that bleedin' ship, and I know I'm going to survive."

"Amen to that," said a sleepy voice nearby where several others rested in the shade.

Cilla spoke in laboured breaths. "I wonder where Ted is. Pat said he'd gone with the first load. Even before the stretchers. I hope he's being very careful. If the Germans find out he isn't supposed to be here at all..." She didn't want to imagine what the Nazis might do if they caught him.

"You'll find out soon enough," said Pip. "Listen."

The old lorry trundled down the cart-path and rounded the corner in a cloud of dust. It ground to a halt, and the planter jumped down.

"All aboard for the skylark," he said and let down the tailgate with a resounding crash.

"Where does he find the energy?" The women hauled themselves off the ground and clambered into the back of the lorry.

Cilla reach back for Pip's good hand. Her arm was still in plaster, and although she insisted she wasn't in pain, she didn't refuse Cilla's help.

Gears grinding, engine roaring, the lorry bumped its way down the narrow path, leaving billows of red dust in its wake.

The enticing smell of cooking meat wafted through the heavy air and tormented the taste-buds. The smell intensified as the truck lumbered into the clearing. Smoke billowed around a huge grill, where sweating natives cooked great slabs of meat.

"I hope to God some of that is for us," said Pip, noticeably salivating.

The lorry stopped, and before she jumped to the ground, Cilla shaded her eyes and scanned the area looking for Ted. The stretchers lay beneath the branches of the trees, and some of the men who had come ashore with the work-party were in the clearing, but Ted was nowhere in sight. Her initial excitement was fast being replaced with apprehension.

Brushing away the thought that he might have already been recaptured, she studied her surroundings for possible hiding places. A number of buildings, some obviously native houses, dotted the jungle, and at the edge of the trees stood a larger wooden house on stilts.

A white woman and several native women, each with towels slung over their arms and carrying a basin, came down the steps from the large, airy veranda.

"Merry Christmas. I'm Caroline Mercer." Her smile was almost as large as her straw hat. "You've met my husband."

The women from the prison ship gaped at one another. "Is it Christmas?" Each day in captivity had seemed so like the one before it, they had no idea what day it was.

"It's Christmas Eve," said Mrs. Mercer.

The word quickly spread from the women to the wounded and the work party. Soon everyone began hugging each other and wishing each other Happy Christmas.

"Please, help yourselves to water or coconut milk." Mrs. Mercer indicated a table covered with palm leaves and piled with chunks of fruit and coconut meat. "The cooked food will be ready shortly."

Only good manners restrained the dehydrated women from gulping down the liquid and falling on the fruit.

The children, having already eaten their fill of fruit, played in the sand at the water's edge or frolicked with the German sailors.

Caroline Mercer turned to the men of the work party. "Right. If you'll take the stretchers to that hut, you should find it ready." She pointed to a small hut with a broom propped against its doorway.

Suddenly, a shout then a gunshot sent thousands of budgerigars into the air. Cilla jumped and pressed her fist into her midriff. "Oh, my God! What's that?"

"Those blasted Germans!" Caroline Mercer started, slopping water out of the basin. "They've insisted my husband provide them with fresh meat. He's had to kill two of our beef already this morning. I wonder what they're shooting at now."

"One of our blokes made a run for it. Poor bastard. Hope he makes it." The big Aussie emphasised his wish with a thumbs-up.

"Good luck to him," said Caroline Mercer. Her big smile had been replaced by a sad frown. She turned her attention to the women. "We have a bit of a problem with too few plates. I've had the native workers open some coconuts, but the fibres need to be scoured out before the shells can be used for food. Sand and seawater does a wonderful job if some of you will do that. I'll just take this water to the nurses so that they can wash the injured men, then the rest of you can get cracking in the kitchen, all right?"

"God bless her, she's really organised." Pip quickly refilled her cigarette tin with water and drank it down in one gulp.

"I'll say. It mustn't have been easy to have this lot dumped on her." Cilla fidgeted. She was eager to search the buildings for Ted. "I think I'll see if Pat and Jean need any help." She hurried after the water bearers.

Caroline Mercer stopped at the door to the hut and frowned at the broom leaning against the door frame. "Where did that young bloke go who was cleaning this hut?" She stuck her head out the door and looked around. "That's funny. Where could he have got to?"

Cilla had a feeling the young bloke in question was Ted.

What little air stirred through the open walls of the hut seemed to make it cooler inside. Cilla rubbed her eyes, adjusting her vision from the bright sunshine.

The stretchers lay side-by-side on the cool palm mats. Pat, bent over one of the wounded, looked up as Cilla came through the door. "Oh, Cilla. I'm glad you're here. We could use some help."

Cilla picked up a sponge and basin of water and turned to the nearest stretcher. The man had severe burns, so she was not sure about getting water on him. She sponged cool water on his forehead. "Have you had a drink?" He seemed familiar.

"Yes, thank you, lass." The man smiled up at her.

"You're Ted Evans' friend, aren't you?" She bent close to him. "I saw Ted leaving the ship with you," she whispered.

He held her gaze a moment. "Aye, I'm Jock. Are ye Cilla, by any chance?"

"Yes, I am." Here, at last, was someone who might know where Ted was. "Where is he? I haven't seen him since I came ashore?" Her voice shook with anticipation.

"Scarpered. Hiding." He winked and tipped his head in the direction of jungle.

Cilla gasped and swallowed hard. The gunshot!

In the clearing just outside the hut, a sudden commotion erupted. Guttural yelling disturbed the birds, and they took to the sky screeching.

"What's going on out there?" Her throat constricted with a premonition.

"Go and see," said Jock. He gave her hand a reassuring squeeze before she slipped away.

Nazi officers waving guns barked orders. The terrified birds, screeching like banshees, flapped around the treetops. German sailors emerging from the jungle undergrowth dragged a man kicking and screaming every derogatory adjective in the English language. His full beard and long hair falling across his face hid his features.

An anguished scream cut through the bedlam. A woman rushed forward, shrieking, "Tom! Oh, Tom. No. Don't take my husband." She fell on her knees in front of the prisoner and took his face in her hands.

She raised his head, and Cilla wilted with relief.

As he curled up in his green hideaway, Ted's pulse pounded in his ears. Each stealthily-drawn breath sounded to his senses like a foghorn in a shrouded harbour. Inside the shrub, the air hung wet and suffocating. Sweat trickled down his back and dripped from his temples into his beard. Insects, drawn by the salty moisture, crawled across his ankles and bare arms. They filed across his neck and into his beard and his long hair.

The minutes dragged by, but the toe of the shoe didn't move. Ted grudgingly admired the man's control as he stood as silent and still as a tombstone.

A gunshot echoed up the gorge—the jungle erupted and Ted's muscles tensed, but he caught himself on the verge of reacting. From somewhere below came a shout. The man beside his hiding place muttered, and the boot toe moved, followed by the sound of retreating footfalls fading down the gorge.

Ted's first reaction was to jump up and slap at the insects nipping him. He could feel them down his back and up the leg of his tattered trousers. The urge to scratch at the welts was almost unbearable, but he forced himself to count slowly to three hundred before he dared move. Then, unfolding himself, he carefully stretched out his legs. His toes tingled, and sharp needles of pain shot up to his calves as blood began to re-circulate through his body. He couldn't run now if his life depended on it. He strained his ears as the jungle grew quiet once more. Tense muscles painfully relaxed. Slowly, he lifted the branches of the bush carefully so as not to disturb the birds and crept out into the comparatively cooler air.

Up. Go up. That was the thing to do. With measured stealth he clawed his way up the side of the gorge until he was above the tree line. Scrambling over large rocks, quite suddenly he stood on the tip of a rocky crag overlooking the sea. Directly below, the three German ships were anchored.

He dropped to his stomach and inched forward to peer down. Children splashed in the water; others played tag with young German sailors. Their excited, high-pitched squeals carried up to him were suddenly overridden by loud yelling. People ran from all directions and gathered near the hut he'd cleaned.

German sailors dragged a man into the clearing, and a woman's scream echoed up the side of the craggy rocks. She threw herself in front of the prisoner, but a German officer moved her out of the way.

As the knot of people started to disperse, Ted finally saw Cilla standing beside Cal Mercer near the tailgate of his lorry. From time to time members of the work crew came briefly into view as they took heavy loads from the native men and loaded them to the truck.

A twinge of conscience prickled, but he knew his prison-mates wouldn't begrudge his escape. Besides, he consoled himself, as a member of the Royal Navy he had a duty to escape captivity by the enemy.

The afternoon was slipping away. The sun hung low on the horizon and would soon set. Tomorrow the hunt would begin again. A flashing light from the Raider caught his eye. The ship was signalling a long message to the German crew on the island. He narrowed his eyes against the setting sun and concentrated on deciphering the intermittent flashes. Finally he smiled and let out a long sigh.

*

"What's happening?" Cilla whispered to Mr. Mercer. She had been watching his facial expressions as he supervised the loading of the meat the Germans had commandeered. He seemed to understand what the German officers were arguing about.

Cal glanced around cautiously then whispered. "They have to leave. They know another prisoner is hiding in the jungle, but they can't wait."

Oh God! That has to be Ted. "But what about the gunshot? Do they think they wounded him?"

"They don't think so, but they aren't sure." He narrowed his eyes at her. "Is he your husband?"

"No. We're not married. He's a British sailor." Tears of frustration burned behind her eyes. If Ted had been hurt, she needed to find him, soon. "When are they leaving?"

"Right away. The ships have been signalling them to return so they can catch the tide." Cal winked knowingly at Cilla. "Don't worry, love. He'll come out of the jungle as soon as they leave. You mark my words."

A German officer stepped up to Cal and, ignoring Cilla, snapped his heels together, sending up little spurts of dust. "You will return us to the jetty," he ordered and vaulted over the tailgate.

Cal squeezed Cilla's shoulder. "Chin up."

A flurry of activity erupted in the clearing. Amid yells and shouts, Germans urged the work crew into the back of the lorry, then climbed in after them. The engine spluttered to life, and the truck inched out of the clearing and down the rutted cart-track.

As soon as the lorry was out of sight, Cilla ran to find Pip. "I'm going to search for him."

"Are you bonkers? It'll be pitch dark in a few minutes. If he isn't hurt he'll find you. Besides, where will you look? Wait until daylight."

"But what if he's wounded? He could bleed to death before morning." Hot tears brimmed before they rolled down her cheeks.

Pip put her arm around Cilla's shoulders. "Don't cry. He'll be all right. If they'd shot him, they'd have found him. He's probably just waiting until the ships sail. Come on. Let's get some of that wonderful smelling food."

The sun had set by the time Cal Mercer returned. The last streaks of light shadowed, held in that final magic moment between day and night. He made himself a place to sit among the women and children gathered around the bonfire. Firelight flickering on his tanned face gave him the appearance of an ancient storyteller.

"I know you've been concerned about getting out of here and now that the Germans have gone, I can safely tell you. They asked about a wireless, and I told them truthfully that we didn't have one on the island. What I didn't tell them is that we have a very good one on the boat. The missionary couple took the boat to Melagong, an island about two hours from here. As soon as the Germans told us they planned to leave you lot here, I sent a couple of the natives in a canoe to intercept the missionaries on their way back. They got a message off to the mainland, and a ship has been dispatched to pick you up."

A cheer that could have reached Ted and must have been heard by the Germans on the ships echoed around the compound, almost drowning out Cal's last words. "It should get here tomorrow, and you'll probably be taken to Sydney."

Cilla's pulse raced. Tomorrow? What if the ship came to get them and Ted still hadn't appeared? She couldn't leave without him. He could be hurt—or dead! Tears burned the back of her eyes. No! After everything he'd been through, fate couldn't deny him now. She made up her mind that as soon as it was light enough to find her way through the jungle, she would look for him.

Day ebbed away in a kaleidoscope of reds and purples. The moon had not yet risen above the trees where Ted waited in the shadows, listening to the sounds of happy voices. Cautiously he crept closer to the dancing fingers of light cast by the flames of a bonfire.

He scanned the dishevelled crowd seated around the blaze. Their animation and laughter contrasted sharply with their physical appearance. A couple of women snuggled infants. Children dozed, stretched out on the sand, or huddled next to women's legs. Cal Mercer sat among them, but no other men were visible.

Ted's pulse pounded with excitement at the sight of Cilla shading her eyes against the firelight. She seemed to be searching as she stared toward the trees where he hid. She lowered her hand, and he could see her clearly in the glow of the flames. Her hair, burnished in the firelight, hung loose around her bare shoulders.

He stepped into the circle of light. "Cilla."

She leaped up and ran, kicking up little spurts of sand as she closed the distance between them.

He opened his arms and enfolded her. "Cilla! at last!"

"Ted! Thank God. Are you all right? I was so worried that you'd been shot."

"It would take more than a bloody Jerry's bullet to keep me from you."

He drew her more tightly to him and kissed her fiercely, hungrily, hardly aware of the applause and cheering from the people around the campfire.

She looped her arms around his neck, her body fitting against his, and returned the kiss with a passion that both surprised and pleased him.

She pulled back and studied his face. "Are you sure you're all right?"

"More than all right. Twenty-four hours ago I wasn't certain I'd ever see you again. Now we're both free and off that flaming ship." He hugged her. "And I don't ever want to lose you again."

"When I get home to England again, that's where you'll always find me," she said, fingering his hair. "I've never known your hair this long. And I like the beard, by the way." She ran her hands down the sides of his face.

He laughed. "Doesn't it scratch?"

"No, I like the feel of it. You look like the matelot on the Player's cigarettes packet."

Afraid that if he stopped touching her she might slip away, he trailed his fingers down her arms and took her hands in his.

The moon peeked above the trees, and for the first time, he could see her clearly, and she was smiling.

"You are real. I can hardly believe the nightmare's over."

"I know what you mean. I keep wanting to pinch myself." She suddenly stopped laughing. "Oh, I forgot. You must be hungry. There's plenty of food."

"Later." He grinned at her.

Intertwining his fingers with hers, he led her away from the people seated around the fire. She fell into step beside him, and as they wandered up the beach, the old familiarity returned. From the campfire behind them, people began to sing an old carol.

"It's Christmas Eve," she whispered.

"Really? I didn't know. Happy Christmas, my darling."

They stopped walking and, as if mutually confirming they were not dreaming, gazed at each other.

"Happy Christmas. Tomorrow will be the best Christmas day of our lives," she said.

"No. There'll be lots more Christmases."

"Not quite as wonderful as this one. We're free and we're going home. Cal Mercer got a message off, and a ship is coming from Sydney to get us. It will be here tomorrow."

"Then we'd better make the most of tonight."

Aware of the prison ship stench still clinging to him, he gripped her hand. "Come on. Let's go for a swim."

"What! Now?"

"Yes. I'm filthy from the jungle, and I can't bear to touch you until I'm free of the smell of that rotten ship." He tore off his ragged shirt and dropped his trousers.

With an impish grin, she unfastened her halter top and stepped out of her shorts.

The moon shimmered across the lagoon like a pool of melted butter as they ran hand in hand into the water.

EPILOGUE

London 1941

The boy set his bicycle against the hedge and let himself through the wrought iron gate. At the front door of the house, he banged the brass knocker and, opening the leather pouch slung around his shoulder, pulled out an envelope.

A tousled woman opened the door rubbing her sleepy eyes.

"Telegram for Evans."

She glanced at the boy, and her eyes widened as her hand flew to her throat.

"Yes. I'm Mrs. Evans." She slowly took the envelope from the boy.

He turned and in two strides, a hop and skip jumped over the hedge separating Mrs. Evans' house from her next-door neighbour.

He landed beside a man crouched below the hedge, digging in the flowerbed. "Hey! Watch it!" The startled man got to his feet.

"Sorry, Guv'. Didn't see you there. Are you Mr. Thornton, by chance?"

"Yes." Dan Thornton looked the boy over, noticing for the first time that he wore a uniform. Dan's heart suddenly became almost too heavy to continue beating.

The boy pulled an envelope out of his pouch and placed it in the man's trembling hand.

"See, ya," the boy said, and by the time Dan Thornton peeled open the envelope, the boy was peddling off down the street.

Dan scanned the message and let out a whoop that brought his wife running from the house to his side. "What is it? Is it one of the boys? What's happened?"

Before he could answer, Mary Evans ran out her front door waving a paper.

"Did you get a telegram?"

Maude Thornton snatched the paper from her husband and read aloud,

"*23 Mar 1941. Mr. and Mrs. Edward Evans married Christmas Day, Remaru Island. Arriving home this p.m. Love, Cilla and Ted.*"

213

Printed in the United Kingdom
by Lightning Source UK Ltd.
93480

Printed in the United Kingdom
by Lightning Source UK Ltd.
93480